Going Vintage

Going Vintage

Lindsey Leavitt

SCHOLASTIC INC.

ISBN 978-0-545-62990-4

12 11 10 9 8 7 6 5 4 3 2 1   13 14 15 16 17 18/0

Printed in the U.S.A.   40

First Scholastic printing, September 2013

Book design by Regina Roff

To Rachel
"Sisters, sisters, there were never such devoted . . ."
(Someday we'll learn the rest of the lyrics.)

Going Vintage

"Losing love is like a window in your heart
Everybody sees you're blown apart
Everybody sees the wind blow"
—*Paul Simon*

Chapter 1

Things I say to distract Jeremy so I can take a break from making out:

1. I need to go to the bathroom.
2. Oh, did I tell you . . . (insert funny thing that happened). It has to be genuinely interesting so he doesn't know that I'm thinking about anything besides This Moment, even though I obviously am, because it's not like my brain just turns off when we're kissing. Well, my mom told me once to be careful because guys turn their brains off and certain body parts on, which was so disgusting I'm sorry I brought it up now.

3. I'm hungry.
4. One time I actually said I needed a break, and Jeremy took it the wrong way, thinking I meant a break from us, when really things were just getting too hot. He knows I have very clear limits and geographical boundaries, no matter how much the kid persists, which is every time we're together, which is every day. So you can imagine how tiring that gets. Another thing my mom once said was, when you're with someone, you give pieces of yourself, and they always kept that piece, or at least a piece of the piece. "Pieces" might have been code for "virginity," I'm still not sure.

We finally made up by making out. Which was great, but I actually DID need to use the bathroom, so I had to go back to that excuse as soon as I was sure he didn't think I was deserting him forever.

This time, I go with Distraction Number 3, partly because I *am* hungry, but I also used the other excuses twice this week. It seems every week I have to use an excuse more and more to end the kiss-off. And actually, every week I use them less and less.

We're supposed to be studying in his bedroom. My parents won't let me have a boy in my bedroom ever, even to study, even if I'm showing off my Major League Baseball bobblehead collection (twenty-three nodding athletes and counting). And they'd issued that rule with parental wisdom, because studying at Jeremy's is almost always code for making out. Most of the things we say we're doing are code for making out. It's not like we're horndogs—we hang out with his friends some, go to the movies or Anaheim Ducks hockey games, maybe the beach. It's just that Jeremy seems to really like kissing, and he's my first bona fide boyfriend, and of the sundry activities I start (and quit), the one that can't be included on a yearbook page is frankly the most enjoyable. So when we're alone, we pretty much kiss each other's faces off.

In a romantic way.

"Really? You're hungry?" he asks. "Even after Pizza Hut?"

"That was lunchtime."

"You had two slices."

"Three." I pat my stomach. "You're right. I should be famished by now."

He swings his legs over the side of his double bed, still covered in a sports comforter from when he was, like, twelve. I sit up and adjust my sweater-vest, purchased at Goodwill last month when I decided my fall wardrobe would be eighties prep, although the itchy argyle and unflatteringly high skirts were making me rethink the collection. Plus, kneesocks did me no favors.

"What do you want?" he asks.

"Chips and salsa with cream cheese, light on the salsa, heavy on the cream cheese. And a glass of milk if you're using medium or spicier."

Jeremy smoothes down his dark, floppy hair. Action Hair, I call it. No amount of combing or hair product can achieve the adorableness of Action Hair. And no one can get it like that but me. "I swear, on the weekends you eat more than the entire wrestling team."

"Four days healthy, three days free. Diet plan of the gods."

"The gods wouldn't touch Meat Lover's pizza. Do you know what's in a pepperoni?"

"Are you calling me fat?"

"Never." He reaches over and pinches some skin on my stomach. "You know you're beautiful. I love every piece of you."

He smiles lazily, and I want to give up all my pieces right then. I kiss him, even though I was the one who needed a break before. He's the one who is beautiful, and I love days like this, days where there is no one but us, and we don't need to talk, because we already know what the other thinks.

It's another five minutes until he gently pushes me away and says, "Why don't you start on our paper?"

"You mean *your* paper," I say. "I'm not even in philosophy."

"But you're writing it. So it's ours now."

"I've always wanted to share a paper with a boy!" I clap my hands. "Can we name him Hunter? Hunter the Paper Boy. Or Boy of Paper, so he's not confused with paperboy paperboys. I'll knit him a sweater, show embarrassing baby pictures to his dates, and scream at his soccer games."

Jeremy stares at me hard. I love when he gives me that look, like all the staring in the world would never unlock my feminine mysteries. "I don't get you sometimes."

"*All* the time!" I call after him. So much for feminine mystery.

I hate when I say things that I think are funny but Jeremy doesn't laugh or understand, and I wonder if something is wrong with me. Sometimes I even text the joke to my little sister, Ginnie, and 84 percent of the time she writes back with a "You're the funniest person on the planet!" which is a million characters beyond a simple "LOL." But that could be because she's my sister. Although Jeremy has been my boyfriend for over a year now, so that should at least warrant a courtesy laugh, right?

To test my theory, I write Ginnie about Hunter, and within a minute she confirms my genius. I love instant gratification. It's been an hour since I've checked my phone, so I have to respond to a few texts. There's not much to say, just that I'll write more later because right now I'm with Jeremy. I love writing that. It says that I'm his and he's mine, and between the lines there is belonging, something I didn't feel at Orange Park High School until we started dating.

I finally settle into his swivel computer chair and spin myself dizzy. I help with his philosophy and chemistry homework, and he teaches me Spanish and history. He gets better grades than me, but that's probably more due to effort than intelligence. Don't tell him I said that.

I click onto his computer to look up essays that could tell me what I'm—sorry, *Jeremy's*—supposed to think about Kant's moral philosophy. Jeremy's Friendspace profile page is open on his computer. I smile at his image, an action shot of Jeremy grabbing my legs. His cousin Oliver is holding my arms and they're about to throw me in the pool on my sixteenth birthday last March.

I don't know much about Oliver, but who does? I think that mysterious aloofness is part of his image. He *was* nice enough to give me a birthday card that night with a twenty-dollar gift card to Outback. Outback? That's the way to get in good with your cousin's girl. Jeremy, on the other hand, got me this ruby ring that we saw while I was selling something for my dad to a pawnshop in Santa Ana. I love jewelry with history, even the desperate history of pawns. I run my finger over the ruby, rubbing the memory until it's warm.

I think about doing something cute—like updating Jeremy's "What's Happening?" section to say, "My girlfriend Mallory is a goddess," but Jeremy's not a big fan of The Cute. I'm about to click off when I see that he was previously active last night at nine.

Which is . . . huh.

He was supposed to be playing basketball last night at nine.

It's not like I'm one of those stalker girlfriends who reads all her boyfriend's texts or combs through his yearbook signatures for hidden meanings. But right now the truth is not hiding; it's straight up in my face. And unless he was Friendspacing on the free-throw line, he obviously lied to me.

Why?

I know the answer before I asked the question.

Authentic Life.

It's this game on Friendspace. You create a character that looks like you, then make virtual friends and get a fake job and furnish your pretend house, making sure your imaginary dog doesn't pee on your couch. There are options for vacation packages, sports teams, and parenthood. Some levels give the user the opportunity to create fantastical worlds, so if you've always wanted to be a warrior goblin princess who likes to shop and compete for the Olympic gold in curling, well, here's your chance.

Authentic Life is probably more fun than that; I've just never gotten into it. Jeremy's not the only one in "the community"—it's the new trend with online games, and even celebrities have avatars. Everyone has an Internet vice, so I can understand a few minutes here or there, but Jeremy is on there A Lot. His usage shows up on his Friendspace feed sometimes, and it's always odd hours—sometimes he'll slip away when we're hanging out to go "check e-mail," but I know it's this stupid game.

One back click and I come to Jeremy's Authentic Life world. Although I know he plays this game, I've never actually *seen* his site. He's designed his own black-and-silver background, and pictures of other virtual people and places splatter the page. There he is on his pretend trip to Mount Rushmore, there he is sticking an American flag on the moon, there he is...there he is with a girl. In most of the pictures. BubbleYum. Her avatar has curly red hair and a black kind of corset, and she's holding a golden lacrosse stick.

She's even next to Jeremy in his profile picture, holding his hand. Jeremy's avatar is totally Jeremy—the dark hair, muscled frame. He's wearing a karate robe with a red dragon, and his handle says TheAmazingAsian.

The Asian part is half real, from his dad's side, but the amazing part I'm starting to doubt. Karate? I don't think he can even do a judo chop. I have no clue why he's virtually living in a walk-up in Greenwich Village when he's always said he wants to leave California for Canada, where people love hockey as much as he does. And who cares where he fake lives when that leather-clad lacrosse cartoon is on his arm?

One word pops out among the list of fake favorites. *Married*. For a moment, a tiny hopeful second, I'm flattered that he's carried me over to Bizarro-World. And then I know. BubbleYum is his main squeeze.

My boyfriend is cheating on me with a cyberwife.

Chapter 2

Jeremy's [Fake] **Profile Information**
MARRIED
Lives in Greenwich Village, NY
Profession: Professional Portrait Artist and Free-
lance Graphic Designer
Black Belt in Karate
Favorite movie: Anything martial arts
Favorite music: Techno
Level: Advanced Lifer

I could click around and talk to this BubbleYum person using
Jeremy's avatar, but I'm sidetracked by his in-box, bulging with
e-mails from his corseted wife. I pause for a moment before
clicking on the messages. Do I want to read this? Of course I
don't. Of course I do.

My hand shakes as I scroll through the trail of words—secrets, confessions, fears. Is this what shock feels like? Like I've jumped out of my body and I'm watching this moment happen, but it's not my moment, it's not *my* boyfriend saying those things to another girl. It's someone else somewhere else, maybe in a movie playing for an entire theater of viewers rolling their eyes because everyone saw this coming. Everyone except that poor girl in front of the computer.

But it is my moment. This is happening to *me*. It's real—authentic, so much more so than this stupid game. I read and read, imprinting that earth-shattering moment into my consciousness until a machete can't even hack it out of my brain.

Bubs,

I missed you today. And your new profile page makes me so happy. I like all the pictures you added of us—we're a good-looking couple. There was this song at the grocery store. Maybe James Taylor? I don't know oldies. But the line is "And if I'm feeling down and blue, or troubled by some foolish game, she always seems to make me change my mind." Babe, I can't tell you how much you mean to me. Ha! I know that sounds cheesy, but it's true.

Looks like our puppy is growing into a big old dog. Stop feeding him the expensive dog chow, LOL! I've got to put in some extra time in the art studio tonight, but maybe you can come in and watch me paint? Or I can paint a picture of you. I want to start studying nudes.☺

—AA

Jeremy, I mean, AMAZING,

I looked it up. That's totally James Taylor. You need to go to some hipper grocery stores.☺ All the songs that make me think of you have really heavy, intense beats. Not to say I don't like a good love song, but you're bigger than that. Bolder. And nudes, hmmm? I'm listening.☺

Sorry about Snoopdoggie! I just can't tell him no when he gives me that look. And thanks for taking out the trash. You're the best hubby around.

You know what else makes me think of you? Everything. I wish I could jump into the computer forever.

Love,

Yum

Everything. Everything out there reminds this girl in a wired box about my boyfriend. She's thinking about him and . . . he's thinking about her. How dare they. Both of them.

I don't read all the messages. There's too many and not enough time. Besides, what I see is enough to make me ill. The talk isn't dirty or about sicko fetish fantasies. This is worse. They talk about *everything.* The day—both the one they had invented together and what was happening in the real world. No mention of Jeremy's ACTUAL girlfriend, though. I am invisible in this alternative world.

Eating Pizza Hut is suddenly not a good idea. Agreeing to write Jeremy's paper isn't a good idea. Being here, in his room, twirling in this chair where Jeremy sits daily to construct his fantasy world that is Mallory-free makes me feel like a freak-ing idiot.

The big question rushing through my ears: Why did he need this?

And the other question—that harsh, scratchy whisper: Why wasn't I enough?

And then it's just a tide, surging along, where every single interaction I've ever had, every kiss, every joke, every truth becomes a wobbly question mark.

Do I need to hack into his real e-mail, check all his phone texts?

Who is this girl, moving in on someone in a relationship? Does she even know he's in a relationship?

Is this make-believe, or is something physical going on?

Does she live nearby? Do they have secret rendezvous?

Eww. Did they cyberconsummate their virtual marriage?

How can some girl, real or unreal, close or far, know Jer-emy better than I do? The same boy who I've been with for thirteen months, the same boy I was, *I am*, in love with?

"It's mild salsa." Jeremy's standing in the doorway, chips under his arm, salsa and a Diet Coke in each hand. "And I got you some gum. You know, for after."

Right. Because after, he wants to hook up some more.

Since Jeremy can't see the screen from where he's stand-ing, I make a snap decision and shrink the page so all that is visible is a blank Word document. I walk around the desk, still amazed at the out-of-body feeling, like everything's all float-ing or slow motion. How can this even be real? When I take the snack from him, I make sure my still-shaking fingers don't touch his. "Thanks," I say. The word is gravel on my tongue.

He flops down on his bed. I bite into a chip but don't chew, so when I swallow, it pokes at my throat.

"Did you start on Herbert?" he asks.

"Who is Herbert?"

"Our paper."

"*Hunter.*" I can't help the shrillness in my voice. "You don't even care enough to remember his name."

"Okaaaay." He pushes his hair out of his face. His adorable, floppy Action Hair. I love it. I hate it. "I didn't know you were so attached."

"Some people still value loyalty," I say.

"Are we still talking about my philosophy paper?"

"Are we?" Now is the time when I should confront him. Ask all the questions pinpricking my skin. And as much as I want to, I also don't want to hear his rationalization, or see him get annoyed/anxious/defensive. Or worse, calm. What if he's Mr. Supercalm and Collected, I'm Glad You Know, It's Best This Way?

I want him to know that I know, but I don't want to know anything. I don't want there to be anything *to* know.

"If you don't want to work on it now, you can e-mail it to me tomorrow when you're done packing your grandma's house." My heart drops when he says *e-mail*, all casual, like e-mails are everyday forms of communication and not vessels for relationship destruction.

"Maybe I'll do that," I say faintly.

In one fluid motion, he yanks me onto the bed with him. My skin, burning with want only minutes ago, is icy from his touch.

"So what are we going to do the rest of the afternoon, then?" He grins.

I squeeze my nails into the palm of my hand. I'm nauseous from his closeness, disgusted with this stranger. "I need milk."

"What?"

"Milk. You didn't bring me milk."

Jeremy rubs the small of my back. "You said you only want milk if it's hot salsa."

"Changed my mind." I squirm away from him.

"You're good at that."

So are you.

He stands. "Be right back. Anything else?"

I shake my head. Jeremy asking what I want, offering me anything at all, is more fake than his virtual trip to Mount Rushmore. He doesn't care about me. I'm his warm body. I'm not the one he's thinking about when a James Taylor song comes on in the unhip (who says *hip*?) grocery store.

The second he's gone, I'm back on his computer, feeling another wave of hurt when I see the page. Part of me hoped the information would disappear. I enter his "world" by zooming in on a little arrow hovering over the map. Fake Jeremy is listening to music in his New York bedroom, lying on a bedspread that I'm guessing his wife picked out. Maybe he's waiting for her so they can whisper stupid song lyrics to each other.

I click on a book and chuck it at his head. His icon starts to bleed. I laugh. This game *is* addictive.

But that's not enough. I want to hurt him like he hurt me.

I click onto his account settings, to the list of applications. Authentic Life has more than one version, and I don't have time to erase them all. That's okay. What I really want is for him to know I was here. I want *her* to know I was here.

I replace his BubbleYum profile picture with the one of Jeremy and me by the pool. I erase the MARRIED part and add CONFUSED. And because *confused* isn't accurate enough, because I really want things to hit home, I leave his Authentic Life page for his main Friendspace page—the real Jeremy. Instead of the cute update I'd considered for the "What's Happening?" section, I write:

JEREMY MUI IS A LYING TOOL.

Sums it up very well.

The first response comment has already dinged onto his page when I push the swivel chair back and run out of his bedroom. I'm downstairs in a second, brushing past a bewildered Jeremy. I almost grab the glass of milk in his hand and dump it on his face, but go for the more old-fashioned approach by slamming the front door.

The thud still isn't loud enough to make my point.

Chapter 3

Six things of interest I find while packing up my grandma's entire life:

1. An old time card of Grandpa's from when he worked at a grocery store in Oakland.
2. A clunky camera on a leather strap. Doesn't work, but makes a great accessory.
3. A gorgeous fifties or sixties seersucker housedress. This garment needs a new home. Dress, meet Mallory's closet.
4. A turquoise ring on a knotted silver chain. Will have to ask Grandma if it's important to her, because if not, I want.

5.   Notebooks filled with lists.
6.   One particular notebook filled with one particular list.

Needless to say, I do not work on Jeremy's philosophy paper Friday night while my dad and I drive up the coast three hours to Grandma's house in San Luis Obispo. I don't answer my cell phone any of the ten times my I'm-pretty-sure-he's-an-ex-boyfriend calls. I also ignore the millions of phone calls from my friends and sister, no doubt in response to my Tool Proclamation. The incident makes me want to detox from the high school gossip loop, at least for the weekend.

On Saturday, I hibernate until eleven, happily wrapped in a dream involving Jeremy's computer, a hammer, and a Smurf. The Smurf was the one with the hammer. It made sense in the dream.

My dad wakes me up so we can get to work packing up Grandma's life. She's already moved into a swanky retirement community in Newport Beach, just twenty minutes away from Orange on a good traffic day, so I'm glad she'll be close. I'm still puzzled why she'd leave the cute downtown bungalow with a wraparound porch and purple shutters. It was always my grandparents' dream to retire here and buy a fixer-upper, but Grandma Vivian quit working on the house after Grandpa Alvin died two years ago. Now Dad and I have to sift through her eclectic collection and decide what is a keepsake, what can turn a profit, and what is junk.

After three hours of de-cluttering, it's all starting to look like junk.

I'd just gone through a box of old electronics when I find an aged spiral notebook. I hold up the discovery in the dim basement light. "Dad, is this anything?"

Dad reads from the first page. "'Juice. Eggs. Bread.' Just another notebook filled with lists. You'll probably find fifty of them. Mom is … was …" Dad pauses, deciding if his mom still makes responsible lists now that she's discovered her second childhood. "… is … She's a lister. Just like you, Mal."

Just like me. Grandma is never compared to me—it's always my sister. Even though I have the same freckled skin as Grandma, Ginnie has her blond corkscrew hair and athletic build. They have the same laugh, same vibrant energy. But listing? That is me. I write dozens a week—things I need to do, books I want to read, teachers at our school I'm pretty sure are serial killers. Lists add a number to randomness, give ideas the illusion of order. Of course, I never follow through on 76 percent of the goal-oriented lists, and some aren't very versatile. (Boys I've said *I love you* to: 1. Jeremy. Tool.)

"I don't even know how to price some of Mom's stuff—there's a tribal spear from Borneo in her office."

"Where's Borneo?"

"Exactly." He opens another box, a puff of dust circling in the air. "Old toys. These I know." He analyzes a train set. "I'm going to check some of my collectors' sources. You good?"

I flash the same fake smile I'd worn all day, intent on covering up the drama that involves things girls don't tell dads. The swallowed secrets are starting to give me a headache.

Once he's gone, I flip through the notebook, stopping at a list that isn't about groceries.

Junior Year: Back-to-School Resolutions:
1. Run for pep squad secretary
2. Host a fancy dinner party/soiree
3. Sew a dress for homecoming
4. Find a steady
5. Do something dangerous

That's it. Nothing on the page before or after. No explanation why such a big list is in such an unassuming notebook. Tasks, dreams really, to be checked off, accomplished. No mention if they ever were.

My knees are raw from kneeling on the concrete basement floor. I stand and stretch, a thin string of sunlight illuminating the paper. "Dad?" I yell up the stairs. "What year was Grandma born?"

"1946. She's a baby boomer. Why?"

Grandma would have been sixteen at the beginning of her junior year, sixteen just like me. 1962—this list is over fifty years old. I bet she wore really cute cat-eye glasses and giggled over milk shakes on Friday nights with her quarterback boyfriend who never cheated on her with someone named BubbleYum.

The punched-in-the-gut feeling returns with the memory. Man, where is that hammer-wielding dream Smurf when you need him? He could be my cartoon hit man and teach

Jeremy a valuable lesson. Nothing fatal. A cartoon hammer would be fine, as long as it hurt.

I click a pen and turn to the next page in the notebook.

Mallory's Junior Year: Early October back-to-school resolutions:

1. Jeremy. Yell at him? Erect a shrine of a marble screwdriver in his honor? ~~Ask him to take me back? Act like nothing ever happened?~~
2. Bury my cell phone in the backyard. One more ring and . . . I don't know. It really is a good thing I don't have a hammer.
3. Be strong. Or at least not weak.
4. Wear Grandma's blue dress somewhere where Jeremy will see me, making him forget BubbleYum and remember yesterday, on his bed, when he called me beautiful.
5. Er, find a hobby?

My list sucks. Every one of the goals accomplishes nothing, just proves how much of my life involves . . . no, *involved* Jeremy. Grandma's list is far more dynamic, more earnest. I bet her life at sixteen was better than mine—simple and carefree. Sew a homecoming dress? Seriously? That's your biggest drama? Golly gee.

I sit down on a rocking chair, rubbing my hands along the seasoned wood. Maybe...maybe my great-grand-pappy whittled soap in this very seat. (Did I have a great-grand-pappy? For this daydream, yes.) The room holds that mildewy sweetness of history, the boxed-up stories and artifacts from a full and rich lifetime, a life spent exploring and traveling and changing the world through Grandma's work at A Child's Last Chance, her nonprofit organization. All that potential was reached because of her uncomplicated adolescent beginnings.

I wonder if she found a handsome, caring steady and if they went on a million dates before they kissed and if they spent all their time talking about life and love and the American Dream. All they had was black-and-white TV, so they probably sat around and conversed all the time. On the phone, sure, but more in person. Not like now, where I go to the grocery store to buy herbal tea for my sick sister and the guy next to me starts discussing what flavor of Rice-A-Roni is best. Of course I answer *chicken*, only to find he's talking to his wife on one of the earpiece thingies. Then he gives *me* a weird look, like talking to the *air* is normal, and buys the beef flavor anyway. Beef rice? Honestly.

I stop rocking. I want to live in a world free of air talkers and technological affairs. Is that too much to ask?

My phone rings for the 1,204th time. I consider my caller ID. Ginnie. My sister is my secret-keeper. If I could tell anyone about BubbleYum, it would be her. It's worth breaking my phone fast to hear her voice.

"Hey," I say.

"Where have you been? Did you lose your phone again?" Ginnie asks. "This isn't a good time to lose your phone."

"Not lost. Ignoring it."

"Your fingers were starting to itch from lack of technology, huh?"

It's not an itch. It's a burn. I'd reached for the phone seventy-eight times in the past twenty-four hours. Half of those were to call Jeremy, but I'd also had that urge to post on Friendspace every little thing I was doing. Dreamed about a Smurf assassin last night! Found out boyfriend is a cyberslut! Unearthed a fifty-year-old grocery list!

Communicative technology is really just listing, spread out through texts and updates to an assortment of friends, a daily reminder to the virtual universe that I exist. And I also have *no* idea what's happened to my friends over the last twenty-four hours. It's like living in a cave and knowing there's a lightbulb directly above but never turning it on. "I can go one day without using my phone, thanks."

"So let's go over the easier things first," Ginnie says. "Did you find pictures of Grandma's hidden lover, Eduardo? And if so, is he atop a horse? How many buttons are undone on his shirt?"

The "hidden lover" line gives me a little jolt, but the connection to my situation is thin enough that it doesn't sting too much. I roll my eyes. Despite the fact that she's two years younger, Ginnie is wittier than me. Brighter. More mature and athletic. Prettier.

Yes, I still like her. Usually.

"Your silence tells me he's either completely shirtless or you're rolling your eyes, which wouldn't be the case, because that was good stuff," Ginnie says. "I thought of it, like, an hour ago. Thanks for finally answering your phone so I could use it."

"Are you done with your monologue? I only had the worst day of my life yesterday."

"Is Eduardo's chest hair that frightening? Gross, was it gray and curly?"

"Were you saving that joke, too?" I ask.

"And now it's out of my system." Ginnie sighs. "Okay, let's discuss the Internet Elephant. Are you the one who called your boyfriend a tool on Friendspace?"

"Yes."

"And you did this because..."

"He is," I say.

"I agree, of course, but what brought on this change of heart?"

I tell her. All of it—the making out, the James Taylor, the karate outfit—everything right down to the salsa brand. She's silent except for a few thoughtful *mmm*s. My voice is mono-tone the whole time. If I can keep the emotion out of my voice, maybe I can keep it out of my heart. When I'm done with my tear-free report, she lets out a breath and whispers, "What a bastard."

"So I'm not off base for feeling bad?" I ask, hoping she says I'm right, but hoping even more that she says I'm stupid and wrong. That the whole thing is in my head, that everyone has a cyberwife on the side. Maybe I should just call Jeremy back and say sorry and ask where he'd like to meet for a let's-make-up make-out session. "We aren't married. And it's really just a game."

"Those e-mails aren't part of the game," Ginnie says softly.

I slip lower in the rocker. "I know."

"I saw this thing on my Yahoo! news feed, one of those ten-ways-to-know-your-guy-is-cheating quizzes." Ginnie's voice has gone matter-of-fact. Two things to know about Ginnie—she's always right. Also, she's always right.

"Just what I want to read now."

"I read it for you. Which is probably better. Midway through the list, you would start making excuses for him because of your Jeremy tunnel vision. You'll see the light now, discover that he's a tool."

"Before this, he wasn't a tool at all. He was always sweet to me, made me laugh—"

"Mallory, he wears deep V-necks."

"He has nice chest muscles."

"And Mr. Plunging Neckline wants you to know it. You can't trust a guy showing off more cleavage than you."

"Why didn't you say this to me before?"

"Because you loved him," Ginnie says simply. "And you wouldn't have listened anyway."

I pick at a splinter in the armrest. I've just given Ginnie a pass to go off on Jeremy, and who knows how long she's held that inside. But I don't think I'm personally ready to bash my boyfriend. Ex-boyfriend? I don't know what I'm ready for right now. "So this article…"

"This article said that you don't have to hook up with some-one for it to be considered cheating. They can have an emotional affair—like, a connection that isn't just friendship. All those things he was saying to her, does he talk like that with you?"

"Well, no, but nobody talks like that. We're sisters, and how often do we say 'you mean so much to me'? It's easier when you're writing it. When we're together, well . . . we hang out, and he does say he loves me—"

"But does he say even some of the things in person that he's saying to *her* in e-mail?"

I flash back to the messages. There were hundreds. "No."

"Plus, you said they're all flirty, so maybe there *is* more. Do you think she lives around here? Maybe he met her when he went to hockey camp this summer."

"She plays lacrosse," I say.

"How do you know?"

"Doesn't matter." I kick at an empty box. "So basically I just wasn't good enough for him.

"No. You're *too* good for him and he's a jerk who says awful things about you." She pauses. "So you need to move on. Eduardo! Let's find you an Eduardo!"

"Awful things?" I ask. "Jeremy never even talked about me on the e-mails. I'm invisible."

"No, the stuff he wrote on his Friendspace."

My stomach nose-dives. "*What* stuff on Friendspace?"

Ginnie is silent.

"I'm getting Dad's computer."

"Mal, now might not be the best time to look."

I'm not listening. I'm scrambling up the stairs. Dad's left his netbook on the counter. I log in to my Friendspace account with shaking hands. My page is filled with comments and questions from friends. I click on a picture of Jeremy, and it redirects me to his page.

There's a feature to list your top five friends and include a bunch of random, inside jokes about those people. So you could have "Hank Inkley—Sloppy Slippers!" and, of course, that probably only makes sense to Hank, but then everyone sees how tight you are. Jeremy's had "Floater Fish" next to my name forever—we were at a party once, and he said I fit in with everyone, that I just swim back and forth between groups like a fish. Which was actually pretty insightful—I've never had a best friend apart from my sister; I've always just had a few goodish friends. And so then whenever he would see me mingling, he'd make a fish face, looking so cute that I'd want to kiss those puckered lips right then.

But now, the inside jokes are gone, and Jeremy's relationship status says two words.

"OVER IT?" I say out loud. When Ginnie doesn't respond, I look around, realizing I threw the phone onto the kitchen counter. "He makes it sound like he broke up with me. But I dumped him. And I didn't even dump him, because we haven't *talked*."

"It's just a defense mechanism. He's trying to save face."

"Did you see the comments?" I ask. "Someone said I hooked up with Corbin Griffin? I don't even *know* Corbin Griffin!"

"Didn't he run track last year?" Ginnie asks.

"And Jeremy's responding to the comments! Joking! Someone calls his girlfriend a slut and he smiley-faces back. What self-respecting human being answers that with an *emoticon*?" I slam the screen shut. "Jeremy elopes with a flavor of gum and *I'm* the bad guy."

"Everyone knows Friendspace isn't real," Ginnie says. "Look, I can see why you're upset. But don't you think this will blow over? Tomorrow Friendspace will be all about some picture of a baseball player passed out with a Sharpie mustache. Jeremy's relationship status will be forgotten and you can heal in peace."

My phone vibrates with a text. "Hold on."

I glance at the screen. Thirty-two texts. Seven are from Paige and Cardin, my two closest friends when I'm not with Jeremy or Ginnie. Paige's texts are full-sentence diatribes. It's a good thing her parents aren't on the pay-by-the-syllable plan. And Cardin's are just...Cardin. Sound effects to punctuate her mood, most definitely as she reads through the Friendspace battleground.

And there are six texts from Jeremy, starting with WHERE DID YOU GO? to WHY DID YOU HACK INTO MY ACCOUNT? to IT'S NOT WHAT YOU THINK. to I'M NOT GOING TO FREAKING STALK YOU to CALL ME to SO THIS IS HOW IT IS.

But some texts? Some are from people *I don't even know*, like someone posted my number on a People to Hate message board. I scroll through but stop reading after the fourth text from a stranger.

I CANT BELIEVE THAT YOU WOULD MESS WITH JEREMY.

I WILL CUT YOU IF YOU HURT HIM ANYMORE!!! TRUST!

The only thing worse than personal anguish is when that personal anguish is grotesquely twisted and broadcast in an untrue light. These people don't know me—they don't have any clue what happened. They're just jumping onto a thread train, gleefully commenting on a topic that happened to pop up on their daily news feed.

"I'm done!" I scream, the rage raw in my voice. "Done with computers and phones and . . . and . . . fake fakeness. I'm talking complete isolation. No networking or chatting or texting or computering."

"Good." Ginnie's voice is encouraging. "That'll be healthy for a couple of days. Focus on yourself."

"Forget that. Try *forever*. I am so over this decade, this century."

"I don't think this century is your problem."

"You're right. Technology is the problem."

"But you're using technology right now," Ginnie says.

I hold my phone out, giving the gadget a look of severe disgust. I switch to speaker, so I don't have to get too close to The Battery-Operated Evil. "Yep. And do you know what cell phones cause? Cancer."

"Mallory."

"And people die texting while driving. They're villainous contraptions. Computers? Oh man, Internet predators lurk,

lurk, online. For all Jeremy knows, BubbleYum is a fifty-eight-year-old pervert in Ohio."

"I hope she/he is," Ginnie offers. "Wouldn't that be poetic?"

None of this is poetic. I slide Dad's netbook into his briefcase. Netbook. A modern version of a *notebook*. Which reminds me of something. Grandma's pen-and-paper, honest-to-goodness notebook. "Wait. I found this list of Grandma's from when she was sixteen. You know what she was worrying about?"

"The still undiscovered effects of secondhand smoke?"

"Learning how to sew. Sewing, Gin. Her life was much easier because it was much simpler. Wholesome. And that's why she's so incredible now—because her past was so perfect. What if we went back to that?"

"You mean, like, wear thrift-store stuff? You already do that with your eighties phase. And remember your forties military trend—ugh, so much khaki."

"I'm not talking about clothes. I want to go back to how life was when Grandma made that list. To simplify. Connect. Get to, I don't know, my core. If they didn't have it around in 1962, I'm not interested. Not just technology, either."

Ginnie gives a low grunt. "But this is kind of your deal. You jump in on a crazy whim but ditch the idea before lunchtime. You need to think of a long-term solution for your pain. Like Eduardo."

"Would you *shut up* about Eduardo?"

"All I'm saying is a list won't fix your problem."

"Of course it won't. That's not my point." I start to pace the room. "I can't fix the past, but I can fix my future, right?"

"How does ignoring your cell phone have anything to do with Jeremy being a tool?"

"If Jeremy didn't have a computer or the Internet, he wouldn't have met BubbleYum. If I didn't have this cell phone, strangers couldn't text me threats. Technology is the reason my life is falling apart." My voice rises. I've never felt this passionate about anything before—the world, or my world at least, is suddenly so much clearer, like everything before was a big surface float, and now, for the first time, I'm diving into the deep end of life. I have to say it out loud, I have to commit, I have to prove that fulfillment is still possible. Unplugged. "If I go back to when people actually talked in person, to when things were real, then maybe it *will* be real. That's what I need. Some good, old-fashioned, legitimate reality."

"You'll be texting by sundown."

"No way. Trust."

"You're really doing this?" Ginnie just as well could've asked if I was scaling Everest in flip-flops. Which, naturally, makes me want to give up technology and do this list even more. To prove her wrong. No, to prove the world wrong.

"I am absolutely committed. I give you my vow."

"You *give* your word. A vow is something you *make*."

"It doesn't matter! I vow. Vowed. It's happened. This time *is* different. You'll see." I have a goal, a purpose. And I'm going vintage until I accomplish every task on Grandma's list.

Chapter 4

Gifts from Jeremy:

1. The Purple Paper Clip: Jeremy and I did this English report together last year, right after we'd started "talking" but before we started "dating," which basically meant we were hooking up but not acknowledging that in front of polite society yet. Jeremy's job was researching nineteenth-century English writers, mine was to put all our thoughts together (read: write the paper), and then he printed out the report and made a poster with selective

works and author photos. Right before class, he handed me my copy, held together by a purple paper clip because, as Jeremy said, "that one time I wore a purple shirt and my friends were laughing about it and you said your favorite color was purple and that shut them up."

My favorite color is actually yellow, for those playing along at home, but I kept the paper clip all the same.

2. Playlists: I'm not big into the music scene, but I know what I like when I hear it. And Jeremy knew (knows?) music so well that if I told him one song I liked, he could find me thirty other bands I would love. One weekend, he stole my iPod and made me playlists with themes like Happy Mallory, Sad Mallory, Studying Mallory. Oh, and Ready-to-Go Mallory, the most commonly played.

I wonder if that weekend, when Jeremy was shuffling all those songs around for me, he was also e-mailing BubbleYum. If he made her playlists. What HER themes were.

3. One of those cologne cards from Hollister with Jake, Jeremy's scent.

I had three or four of them: in my desk, in my purse, by my bed. When I missed him, I'd sniff. Yes, I'm a lame little sniffer.

4. The ruby pawnshop ring: I'm going to sell the ring next time I'm at the pawnshop, let someone else build a better history with it.

5. A broken heart. Nonreturnable.

Dad and I go into a packing frenzy. It isn't moving-to-a-new-house packing—Grandma Vivian doesn't plan on keeping most of her stuff, and the furniture stays for the new renters. A third of the boxes will go to Goodwill, another third Dad deems "of value" and will be stocked in our garage and inventoried. The rest is the good stuff, the pictures and journals and knickknacks that make my grandma's life her life. All I have to do is weed through baby pictures of my dad and his siblings, through the family reunions, to teen Vivian. Even one picture will help.

Despite boxing up his childhood, Dad's benevolent enough to offer Morgan's Steakhouse. We rarely go somewhere expensive, only on birthdays or when he's sold a house. Lately, birthdays—which, as you know, are *annual* events—feel like the more common occurrence.

That remark is the kind of thing my mom grumbles to herself when she's paying the bills. It's an unfair jab, especially since the man is offering me steak.

"Get the steak if you want," Dad says. "Surf and turf this baby. I know Rodney's train set will get me five hundred, easy."

"Get *you* five hundred dollars, or Uncle Rodney?"

Dad tears off a piece of bread and slathers it with butter. "Uncle Rodney makes more in a month than I do a year. He's not going to miss the train set."

"Even for sentimental purposes?" I ask.

"If he was sentimental, he'd be down here helping me." Our waitress appears and Dad beams at her. "Two wedge salads and two surf and turfs. Bloody on my steak, burned on hers."

"Petite filet. I don't need the surf," I say. "And don't burn the steak, just sear it before it's cooked. I like a little pink." The waitress nods and starts to walk away. "Wait! And can I also have some sautéed mushrooms, but not, like, soaking in butter." The order reminds me of the time Jeremy and I went to a pizza place called Mellow Mushroom, even though he hated mushrooms, and he picked them all off, until it was pretty much just bread. "Wait, again. Never mind on the mushrooms."

I haven't eaten since Pizza Hut the day before, and steak probably isn't the best stomach filler, but dad looks happy and hopeful and he's selling his brother's train set for this meal. I dig into the wedge salad and hope the stomachaches I'd had all day are due to hunger and not the waves of heartsickness that come every time something reminds me of Jeremy, which is nearly everything because we dated longer than most celebrities are married. Unlike him, I cherished moments beyond our lip locks, like de-mushrooming a pizza. I know that's not deeply romantic, but at least I thought it was real.

"So!" Dad plunges his knife into the butter, bringing the bread to butter quota to 1:1. "Find anything interesting today?"

"You mean Dad-wants-to-sell interesting, or Mallory-wants-to-keep interesting?"

"Either. Both. Selling does pay the bills."

I play with the cloth napkin, consider telling Dad about The List. But then he'll ask why I need The List, or act like The List isn't important, and either way I know he just isn't going to understand, bless his butter-eating male heart. A moose head looks down from the fireplace, sternly rebuking me for the lie I'm about to tell. "No. I didn't find anything interesting, except for a dress I'd like to keep."

"Done. Now. Let's inventory. Mom's antiques are going to bring in the bulk of the cash, but I want to hold on to those and make sure she really wants to sell. Dad's old tool set is a collector's year. I'll have to check its condition, but I know a guy up in Fresno who specializes in vintage tools..."

So my dad. He's technically a real-estate agent, but I think he's only still in that gig so he can have something to put on his business cards. What he really does is buy and sell crap, but "crap dealer" doesn't look great on a card, unless you add an *s* to *crap* and work at a casino in Reno.

Actually, that's where we used to live, until three years ago, when Lady Luck turned on the economy. After working on too many foreclosures and short sells, Dad quit "the most depressing job on earth," and we moved to Southern California for a fresh start. Now we rent a tract home for practically free from my rich uncle Rodney, who owns more homes than most people own shoes.

In Orange, with the large metropolitan area and a healthy antiques industry, Dad can finally go for his dream. Garage sales, antiques malls, estate sales, abandoned storage units—he picks through all of it. As a result, he always has this musty smell about him, aged books and polished wood. Add in his shaggy hair, the sleeve of tattoos on his right arm, his wiry frame, and his collection of old neckties, and my dad is quite possibly the most lovable person I've ever known.

"Hey, Dad?" I interrupt. "As much as I love me some talk about old radiators, do you think I can have more than that dress?"

"You're not giving me a hard time about the train set because you want it, are you?"

"Of course not. I'm . . . I'm really interested in the early sixties right now. I'd like more clothes from then . . . more accessories?"

Dad points at me. "Is this your new phase? Because early sixties vintage is expensive. Yes, it's classic, and I'd rather my daughter dress in knee-length skirts than what most of your friends are wearing, but I can get a lot of money for those clothes."

"It's not like I'm asking you to take me to Rodeo Drive. I just want some old clothes."

"Highly sought after *vintage* clothes."

"And, maybe, I don't know ... pictures? Of Grandma?" I'd started to consider how I was going to research without the Internet. Our library would have plenty, but better to connect with more personalized information, more of Grandma's small-town, big dreams. "And any, um, keepsake things she left from when she was my age? Like journals or yearbooks?"

"Oh, Mal." Dad puts down his fork and reaches across the table. "This is hard on you, isn't it? Don't worry. Mom's going to be happier at Sunshine Villa. It's very state-of-the-art ... tennis and golfing and a spa and lots of activities. That house has been haunting her ever since Dad died, and she's just getting a fresh start, not giving up, okay?"

I blink at my dad. I haven't been worried about Grandma Vivian—I haven't even worried about Dad. Five-hundred-dollar train set or not, this isn't easy for him. And here I am asking for all of my grandma's memories, just so I can be a little more authentic. I'm not thinking straight, or maybe I'm thinking too straight and not considering anyone else. That's what pain will do to a person.

Pain. Why did it feel so big? Is Jeremy hurting? I hope he is. I hope he's writhing. I bet it would hurt less to know he felt even an ounce of this. I look down at my wedge, and notice the head of lettuce looks like Jeremy's head, that the bits of bacon could easily be his eyes, the tomatoes his mouth, and—

"Honey, why are you attacking that salad?"

I set my fork down. "I'm fine. I'm fine. I'm—"

"Fine. You mentioned that." He folds his napkin in his lap for the fourth time. His lap is fully protected from crumbs or spills. As for me, I'm pretty sure half the blue cheese is on my sleeve. "Anything you want, you got it. I found a small bin of old pictures from when she was young. I'm sure she won't mind if you bring it home—"

"Yeah?" I'd thought I'd have to wait, have to pillage through her boxes next time. Now there is a bin back at that house that might have a small answer, a clue how to find my vintage self. "We can bring it back later. I'm just . . . I want to connect with her maybe? You know?"

He smiles, kind gray eyes crinkling. "Makes sense to me."

It would make sense. If that were the truth.

We get home late Saturday night, and it isn't until I've had all of Sunday morning to methodically erase Jeremy from my bedroom that I feel prepared to look through Grandma's stuff. Part of my detox involved bending all the bendiness right out of that smug little purple paper clip, but of course it pokes my hangnail, and now I have a mutilated thumbnail *and* a cheating boyfriend.

I suck on my thumb as I open the bin and lay Grandma's life across my floor, from baby to adolescence. It's so different now—I could fill this room with all the pictures Mom takes of Ginnie and me at every mundane moment of our life, even if most of those pictures never get printed off her computer. All I have of Grandma's teen years fits in this box.

My favorite picture is of Grandma at sixteen in the seer-sucker dress, the sun behind her, face splattered with freckles and exploding in a grin. This picture hung in her hallway gallery, and as a child I wondered when Grandma stopped looking like that girl and became the wrinkled but elegant woman I've always known. I stick this picture on my desk with no intention of giving it back.

Beyond the framed pictures are childhood gifts from my dad and uncle, a shoe box of loose photos, and the mother lode. Her yearbook from junior year—1962–1963. I run my hand over the silver embossing. Grandma went to Tulare Union High School in a central California farm town that smells like manure but is that wholesome kind of place where you know the names of the butcher and the baker and the guy sitting on his porch across the street. I mean, I only visited Tulare once when I was six, but that's how I remember it.

I close my eyes, imagining what I'll find inside the yearbook pages. Pictures of Grandma at dances and pep club meetings. Pep club is the list item most foreign to me. What do they do at meetings, practice peppiness? Do they compete with other schools, try to out-pep each other? Before I can solve these mysteries, someone tries to twist the handle of my door.

"What?" I yell.

"I have an offering." Ginnie's voice is muffled through the door.

"You alone?"

"No. Eduardo is with me. He's the offering."

I unlock the door and Ginnie holds out a bowl of milk toast. Milk toast is the most perfect breakup comfort food ever, and since it's Sunday, my "diet" allows it. You line a bowl with pats of butter. Add about five slices of buttered toast. Add warm, almost-boiling buttered milk and two poached eggs. Oh, and then add more butter. My dad's recipe, of course.

"This is better than Eduardo," I say.

I sit down at my white desk Mom bought at a Pottery Barn outlet. Ginnie paces back and forth, watching Grandma's childhood follow her forward and in reverse. "Were you playing the song 'Survivor' earlier?"

"I was deleting Jeremy." I wipe some butter off my chin. "I needed motivation. But no more iPod, not when we start The List tomorrow."

Ginnie sits on the rug, folding her legs underneath her. "*We*?"

"Beyoncé still had Destiny's Child when she sang 'Survivor.'"

Ginnie laughs. "Fine. Fine. I'll do your stupid list. But I'm not giving up technology too. I can't do my homework without music. And I order my moisturizer online. And—"

I tap my bowl with my spoon. "Okay! I'll go one hundred percent 1962, and you can just be the vintage sidekick."

"I play center forward. I'm never a sidekick."

I groan.

"Sorry. Soccer humor." She picks up a picture of Grandma in college at an antiwar protest. Grandma's waist-length hair is as wild and defiant as the scowl on her face. I don't like this one as much as the seersucker picture, don't like the obvious absence of a bra underneath Grandma's T-shirt. Plus, who *yells* for peace? "What do you want me to do on the list? The dinner party one? Can we do organic?"

"This is 1962 we're talking about. A can of green beans was considered organic," I say.

"We'll have to try out some recipes first," Ginnie says. "Maybe I'll make some family dinners."

"Whatever you want." My sister is helping me! I am not alone in my list mania, which is especially vital because there is one item I cannot do alone. "You can invite your steady over too."

"That item is stupid. No one has 'found a steady' in forty years."

"If it's on the list, we have to do it. And I've already been there, done that, got that I WAS TOOLED BY JEREMY MCTOOLER-SON T-shirt. And look what good came of it," I say.

Okay, *some* good came of it. Maybe sometimes Jeremy thought of me instead of BubbleYum when certain songs came on. Like all the songs he put on my iPod. And the song we first danced to. And the music we sang in the car, when we were driving home with the windows down and it was just us. We couldn't really hear the melody over the wind, just our own voices shrieking in out-of-tune ecstasy. I had to believe those moments were real, that they were mine.

But hey. I had The List, so I wasn't giving Jeremy much thought anyway. Only thirty-eight minutes of every hour.

Forty-seven, tops.

Ginnie squints up at me, chewing her lip. "You really need to do this? I mean, I know I give you a hard time, but how are you feeling?"

"Like I don't know who I am and I've lost all hope in humanity. You know. Same old."

"Seriously, Mallory. I get it. This Jeremy stuff, how it all went down... it's a big deal."

It is a big deal. I know there are worse things happening in the world. I recognize how good I have it. After all, I'm sitting in my cozy home eating warm milk toast. But knowing something is different from feeling it, and right now, losing Jeremy, especially in the shocking, incomplete way I have, feels like it will never stop hurting, that this new pain is as much a part of me as my arms.

I'm still so numb I haven't even cried.

"I'm going to have to see him at school tomorrow," I whisper.

Ginnie crosses the room on her knees and hugs my lap. "See him, but you don't have to talk to him."

"He's going to want an explanation," I say.

"An explanation? *You* don't owe *him* anything. If you don't want to talk to him, don't. If you want to yell at him, do. If you want to slash his tires—"

"Ginnie."

"I was going to say don't. Or do. Whatever helps." She perches her chin on my legs and looks up at me from underneath thick lashes. "And since you obviously haven't gone completely vintage yet, I think you need a farewell marathon. So what'll it be? British chick flick or vulgar comedies?"

I smile. "Vulgar, please."

She shakes her head. "I hope you don't think once we go vintage that I'm watching some stupid show like *Bewitched*."

Chapter 5

The things a random passerby at Orange Park High thinks of a teenage girl who supposedly hacked into her boyfriend's Friendspace account, proclaimed him a tool, and abandoned all technology, thus allowing an entire weekend of Internet rumors to breed:

1. *Insert any and all derogatory words used toward women, including creative combinations thereof.*
2. How long do I need to wait until I can hit on her ex?
3. How long do I need to wait until I can hit on her?

4. I would delete my account.
5. I would move.
6. Why is she wearing that remarkably chic seersucker dress with bobby socks to school? What does she think this is, 1962?

Or maybe it's not so bad. If my classmates think anything when they see me, it's a fleeting thought. I'm not that high up on the People to Care About scale at this school. And they all have their own lives and own worries and own insecurities. Granted, there might be major Mallory drama brewing on Friendspace, but I feel so fabulous in Grandma's dress, I soldier on with my chin high. I also have the scavenged turquoise ring on a chain tucked under my dress, over my heart. I've decided to keep it, just for a while, so I can have something tangible to connect me to Grandma's teenage spirit.

Clearly, it was not Grandma's intent when writing her list to alter the course of her future granddaughter's life. The List might have been her creation, but this is my experiment. Here's my hypothesis: life—social life, at least—was simpler and easier in 1962. I want to see what kind of girl I am without technological crutches. It might take me a while to find the answer to that question, because I don't have much of a battle plan. For day one, I set out to:

1. Wear the seersucker dress.

2. Abandon the twenty-first century.

3. Avoid Jeremy.

I manage one out of three. Jeremy is waiting for me outside first period.

The worst part is not how cute he looks in his black V-neck (which, okay, is slightly plunging), or the curious looks everyone gives as they walk by. Or the fact that the navy seersucker dress, although fabulous, is living up to the sucker part and doesn't give me enough room to gulp in much-needed air. No, the *worst* part is that my stomach does that flutter, an unintentional that's-the-boy-I-love butterfly jump. The feeling I always get when I see him, like my stomach has no idea that BubbleYum even exists. And neither does my heart.

His expression clouds over when he sees me. "Mallory." His voice is hard. "I've called you *thirteen* times."

I'd planned to not talk to him, like, ever. Not the most realistic plan, but a hopeful one. I've learned over the past weekend that I don't know Jeremy as well as I thought, but one thing I do know is that Jeremy's persistent. If this doesn't happen now, he'll be outside my next class, and my next. I breathe out, the crisp dress constricting my ribs. "I haven't checked my phone."

"You check your phone every three minutes."

"No, I don't. I mean, not anymore. My cell phone is gone."

I push past Jeremy and make it to my desk. We only have two periods together this year, which was distressing a few weeks ago, but a blessing now. I can get through two periods a day, until he stops talking to me, maybe even stops talking *about* me. Eventually, he'll be that one boy in my class. That one boy who was also my first love. That one boy who made me feel like an idiot. That one boy who . . . is wearing Hollister cologne.

Jeremy sits down in the seat in front of me, even though that's Bradley Pittmore's seat. Bradley hates when Jeremy sits there before the bell rings. Right now, Bradley is talking to Mrs. Yee, but his eyes bug out when he sees his occupied seat. Jeremy leans into me, like we're still together, like he didn't say all those things to BubbleYum, like we're discussing our plans for the afternoon and not like we just broke up, albeit unofficially. "What happened to it?"

"What? My phone?" I avoid Jeremy's gaze, instead focusing on Bradley, who needs to get over here and kick Jeremy out of his seat. "Nothing, I just don't use it anymore."

"Well, what about my e-mails?"

"I'm not online anymore. I'm going... I'm taking a break from all of that."

"'All of that'? You mean communication with everyone, or just communication with me?"

Intoxicating cologne is an unfair battle strategy. "Both."

Finally, Bradley crosses the room and taps Jeremy on the shoulder. "I hate when you sit in my seat."

Jeremy lowers his voice, and when he speaks at this softer level, he's tender and husky. It's a voice just for me, the voice that always does me in. "Mallory, it's not what you think."

Wouldn't it be wonderful if he was right? Wouldn't that be magical if there really was some justifiable reason to have 353 e-mails from another girl? Or maybe someone had hacked into his Friendspace account and invented the whole site? "What *do* I think?"

"That's what I want to know."

I swallow. "That you're cheating on me with an online cyber-wife."

"Cheating?" Jeremy's thick eyebrows arch in surprise. "It's just a game!"

"And this is just my life. My *real* life."

"So what? You're flaking, just like that?" He slaps his hand on the desk. "Figures."

I don't have the energy to point out that *he* is the one who flaked on *me*. That this is *his* doing, that my emotions are completely valid, that 353 e-mails filled with romantic song lyrics makes him the mayor of Cheatsville. I wish with everything that I respond with conviction, but the bold statement comes out with a question mark at the end. "I need a break from you?"

"Dude, talk to your girlfriend after class." Bradley jabs at Jeremy harder.

Jeremy stands, never breaking eye contact with me. "It's cool, Bradley. I don't think she's my girlfriend anymore anyway."

I spend the rest of the period looking away from my officially ex-boyfriend and brainstorming ways to accomplish The List. If every day is going to be like this, then Jeremy's Hollister cologne is going to Do. Me. In.

Fourth period isn't as hard, because Jeremy doesn't try to talk to me again. Okay, so maybe this makes things harder. I can't decide. Most likely, I've hit the terminal velocity of hardness. The stares from my classmates continue. I brainstorm more

heinous things that could happen in life than a cheating boy-friend. The list, really, only depresses me. And the stares...
why are you staring?

Mr. Hanover tells us that we're working on our virtual industries today and to go log on to our computers with our partner. The problem here is twofold because:

1. Jeremy is my partner.
2. I've sworn off the Internet.

And of course everyone knows Jeremy and I are computer partners, so now there are dozens of eyes on me as I raise my hand. "Mr. Hanover? Can I speak with you for a minute?"

"What is it, Mallory?"

I do not give anyone the satisfaction of making eye contact right now, most of all Jeremy. "Um, it's private."

Mr. Hanover looks at the door, then back at me, probably wondering if discussing anything in "private" can get him into trouble. "Okay, class, get on your computers. Mallory, outside."

We step into the hallway, door open. Everyone thinks I'm telling Mr. Hanover that I need a new partner, but it's worse than that.

"I can't do this assignment."

Mr. Hanover scratches his peppered beard. I probably shouldn't have used the word *can't*. Mr. Hanover is all about having a can-do attitude. "Are you feeling ill?"

"No, it's just...I can't use the Internet. I mean, I *can* use the Internet, but I've made a choice not to."

"Is this some new homework cop-out?" Mr. Hanover glances back into the classroom. The buzz inside is quiet—everyone is already online working on their Industrial Revolution projects. We had to choose an industry like steel or cotton and build a mill and hire workers, all virtually. Jeremy, big surprise, is already the tycoon of the project—we have the cleanest working conditions and greatest growth. I wonder if he's duplicated BubbleYum in our project. She's probably his secretary. "I don't think you even have much more work to do on it. Your partner has been so dedicated."

"No. I just . . . I can't do this assignment. At all."

"Do you need a new computer?" I look of realization spreads across Mr. Hanover's wrinkled face. "Ah, or a new partner?"

"No, it's not about my partner. Bottom line is I am morally opposed to using the Internet in any capacity. It's a deep personal belief, and I would like an alternative assignment." I swallow. "Please."

"I don't think that's enough of a reason to let you out of this." Mr. Hanover is quiet but firm. It's a big deal that we got these computers. Mr. Hanover had to apply for a million grants and change his whole curriculum after years of teaching to fit in the technology-heavy unit. And I *so* wanted to take this class—the entire junior class did—and not just because of the projects. Mr. Hanover is interesting, funny, and fair. He's that teacher who will have a book dedicated to him someday by a former student. "You knew when you signed up for the class that most of this unit involves the Internet."

I feel close to tears. When I made my oath, I didn't think about schoolwork or other justified reasons to use technology. I don't think NASA should pull every satellite out of the sky that's monitoring... whatever the satellites monitor. This isn't a crusade for everyone, just my personal battle. "Can I write a report instead, or make a stick model of our mill or ... oh! Trains were big then, I can bring in a train set my dad just found and, uh, tweak it to fit the right century."

"If I give you an alternative assignment," Mr. Hanover says calmly, "where are you going to get your research?"

"Books. Remember, those things we used before Wiki-pedia?"

"Mallory—"

"It's history, not computer science. I'm being historical. And I promise you, Mr. Hanover, there is a really noble and sane reason why I can't do this."

There's laughter and yelling in the class. Mr. Hanover pops his head in and with one frown the class quiets. He cuts me a hesitant glance. "Fine. We'll keep it simple. Write a paper on how the Industrial Revolution shaped modern society. Four pages—"

"Four?"

"Five." Mr. Hanover barks a laugh. "I'm giving you a break. Take it and be grateful."

I think of Jeremy. I can't take a whole semester of sniffing his delicious sniffiness. "Sorry. I *am* grateful. Thank you."

"I want that typed, of course. Is it just the Internet that offends you, or are word processors also off-limits?"

Oh. I don't know. They didn't have word processors then, but I don't have a typewriter. Can I fudge on this point? Write it out and make Ginnie type it for me? "Um, I'll type it. Somehow."

"It'll be due next week, when everyone presents their virtual industries. And you can turn in a note tomorrow from your parents or doctor or church leader or some legitimate authority figure explaining why you've gone medieval. Got that?"

Good thing Ginnie is a champion forger. "Got it."

He pushes up his shirtsleeve. The gray fuzz on his arms looks like a sweater of hair. "You do know that people literally gave their lives back then for advancements in transportation and technology."

Exactly. They were so busy working on the railroad all the livelong day that those early-nineteenth-century folk did not have time for computer indiscretions. *That's* a lesson learned.

Jeremy and I always sat together at lunch. Not by ourselves—we kind of worked our way around the different tables and benches, but always together, especially this school year. Junior year was to be Our Year of the Couple. I'd mentally dubbed it as such when Jeremy told me he loved me in July. He even cried when he said it. *Cried.*

I can sit most anywhere and be fine. Relatively fine. There *is* the dilemma of trying to find something 1962-ish to eat from a menu filled with Papa John's pizza and vending machines. I finally give up and grab an apple, not overly hungry.

I survey the quad, considering the large trees, circular tables, and rows of bleachers facing the outdoor theater. If I really wanted to avoid people, I could head inside to the actual cafeteria, since no one eats in there, not in sunny California. Well, no one *worth* sitting by.

There aren't Imperial cliques at our school, not like you see in old teen movies with jocks and nerds and cheerleaders. I mean, we have all those, but most people aren't just that one thing, so all the groups bleed into one another. You can be an A student (The Stars) who also does drugs (Burnies, which, if you include dabblers, is almost half the school) and plays the harp (Unusual Instrumentalists—ha, just made that one up). I guess the exception would be the handball courts on the east side of the cafeteria where lots of Hispanics hang. Jeremy always called that Little Tijuana, which I never liked, but he also called the Asian table Chinatown and he *is* Asian and we always sat there, so maybe that makes it okay? Maybe not.

So, lunch. The dominant identifier—whether that be a talent or religion or family income—usually decides table selection, which is why I spot Jeremy sitting with The Kids With Nice Cars, a group we didn't usually visit, since Dad's 1994 Ford Escort I occasionally get to drive would not suffice.

"I heard about the breakup. How's it going?" My friend Paige Santos is next to me, a turkey sandwich in one hand, a Coke Zero in the other, and a severe look of concern on her face.

"Fine." I'm still staring at Jeremy. He's laughing at something his cousin Oliver said. He never laughs like that with Oliver; he never even *sits* with Oliver. Oliver drives a fricking Nissan that's older than he is, so he's breaking the social-class table rules anyway. Jeremy thinks his cousin tries too hard to be indie and quixotic, not that Jeremy would ever use the word *quixotic*, and . . . what do I care? The thing that really bothers me is that Jeremy can laugh at all right now, that he can even so much as fake a smile after what he did to me.

How can I hate someone and still love him at the same time?

"Your dress is adorable," Paige says. "Did you get it at the Circle?"

Orange Circle is the old town shopping area, sort of a Main Street USA that's been frozen in time. My dad has a small booth in one of the antiques malls. All the hipsters shop in the vintage stores, but it's expensive, so I usually pray for a find at Goodwill. "It's my grandmother's."

"Wow, that's even better." Paige tugs at the sleeve. "Good for you for looking so put together after being dumped."

I shoot her a look. "Don't believe everything you read on Friendspace. I didn't get dumped."

"Then what happened? I texted you and tried calling."

"I got rid of my phone."

Paige recoils, her long black hair swishing behind her shoulders. "Got *rid* of it? Did your parents take it away? I was over my text limit once and my father—"

"No. It was, uh, voluntarily retired. I'm simplifying my life by giving up modern technology—"

"What?"

"—and trying to live more like teens did fifty years ago, when communication was more, uh, communicative," I say.

"So, this is a sort of social experiment then?" Paige bites at a hangnail, calculating. Paige is more interested in high school hierarchy than anyone I know—last year she had a slumber party with a purposefully random group of girls, hoping it would be all Kumbaya, we understand each other now. What resulted was an awkward night of ranch dip and half-sipped sodas that ended around nine. Experiment = failed. "So it's a commentary on technology's hindrance of interpersonal inter-action? That's brilliant."

"When you say it like that, sure." Telling this to someone besides Ginnie, even someone like Paige, who I know I can trust, makes me a little self-aware and unsure. "But this might be the stupidest thing I've ever done. It's not really planned out. I'm winging it."

"Can I interview you?" Paige's thinking wrinkle between her eyes deepens. "I need to write an opinion piece for the school newspaper, and a debate on the pros and cons of social networking could be award winning."

"No." Leave it to Paige to create a silver lining to my little crisis that also conveniently pads her college application résumé. "Just do a screenshot of Jeremy's Friendspace page. That says plenty."

Paige touches my shoulder. "I'm sorry. I can be callous when I'm excited. Tell me what happened with Jeremy. After the rumors I've heard, I need a first-person account."

The problem with the breakup is I look stupid no matter what. If word gets out about BubbleYum, it'll look like I wasn't enough for Jeremy, which might actually be the sad truth, but no one else needs to know that. If I stay quiet, the rumors will keep eroding my reputation. My reputation that really only exists because of Jeremy.

Although we left Reno when I was in middle school, we stayed in an apartment in Anaheim first, so we didn't move to our house in Orange until the beginning of sophomore year. After only a month at Orange Park High School, I met Jeremy. My life here is wrapped all around him, and now, thirteen months later, I am still the new girl. No other title or description besides Jeremy's girlfriend ever really stuck to me. He was the one thing I ever fully committed to. With that banner stripped, now I'm … just the girl who won't answer your texts. Legend.

I'm suddenly tired and need to sit. I ignore Paige's question and plop down at her table, the meeting place of many of The Stars, that overachieving subgroup combating for the opportunity to pretend to read a book in the "Most Likely to Succeed" yearbook photo. I'm bright enough to be in their presence, but not so exceptional or talented that they see me as a threat. That's the trick with floating—being enough, but not too much. Today, especially, I appreciate my mediocrity, and that I can crunch my apple in peace.

Speaking of peace, Paige is already talking to the group about the Peace Corps, and since I'm pretty sure that was around in the sixties, I listen. Her eyebrows are knit in calculated concern as she brainstorms ways to raise funds for a primary school library in Malawi.

I should note how dim The Stars can unintentionally make me feel. If I had my phone right now, I would figure out where Malawi is.

"We should all join the Peace Corps together, after college," Paige says. "The summer before grad school."

"Screw grad school," I mutter.

"You mean you'd rather go *before* college?" Paige asks. "But what about early enrollment and internships or—"

"Oh, no. I wouldn't do the Peace Corps, period," I say. "Too much khaki."

"They have Peace Corps units all around the world," Peter Unger says. "You can find a khaki-free assignment."

I'm in a mood. They could propose any cause or educational goal and I would be crusty about it. Just because the Peace Corps was around in 1962 doesn't mean I have to join, right? I only gave up my cell phone yesterday. Baby steps. "I just meant, you know, screw grad school. Higher education is high enough for me."

Yvonne Garcia pats my hand. "Sure. Some people just aren't into grad school."

She says *some people* like I've just doomed myself to a career sorting doughnuts on an assembly line, which is funny because although Yvonne gets straight As, she is one of the densest girls I know.

Another one of my friends, Cardin Frampton, shouts my name across the quad.

I cringe. Cardin is a girl who can't help but draw attention to herself. And I don't need that coming my way.

"Mallory!" She maneuvers around one of the stone benches, all donated from previous classes. The boys at our table go quiet as she bounces over, no doubt imagining her advancing in slow motion, possibly in a bathing suit. "Dude. I texted you until my thumbs got numb, but I heard nothing back."

"I know," I say.

"Are you going to give me details or what?"

"Yeah."

Cardin squeezes into the seat next to me and bends low until our foreheads are touching. Peter Unger's mouth is open, and I'm pretty sure he's panting. "Okay," she says. "Spill."

"Later. We're talking about the Peace Corps." I wave my hand toward the group. "It's a really heated discussion."

Cardin seems to notice everyone else for the first time. "Oh, hey, guys. Peter, I like that shirt on you."

"Thanks!" Peter pipes. He's little and his voice is high, so he's been cursed with the nickname The Pied Piper since before I lived here. "Er, we don't have to talk about Peace Corps anymore. Maybe Mallory can dispel this Jeremy Mui rumor I heard. Did you really drop his computer in the toilet because he changed his security password on you?"

My heart sinks. Give it up to The Stars for fitting gossip into their academic schedules. Can't a girl just enjoy her apple in peace? Corps? "No. He changed his Internet home page. Jerk."

They laugh, nervously, like they're pretty sure I'm kidding, but only pretty. Given how dependent they are on their phones and spreadsheets and e-readers, word of my vintage crusade would be more blasphemous than my grad school jab.

Cardin squeezes my hand. "I'm sure, whatever happened, it was tough for you."

"Right, and"—Paige speaks slowly and pointedly—"*we* don't need to talk about it right now."

I love you, Paige. And Cardin, even if she's the one who sparked this line of questioning.

This time, Yvonne pats my elbow. "Just know we don't believe all the rumors. I mean, who would really hack into someone's Friendspace account? That's evil. Unless there was something"—she goes from patting my elbow to rubbing it in slow circles—"interesting on there?"

"Just our amateur sex videos." I pull my arm away. Who decided that elbow touching is sympathetic?

Yvonne gasps, then giggles. "You're joking, right?"

"Of course she is." Paige smacks Yvonne's arm. "How are you in the running for valedictorian, anyway?"

Cardin hops up. "I don't care what happened. Jeremy *is* a tool, and you deserve to be happy. Will you please text me later?"

"Um." I can't say anything about going vintage in front of this group. "Sure."

"I need a Diet Coke before the bell rings. Bye, girlie!"

"Bye!" Peter pipes. There's a pause in the conversation as Cardin exits, which is just as enjoyable for the boys to watch as her entrance. Then every Star turns their laser focus on me. I feel like I'm an exam that they're all trying to ace. I miss silence. Jeremy used to wolf his food down so fast that he designated the first five minutes of the meal as quiet time. Wait. I guess he still does eat fast. I'm just not there to witness it.

I stand and toss my apple into the trash. All these snarky lines are in my mouth, ready to be spewed. But I'm also mad at myself for getting mad at The Stars. At least they came to the source; that's a lot better than I can say for others. And curiosity isn't malice—I mean, it *is* a good story. It gets better every time I hear it. By the time I finish The List, I'm sure the whole school will think I left Jeremy for a web-footed troll. With mind-reading skills. And magical kneecaps.

The List. That's what I should worry about, not rumors or an attractive ex-boyfriend sitting across the quad, chugging an energy drink, not that I'm noticing. I need to stay busy, stay focused, and prove to my sister (and myself) that I really can go vintage.

I should be thinking about pep club. And if this school is ever going to get a pep club together, I will need the power and connection of The Stars.

"So. Subject change." I stick both my hands on the table with what I hope is presence. "I know you all are the people to come to about this. I have an idea on how to increase community togetherness."

"I thought you weren't interested in the Peace Corps," Peter says.

"I'm not. What brings a community together is organized pep. We need a pep club."

"Pep club?" Paige balks. "That's so ... archaic."

I point at her. "Exactly. Think of it as a sociological experiment."

"Touché," Paige says.

"So, uh, how do I start one?" I ask.

"You want to *start* a pep club," Peter repeats.

For being the smart kids, these folks are a little slow on the draw. "Well, I'd join one if we had one, but we don't."

"But there's key club," Yvonne says. "And honor society and ASB and spirit week and—"

"ASB is just glorified student council. Not enough pep," I say.

Peter leans back in his chair. "Ask Oliver—he's in ASB. He'll know. Hey, Oliver!" Peter hollers across the quad. Several tables look over. Including the table where Oliver is sitting. Including the table where *Jeremy* is sitting. "Come over here. Mallory has a question!"

What I should do is have the brain trust get their heads together and invent a bench that can swallow me whole. Oliver brushes past the other tables. The rest of the quad has lost interest, and I am extremely intent on Paige's folder—plain old red two-pocket, figures—but I know Jeremy is staring now, because I know what his stare feels like on me.

"Yeah?" Oliver asks Peter.

"Mallory wants to know how to start a club," Peter says. "Do you know?"

I sneak a quick look at Oliver. He's looking back at his table with a bored expression, like this visit is a complete waste of his time. "Not really. But it's in the student handbook."

"Great, I'll look in the student handbook." I speak to Paige's folder, which is far more friendly than Jeremy's cousin. I wonder what crap Jeremy told him about me. No, I don't. Because I don't care. Oliver doesn't know me. Let him stand there all bored and judgy.

Oliver sticks his hand on top of Paige's folder so I have to look up. His gaze is still indifferent, but it's direct. "If you're starting a club, you'll need to petition the ASB, mainly the student body president."

"Fine." Great, now he's decided to help me. Even if the bench can't swallow me, maybe I could be invisible. The whole table is watching us. Are they connecting that Oliver is Jeremy's cousin too? Do they think I'm making up a stupid club just because I broke up with my boyfriend?

Okay, that kind of *is* why I'm starting a club.

Oliver has his smartphone out. He's already looked up the student handbook. "Found it online. Do you want me to send you the link?"

"No, I'll . . . I'll just find it on the website." Or dig it out of ancient school scrolls.

"Are you playing ball tonight?" Peter butts in.

"Yeah, you coming?" Oliver asks.

"Regular or spandex?"

City basketball league. Oliver's team dresses up like the eighties rock band Mötley Crüe, complete with wigs and vintage high-top sneakers. I don't think they play to win, just for the spectacle, which I for one can appreciate. Jeremy won't play with them. He thinks it's embarrassing.

"I found some neon suspenders," Oliver says. "Of course I'm wearing spandex."

The table laughs and Oliver's about to walk away, but pauses and leans over my chair, so close I can feel his breath. "Let me know if you need more help with your club." He winks. "We're practically family, right?"

Seriously, right after our breakup? Is he heartlessly trying to tease me in front of my friends? The anger that I thought was tamed spurts out of my mouth. "Shut up," I whisper.

Oliver's expression goes from confident to confused. "Not like that, I meant . . . really, I can help you. Since you're Jeremy's girlfriend—"

I cut him off with a look of steel. Even though our voices are low, I know the rest of the table is listening. I might not have had the inclination to punch Jeremy earlier, but Oliver is another story. "You're a jerk, Oliver. Just like your cousin."

I hope Friendspace blows up with that.

Chapter 6

Why Ginnie is so healthy:

1. She's an All-American athlete.
2. She watches too many documentaries, reads too many articles.
3. She fell in love with Grandma's garden and adopted her green thumb.
4. Biggest reason? I think she goes hard-core with the food education because I don't, because half of the time I care, but the other half I'm dunking Oreos. She goes all the way, I'm midline at best. And that aspect of our relationship can probably

be applied to every other detail in our lives.

Ginnie makes our family meat loaf that night from Grandma's old Betty Crocker cookbook. Let me rephrase that—Ginnie *tries* to make meat loaf from the Betty Crocker cookbook, but she uses brown rice instead of white and soy substitute instead of hamburger. It's chewy and grainy, but at least there's ketchup to cover up the flavor. And even if she went all granola on a classic comfort food, she tried. She's trying.

Mom is at book club, and Dad called to say he had to show a house, so Ginnie and I eat alone. She drums her fingers on the table. "I know I sound like an angry housewife, but I cook and slave and they can't even be home for dinner?"

"Mom says that all the time, that we never eat dinner as a family."

"Exactly. That's the problem." She brightens. "Hey, we should go take some to Grandma. Like a housewarming present. And we'll reminisce with that yearbook you found, and it will be like a Hallmark card."

"Dad said she didn't want anyone to come visit until she was settled."

"And what's more settling than meat loaf?" Ginnie asks.

She has a point. Too bad there is no actual *meat* in our dinner.

I change out of Grandma's dress on the off chance she wants it back.

Thirty minutes later, we are at the front desk of Sunshine Villa Senior Lifestyle Community, the five-star jewel of geezer joints that looks out over Newport Bay. The brochure boasts tennis courts, swimming, horse stables, a theater for community plays, a garden, and fully furnished condominiums. Grandma and Grandpa had always done well, but this place? This place was cashing it up. I wonder if Uncle Rodney financially helped this dream come true.

Ginnie sets the disposable Tupperware tower on top of the granite desk, right next to the fresh floral arrangement. I once went to an assisted-living home with Jeremy and his church youth group, and it smelled of decay and loneliness. This air here is scented by a peaches-and-cream candle, with soft music playing in the background, some older but not ancient men watching football on the flat-screen. Seriously, I want to move here. That's vintage, right?

"Hi, what room is Vivian Bradshaw in?" Ginnie asks.

"We don't give out that information without consent from the resident."

"We're her granddaughters." I slide Grandma's yearbook onto the counter, the aged leather out of place in this glossy palace.

The woman types something on her computer. "She doesn't have a list of approved guests on file."

"Oh, she just moved here," Ginnie says. "So she probably hasn't done one yet."

"She has to fill out the information to move here. She's done it." The woman smiles apologetically. "I'll try calling her room. Please hold."

Ginnie drums her fingers on the counter while the woman calls. "No answer. She could still be somewhere in the community, though."

"Well, can you just tell us where she lives so we can drop this food off?"

"You can try calling her, but I can't release her address."

Ginnie whips out her phone. "It's dead. Do you know Grandma's number?"

"It's in my phone." I pat my pocket, and at the same moment Ginnie and I remember that my phone is at home, along with all the other technology I can't use. She doesn't say anything, just grabs the tower of leftovers and storms to the door.

I hurry after Ginnie, past the fake lamplight road. "Hey! It's not my fault!" I yell.

"Forget it," she says. "You not having a phone isn't as annoying as our grandma banning us from her home."

"She's not." I hug Grandma's yearbook close to my chest as I scuttle down the pathway. "Banning us. Like Dad said . . . she just needed . . . some time to . . . adjust."

Ginnie waits for me to catch up to her. She's already taller than me, and one of the best soccer players in the state, so occasionally she forgets that some people, *normal* people, get winded when they eat a bunch of fake meat loaf, then have to race across a vast retirement community. The light from the nearby tennis courts casts a shadow across her face. "I just think it'd be good for our family if we were together more. Mom and Dad especially."

She's being dramatic. One missed soy-loaf dinner doesn't a

family break. "That's why we are returning to simpler times." I take long, slow breaths. "Back when families *mattered*."

"You sound like an ad for a hard-core conservative group."

"Thank you."

"Forty love!" one of the players on the court calls out. Ginnie and I turn to watch through the green mesh. The server lobs a ball over the net. The other player holds up her racket, almost in self-defense. The ball bounces right past. "Sorry, Linda! I'll get in next time."

"Grandma?" Ginnie whispers.

"If you could hit *one* ball back, I'd be happy! Try this." Linda swings her racket all the way through.

"Grandma!" Ginnie waves her arms. "Hey, Grandma! We brought meat loaf!"

"We brought meat loaf?" I ask. "That's how you get her attention?"

"Shut up."

Grandma jogs over and peers through the fence. She's in classic tennis white, with a skirt that shows off her thick, athletic legs. A ridiculous sweatband makes her short blond curls stick up higher than usual. "Girls? What are you doing? Here, let me finish this match and I'll come talk."

"Don't bother." Linda swats Grandma lightly with her racket. "Being as you have yet to score, I think it's a safe bet that I was going to win."

Grandma shoots Linda a look. "Rematch. Just as soon as I take a lesson."

"Lesson, Vivian? *Lessons*. Many, many lessons." Linda laughs and strolls over to the watercooler.

"Lesson this." Grandma smacks her butt at Linda's back. Ginnie giggles. "Come on, girls. Since you're here, I'll show you the digs."

Grandma walks at a much easier pace, past the clubhouse and up to her seventh-floor condo. The living room feels like one of the model homes Dad shows—new furniture, bland art, neutral colors. Her office before was mustard yellow and purple with a rainbow of accents. Grandma *is* color, and all this beige just screams defeat. The only familiar item is the sewing machine set up on the kitchen table. She changes out of her tennis clothes and into a velvet jumpsuit with jewels on the front, clearly a gift from my mom. She makes herself a small plate of Ginnie's dinner and flops onto her microfiber sofa.

"So, you brought me meat loaf."

"Soy loaf."

"Soy. Even better." Grandma pats the couch. "To what do I owe this great honor?"

"Why weren't we on the list?" Ginnie demands. "Are you mad we came to visit?"

Grandma presses her lips together. "Not at all. I told your dad, I just wanted a chance to get moved in, but now I have and you're here and all is well."

Ginnie takes this and curls up next to Grandma. I'm not upset like my sister was about Grandma's recent changes. Her life, her business. Although I *was* there when Grandma talked to Dad about the packing and she couldn't have cared less what happened to her stuff.

I don't know. Maybe the family just feels like more stuff.

"Mallory found one of your high school yearbooks," Ginnie says. "We want to hear stories about the good old days."

I hold out the yearbook, which I'd been toting around like it is the bible of all things 1962. Grandma's eyes widen. "I haven't looked through this thing in ages."

She thumbs through the pages. I'm so glad I've waited until I'm with her to open this book, like we're entering the past together. The embossed cover says TULARE UNION HIGH, 1962 with a gold "redskin" raising a tomahawk that has long passed its PC threshold. Grandma flips right to the back and starts reading signatures. "'Nice Legs.' Bill Culver. That boy was bad news."

"Show us his picture," Ginnie says. "And how did he know about your legs?"

"I'm sure he wrote that in every girl's yearbook," Grandma says primly.

"I want to see what pages you're on first," I say.

Grandma turns to her junior picture. The girls all wear black dresses with pearls. Grandma's freckles pop out in the black-and-white picture. She's adorable, but her hideously high hair finally makes me understand the term *rat's nest*. It's a less flattering style than I've seen on sixties-era TV shows, and looks especially bad on Grandma's corkscrewed locks.

"What's with the hair?" Ginnie asks. "Mallory, I won't let you do that to yourself *or* the ozone."

"It's a bouffant," Grandma says. "That was the style. My mother would do it for me every other day. I grew it out after high school, wore it really long and wild." She flips to another page, this one with her wearing a red-and-gold sweater with the letter *P*. "Pep club. I ran for secretary, barely made it. That's our homecoming float."

On the adjoining page was a little trailer draped with crepe paper and balloons. The pep club girls, all wearing long skirts and sweaters, hold up a sign: SLAY THOSE KNIGHTS!

I run my finger over the glossed page. After I get a pep club, I'll need to do a float. And I'll need to sew a homecoming dress. Both tasks feel so impossibly far away, it makes me wish Grandma's list instead said "Buy a pet goldfish" or "Eat a large banana split."

Not that I'm thinking about quitting. This yearbook cements my resolve. That and Ginnie's nonstop smirking. "That float looks like it was *really hard* to make, Grandma," she says. "Pep club must be a club that takes *lots of time*."

"Oh, it was fun. We lost the float contest to 4-H club," Grandma says. "But I still think we had more spirit. Here's the dance..." One more turn and there's Grandma in a cloud-white dress. On her arm is a boy with black rimmed glasses, a slim suit, and a huge smile.

"I never knew you were homecoming queen," Ginnie says.

"I wasn't. I was the junior princess."

"Who is the boy?" I ask. "Did you know him?"

Grandma's lips tighten. "I did. He was my date."

"'Clyde Walters,'" Ginnie reads. "The glasses are dorky, but he was cute."

"He was your date?" I nudge Grandma. "Was he your steady?"

"Ooh!" Ginnie jabs at the poor boy's face. "A steady! Grandma had a *steady*!"

Grandma takes a long look at the picture. "Yeah, he was my steady. I wore his ring for almost a year. My first boyfriend, actually."

The ring on the chain around my neck had to be from him. I almost pull it out, ask Grandma if it was Clyde's, if she wants the little memento back to remember her first boyfriend. But I don't want to give it back, not when I have something so solid to connect me to her past. I'll return the ring after I finish The List. Fifty-some years, it's not like she'll miss it. "What happened to him?" I ask.

"Nothing. We dated. We broke up."

"Was it a bad breakup?" Ginnie asks.

Grandma rubs the back of her neck. "I don't know of many good breakups."

That's the truth.

"He left California after high school," she says. "I stayed here."

"Was it tragic?" Ginnie asks. I'm glad she's pushy. I would never ask, but I want to know.

"You could say that." Grandma pauses. "But I got over it eventually. We didn't have a grand romance, girls. I have much better stories about your grandpa. Now *he* was the real thing."

I try to create a flesh-and-blood reality from these black-and-white glimpses. What did Grandma's bedroom look like? What was her morning routine? What did she do with her friends after school? What were her fears, and what did she want to be when she grew up?

Because Grandma? She *lived* her life. She was a San Francisco hippie in the late sixties, met Grandpa at a Berkeley peace protest and married him in two weeks. After spending the seventies as an advocate for this and that—women's rights, the environment, literacy—she started her own non-profit organization for global children with life-threatening diseases. Grandpa quit his banking job to go back to law school and work for her organization. He liked to tease that she was the boss. And she was. For, like, a hundred people.

A few years ago, she won some California lifetime achievement award and the rest of us had to wear dresses and eat chewy chicken breast while they showed a documentary of her achievements. I remember looking across the table at my mom, who kept readjusting her dress and fiddling with her cell phone. My mom...she's very different from her mother-in-law.

But I remind myself now that Grandma wasn't any of those things when she was my age. She was just a girl with a little list and big dreams.

"Where's your senior yearbook?" I ask.

"Never got one." Grandma closes the book and pushes it

onto my lap. "That's enough of that. Mallory, you can stick that with the rest of my junk you cleaned out." She stands and heads toward the kitchen. "I think I'll have another helping. Ginnie, what'd you top this with?"

"It's just ketchup," I mumble.

The two of them go into a lengthy discussion on organic condiments and the evils of processed sugar. I feel like the heel end of a soy loaf that's been tossed under the table to the dog. As much as Ginnie is an asset to Total List Domination, I need Grandma all to myself if I'm really going to find whatever it is I'm looking for. When they start in on the health advantages of raw beets, I tug on Grandma's sleeve and say, "Sorry to interrupt, but, Grandma, I have to learn to sew."

"Um, okay. Is this . . . for some class?"

"Sort of."

"No it's not." Ginnie shakes her head. "It's because of the tool."

I shoot her a murderous look. She takes it with a scowl.

"And . . . are you asking me for help?" Grandma asks.

"Yes. I want to sew my own homecoming dress," I say. "And I was hoping you could teach me how."

Did I mention Grandma is also a master seamstress and does period costumes *just for fun*? She made Ginnie and me Easter dresses for the first ten years of our lives. Seriously, The Stars would die of jealousy if they ever saw this woman's résumé.

"I'd love to help." Grandma starts pawing through one of the boxes of patterns next to her machine. "I don't know what kind of fit you want, but there's a fashion website with patterns for Oscar rip-offs."

"Oh, that's the other thing," I say. "I'm, ah, kind of on a vintage kick right now."

Ginnie clears her throat. "I'll say."

I should have waited until she was in the bathroom to bring this up. She's overdosing on The Smug. "So I'd like to do a style from the early sixties? Like when you were in high school? That's, uh, why I wanted to look at your yearbook. For ideas."

"Really?" Grandma stops shuffling through the patterns and peers over her reading glasses. "You don't want something slinky? I bet Jeremy would appreciate a sexier style."

"Jeremy isn't—" Ginnie says.

"Into sexy. Um, obvious sexy," I say. Grandma doesn't need to know about Jeremy. You know, it'd be nice if someone in my life didn't know all my business, or think they know all my business, or know how messy my business really is. At least when I come to see Grandma, my life can be viewed as put together. "He'll be fine with vintage. We'll find an old pattern to use. But will you help? Please?"

Grandma crosses the room and gives me a hug, her jasmine perfume strong as ever. Even in this new space, with her boring furniture and painfully beige walls, at least she still smells like the old Grandma. "Of course. I'll fit you into my schedule." She laughs. "Right after tennis."

Tuesday is another school day of whispers and questioning glances, another lunch, this time spent with Ginnie on the theater bleachers. We discuss list battle strategies, which to Ginnie means recipes, and I point out boys who would make good boyfriends. She's so against the idea that I decide I'll have to go covert in my steady search. Drop a boy bomb on her when she isn't looking.

After school, I escape to my room so I can comb through a set of encyclopedias I found in the garage. They're twenty years old, so most of the information is outdated, but luckily history stays the same. I find *the sixties* in the *S* encyclopedia and skim through the stuff on hippies and Vietnam in hopes of getting a feel for the earlier, more innocent years of the decade. Like boy bands in slim ties and Jackie Kennedy wearing a pillbox hat. That's another thing wrong with this century—no one wears dressy hats anymore.

There's a knock on my door. "Mallory?" Mom calls. "Can we talk for a minute?"

I still have Grandma's row of pictures on the ground from Sunday. Rather then shove everything back into the bin, I lay a blanket over the mementos. I do not want my mom to see this as a reason to discuss Grandma and the next phase in her life. She'll try to make it this big moment, all sappy close-ups with one tear rolling down her cheek. My room/life is a mess right now, not something she can fix with some feigned empathy.

"Yeah?"

"Ginnie told me you and Jeremy broke up? I thought she

was joking, so I got on Friendspace and now I'm blocked from your account. What's going on?"

I tilt my forehead against the door. Ginnie blocked her. Good move. But I wish she hadn't told Mom about the breakup. I'm not ready for the inevitable mother-daughter bonding. "Ginnie told you. That's great."

"I'm hurt *you* didn't tell me," she says. "Are you okay?"

I unlock the door, only opening a crack. I swear I love my mom, but that doesn't mean I want to do this now. My mom has the ability to take the tiniest bit of drama, explode it into a catastrophe, then somehow make the problem all about her. She's got to be salivating over breakup news. Prime opportunity for a parental lecture.

"No, I'm not okay. But talking about it won't change that. And I have homework."

Mom's face is shadowed, her hair backlit by the hall light. There's a look of firm resolve on her face, never a good sign. "I'm not going to let you push me away. You're in a crisis, and I'm your mother. It's my job to help."

Her actual job is to get all up in my business, and she's a model employee when it comes to that.

"There's nothing to help with. What happened happened."

"You know what you need? A break. You need to go somewhere fun."

"I'm not in the mood for fun. I just want to sit in my room—"

"And mope. Which is why we're going to the happiest place on Earth instead."

"No!" I try to shut my door, but Mom's already wedged in her foot. There's no escaping her when she gets an agenda. I put my hands up in surrender. "Fine. I'll get my Mickey Mouse ears."

Chapter 7

The Bradshaw family's favorite Disneyland attractions:

1. Space Mountain: BEST RIDE IN THE PARK, especially at Halloween, when they haunt that beast.
2. Splash Mountain: except when Mom doesn't plan ahead and wears a white T-shirt. She gets soaked, guys ogle her chest, and she ends up buying a new T-shirt that she passes down to Ginnie or me even though:
   a. gift-shop shirts are expensive.
   b. the shirt is always stretched out.

3. The Tiki Juice Bar: Dole Whip sorbet treat. Healthy enough to justify because of the pineapple, delicious enough because of whatever makes it "whip."

4. The teacups: you don't have a soul if you hate the teacups.

5. It's a Small World: but only in the summer. It's the most air-conditioned ride in the park. Dad brings those little orange earplugs and we get a nice, cool fifteen-minute nap.

Another great thing about having a rich uncle Rodney who has lots of money but little time for family is that he gives us the same Christmas present every year: season passes to Disneyland. When we lived in Reno, our family made a yearly pilgrimage to my mother's mecca. Now that we're next door, we're here at least once a month. And yes, we all wear Disney shirts and pins and fanny packs and the whole bit. You can't have much style pride when it comes to The Mouse.

I wait until Ginnie and I are on the Jungle Cruise, rows away from my parents, before giving her a stern talking-to. "I can't believe you told Mom about Jeremy."

"It's been five days."

"We only broke up yesterday!"

"Officially. You should be thanking me for blocking her on Friendspace. She doesn't need to see how unfriendly a space it can be."

"Is it bad?"

"Posts on your page have trickled down, but you two are still big news." Ginnie chews on an organic granola bar. Her fanny pack is stuffed with healthy snacks. "There's probably a Save Jeremy fan page by now."

"Save him from what?"

"The evils of the world. Or you. Same same. Crocodile." She juts her chin in the direction of the menacing, robotic crocodile. We have a song listing all the animals we see, in order, on the Jungle Cruise.

"Bengal tiger," I add.

"Dancing cobra!" Ginnie sticks her hand out of the boat, gesturing excitedly. Two tourists in front of us snap a picture of the snake. Extra points when we prompt a photo moment.

I hate to say it, but Mom is right. You can't stay mad in Disneyland.

Ginnie sits back in her seat. "I can delete your site if you want."

That makes the most sense. Wipe the whole slate clean, like what I'd just done on my iPod. Except…except, I have over six hundred friends on there, and some of them—like Reno friends—I only ever really communicate with on Friendspace. And all those pictures—I don't think I've saved them anywhere else. And Ginnie and I have an ongoing Scrabble game through the site, and I can't just let her win after two months. Then we'd have to play in person, and I don't even know where Mom stores the board games.

Which I guess was the point of my social experiment, but

what if . . . the end of the world happened, and the only way to access information on how to avoid the end of the world was posted on Friendspace. Surely then, *then* I would make an exception. Best to have the site there, just in case, so I don't have to use precious end-of-the-world minutes creating a new account.

I still have to think *practically.*

"I'll do it later," I say vaguely. "But can you, like, do some damage control first?"

"Now wait a second—" Ginnie starts.

"Elephants!" I clap my hands together. A baby elephant squirts water into the air. Another elephant, Bertha, splashes in a waterfall alone.

"Insert cheesy joke," Ginnie monotones. As if on cue, the "guide" says, "Bertha's been hogging that shower for thirty years now! If you don't believe me, just look at all those wrinkles."

We fall quiet as we pass the apes, go under the waterfall, hear another awful joke. Ginnie pokes my side. "You distracted me with elephants. I was going to say, isn't telling someone else to partake of the Internet Evil just the same as you using the evil yourself?"

"More elephants!" I point.

Mom leans across the French tourists in front of us, sticking her head in between the annoyed couple. "What's evil? Jeremy? Are you two talking about Jeremy?" My mom has this uncanny ability to butt into any conversation with one easily misunderstood word. "What did he do that was evil?"

"Nothing!" I yell back, just at Ginnie offers, "He tooled out on Mallory."

" 'Tooled out'?"

More cruise buddies are staring at us now. Ginnie goes on like we're having a conversation about the weather in our kitchen. "Or tooled up. His ability to tool knows no bounds."

"Is there a new meaning to the word *tool* I don't know about?" Mom asks.

"Switch?" the tourists between us ask.

"Oh, thank you, yes! Come back here, Kevin." She grabs Dad's arm and there's a scuffle as they maneuver to new seats. The tour guide stops his rehearsed commentary. "Sir, in the Donald Duck shirt, don't fall overboard. Those hippos look hungry."

Everyone has a good laugh, except us, because this guide is stupid and so is my mom for picking this precise moment to scour for details. Dad turns his attention back to the guide, but my mom huddles up to Ginnie and me, her eyes big and expectant. "What were you saying about Jeremy?"

"Look, Mom. Jeremy and I . . . just grew apart," I say.

Ginnie snorts.

"So he didn't dump you?" Mom asks.

I cross my arms over my chest. "Why would you assume Jeremy dumped me?"

"I didn't," Mom says a little too quickly. She adores Jeremy. She bought him a Baltimore Orioles baseball hat online. Yes, the Orioles, the most boring team in the major leagues. That should have been an indication he was a bad seed to begin with, right up there with the deep V.

"I just don't see why you would break up with him."

"But you could see why *he* would break up with *me*?" I ask. Ginnie gives a low whistle.

Mom readjusts her Cinderella T-shirt. "No, of course not. I just know how much you like him and I want you to be happy. He's a smart boy, ambitious and nice—"

"And he's a tool," Ginnie says.

I am *this* close to adding "and he cheated on me with a girl named BubbleYum." But then I would have to give Mom the details, and I've been burned enough by her lust for news. Like when I told her about my first kiss with Cameron Steeples in seventh grade, and the next day I pick up the phone to hear her dissecting the kiss with Cameron's mom. She thinks she has a right to know my everything just because she had a forty-hour natural labor with me. My life would be so much easier if she would have just taken that stupid epidural.

"Villagers," I say.

We boat past a village of natives, blow darts sail past us, we narrowly escape, and Dad lets out a hearty chuckle at another lame tour-guide joke we've heard 49,023 times. He twists around. "So your boyfriend is a tool. Is that what I'm hearing?"

"Dad! The entire Amazon rain forest does not need to know the details of my love life."

"Did you break up with him?" Dad asks.

"Thank you!" I say. "See, Mom? Did *I* break up with *him*."

"Well, I have to make some sort of assumption when all you give me is, *you grew apart*. I've used that excuse before; I know how it is. You never tell me anything."

"I wasn't a fan of Jeremy," Dad says. "Shifty eyes."

Mom sticks one hand on her hip. Her shirt has dipped low again, and I catch the French guy giving her scoop neck a look-see. "Kevin, shifty eyes?"

Dad wiggles his eyebrows. "Doesn't make eye contact. Cannot trust a kid who can't manage eye contact."

"He always made eye contact with me," Mom says.

"Are you kidding me? That kid was always checking you out. Bet he would date you both."

"Now you're being ridiculous," Mom says. He is, but not in the way she means. They've forgotten that we're talking about my fresh breakup and moved onto some bizarre foreplay. Mom swats Dad on his thigh. He grabs her hand and pulls her close. Ginnie gives my hand a little pat and I squeeze back. Having Mom take Jeremy's side is one thing, but having Dad joke about my breakup and move on the next second almost hurts more.

Grandma says my parents are the perfect example of what passion will do to a marriage, which sounds romantic enough, but it's not meant to be a compliment. I don't know if they've always been that way. It seems when I was a kid they fought less, but I also don't remember the PDA being quite so public or affectionate. Then again, I could have just blocked it all out. There's a little girl dressed up like Ariel staring as my parents nuzzle. Nuzzling is never right, but especially when you're old and *especially* in a theme park.

We pass the final elephant and Ginnie mouths along with the tour guide. "Many of you think that's water coming out of that little guy's trunk. Don't worry. It's snot." She yawns and closes her eyes. My parents finally unglue from each other as the boat ride ends.

"Splash Mountain?" I ask.

Dad grabs Mom's hand and pulls her out of the boat. "You girls can. I want to walk around with your mom for a bit." Walk around equals make out on a paddleboat like they're sixteen-year-olds. I should know. Jeremy and I have "walked around" on every ride in this park.

Even Winnie the Pooh. I know. I'm not proud.

Mom kisses Dad on the cheek as we shuffle through the exit and into the main part of Adventureland. "I can't stay much longer. I have too much work today."

"You could do it tomorrow." Dad swats at a fly. "Those Internet thieves aren't going anywhere."

My dad might love his job, but my mom hates hers. When we moved from Reno, she was really big on quitting part-time retail to "stay home with her girls." This really meant girl, and that girl was Ginnie, who needed an escort to her endless soccer tournaments and camps. I am totally fine with this, by the way. I'm stifled enough by Mom's love and attention; I don't know how Ginnie deals with Mom knowing everything about her all the time.

But the full-time-mom stint didn't last long. Dad isn't very tech savvy, and what he made from selling houses and running his little booth at the antiques mall wasn't paying the bills, so Mom took over the Internet sales. Even though she's still (too) involved in our lives, she spends most of her time on the computer now—running the website, e-mailing, posting stuff on various online auction sites. Sales, especially international deals, have increased since Mom got it going, but it's just not her thing. She's a different kind of bargain shopper, the one who scours sales, clips coupons, and relishes sticking it to the man/corporation/soccer moms who would dare spend full price.

"If I don't work tonight, then I'll have to do double tomorrow," Mom says. "And we're having a bad month. The last two storage units you bought were a flop."

A family of thirty, all with GIBSON FAMILY REUNION shirts on, weave around us. Mom and Dad are frozen in front of the Tarzan's Treehouse line. Ginnie nudges me with her shoulder and whispers, "Here we go."

"I make most of our money on a quarter of the units," Dad says. "And using the word *flop* suggests failure."

Mom unzips her purse—she's severely anti–fanny pack—and globs on some lip gloss. "I'm just saying, I devote as much time to this business as you do, but it's starting to feel like too much of a gamble. Back when you were selling houses, we made twice the money and you worked half as much."

"And I was miserable! And you know the housing market is stale right now."

I don't hear blame in Dad's voice, but Mom jumps on the defensive. "Sometimes, Kevin, you have to do something you don't like to make life work. All this junk shopping takes up so much time, and you could be—"

Dad's face flushes. "Junk?"

"You guys want to go on It's a Small World?" Ginnie asks. "Little repetitive music and clapping puppets is very calming."

"Yes, Kevin." Mom raises her chin. "Junk."

I slump down on a nearby bench. Ginnie calls these fights left fielders, because we never see them coming. "Wake me up when they're done."

Ginnie tries again. "Maybe we should get a frozen banana."

Dad leans over and with a voice soft but razored says, "It's my job. Not junk."

"It's junk if we aren't making any money." Mom jabs her finger toward Tomorrowland. "If you'd do something more stable, we could pay off some of that credit-card debt you took on even though I *told you* the interest rate was sky high—"

"It was the only card we could qualify for because you spend all of our money on the bargain bin—"

Ginnie jumps up and waves her arm in front of my feuding parents. "Hey! Hello! Your daughter is okay."

Mom blinks. Dad rubs the back of his neck.

"Remember?" Ginnie says. "That's why we came here? To give *Mallory* a little post-breakup sunshine?"

Oh, right. Mallory.

Mom covers her forehead like she has a headache. "Of course. I'm sorry, Mallory. Your father and I are here for you anytime, whatever you need."

"Do you want to talk about it?" The edge is out of Dad's voice now. "For real?"

"No." I look back and forth between my parents. Dad's face is flushed; Mom's is white. Money is the *worst* topic for them. Which is too bad, because money is something they think of every day, especially when we don't have it. Especially when we *used* to have it, and the stupid economy barreled right into our living room and shoved us out of town. "Don't worry about me."

Ginnie grabs my arm. "Mallory is going to do a little, um, activity to help her, you know, stay fine after the breakup. And I'm going to help."

"What?" I ask.

"Yeah, we're just getting to our roots. Details to follow." Ginnie pulls me toward Frontierland. "You guys are great parents for caring. You should go celebrate your parenting skills with a paddleboat ride! Or one of those ten-foot corn dogs. Or . . . Peter Pan. That's romantic. Be together. Be happy. *Don't talk.*"

Mom gives Dad one of those looks that is a conversation in and of itself. I'd guess this one says, *Oh, we're fighting in the middle of Disneyland in front of our daughters, one of whom is emotionally fragile. Let's call a truce to save face.* "I guess I can wait another hour if you two want to go on some rides together."

"Yeah." Dad kisses the top of Ginnie's head. "Meet us at the carousel at eight."

"Wait." Mom digs her camera out of her purse. "For posterity."

Ginnie and I automatically wrap our arms around each other and smile. Only my photo-freak mom would take a picture at a moment like this.

"Bye! Love you! Have lots of fun!" Ginnie calls.

She yanks me into a Moroccan-themed gift shop and cranes her neck out the window, watching Mom and Dad. If there is one ounce of parental tension, Ginnie bursts in with all this sunshine before running away, like that fixes anything. Besides, Mom and Dad were just arguing about money. What couple doesn't argue about money?

Our parents stay in the same spot, and although their body language isn't friendly, at least they're not scaring the little children. They finally leave, Mom a few steps in front of Dad. I pick up a plastic genie bottle and peer inside. They'll be happy again in five minutes. It's how they are.

Ginnie shakes her head and storms out of the store. So, I guess I'm supposed to follow, then. Pity. I wanted to bum some money so I could buy the genie bottle. Ginnie saves all her money; she's always rolling in cash. And three wishes could do a lot to Jeremy. Actually, do they sell voodoo dolls in New Orleans Square?

Ginnie's nearly to Critter Country by the time I catch up with her. "Where are we going? Some ride to get us back to our roots?"

Ginnie doesn't answer at first but keeps walking until we reach the bridge that overlooks the Splash Mountain ride. She dangles her arms over the rail. "I didn't know what to say. I just hate when Mom and Dad fight."

I shrug. "They were arguing. So what?"

Ginnie cuts me a glance. "You don't worry that they argue too much?"

"They're a married couple. That's totally normal."

"I don't think you're a relationship expert," Ginnie says.

"Hey. Still fresh, Gin."

"I just hope there's a way to multitask with this list. Help you get over your relationship, sure, but maybe have Mom and Dad improve theirs."

I stay quiet as a log filled with screamers crashes down the drop. There are only so many purposes The List can fill, but I don't have the heart to tell Ginnie that.

Chapter 8

The five things I need to do to start a pep club (information from student handbook in the office, unearthed by the fourth secretary I asked):

1.   Find an adviser: Mr. Hanover:
     a.   He has a soft spot because he was in pep club as a teenager.
     b.   He has to be involved in name only.
     c.   He has a thing for pocket watches, and I know my dad has five in inventory.
     d.   And there may be some tears, just to cement him in?

2. Find five charter members: Ginnie, Cardin, Paige, Yvonne, and me.
3. Write a mission statement: Prepping Orange Park High for the next level of pep!
4. Approval from student body president: Blake Mickelson.
5. Approval from principal: Mrs. Gonzalez loves Blake, so once ASB approves, she won't even glance at the sheet before signing on the line.

My true-to-period outfit is purple gingham capris paired with a white oxford, Grandma's necklace with the ring, and my hair in a high ponytail. No way am I rocking one of those hideous beehives—some sixties girls maintained hair sanity. I need to go shopping and pillage through Dad's inventory tonight, or that seersucker dress is going to have to make a repeat appearance very soon.

I'm wishing I had a dress or something more professional as I enter the ASB room, short for Associated Student Body, our schools' student government. The members sit on one side of the table, and a drop of sweat slides down my back as I approach what looks like my parole hearing. Blake Mickelson sits in the middle, and seriously, there is a *gavel* in front of him. I thought ASB was a way to proclaim your (albeit geeky) popularity, not an actual organization of power. The girl who won secretary tried to rap her speech. True, these kids got out early for assemblies and school activities, but the authority of a gavel? Really?

Blake motions to the seat directly across from him.

"Go ahead and have a seat, Mallory." His smile isn't overly friendly, more professional, but the girls on the council narrow their eyes in dark jealousy.

Blake Mickelson is an accidental president. He ran because of a bet, won on his charm, and ended up being the most diligent leader to date. He actually *did* get a new vending machine, with organic snacks nonetheless. No one uses the machine, but it's there, and that was enough to catapult Blake into political infamy. His hair helped his cause too. The boy has serious dreads, and you needed something distinct to stick out in a school as diverse as ours.

He glances down at his paper. "So, you want to start a club?"

I sit up tall in my seat. If they want to do this legit, I can play along. "Yes. A pep club."

"Prep club?"

"Pep. You know, like rah-rah?"

"Don't we already have that club?" Blake glances at his posse and a wall goes up like I'm not there. Like I wouldn't have checked if a club existed before trying to start one.

The vice president, Chelsea something or other, pipes in. "ASB focuses on school spirit, so do the cheerleaders, color guard, and drill team."

I do not roll my eyes. I do not point out that "spirit" is not the same as "exposing skin." I keep the sarcasm out of my voice, but only barely. "But none of those clubs are called pep club."

"Lauren is the commissioner of pep," Chelsea adds.

Lauren folds her arms across her chest. There are ASB commissioners for sports and publicity and apparently pep. "Right, so I should probably be a part of this."

"That's fine," I say. Lauren must have waited for this moment for eons. How often does she commission anything? "But the point is pep *club* does not exist at this school."

"Maybe there's a reason for that," Blake says.

There's a laugh at the end of the table. "A reason?"

Oliver Kimball. The literal outlier in this council of Blakein-ites. I knew he'd be here, but I'm trying hard to not let his presence have any impact on me. He has a halfway grin on his face, like he's really enjoying this meeting, but in an ironic way. I'm sure he told Jeremy that I was starting a club and that I'd be at this meeting. He probably planned to build me up with club guidelines before shooting me down in front of the ASB.

"What, you think a pep club would create an unbalance of spirit at our school? You think the other peppy types would rise up in rebellion because this girl…" He points at me. "What's your name?"

"*Mallory.*" Like you don't know my name. Gah, is tooli-ness hereditary? Passed on through the mother's genes, like baldness?

"Because Mallory wants to start a club that'll probably get five members and a thumbnail-size photo in the yearbook? Let her have it."

Let me have it? Now I'm confused. Is Oliver Kimball on my side? The same Oliver who only listens to bands that haven't been invented yet, who is anti-industry or -establishment or whatever is underground to be anti about, is promoting *pep* club?

No, it's a trap. Guard up, Mallory.

The rest of the ASB stares at him. He pushes back his horn-rimmed glasses in response. I wonder if he has a prescription or if he's just wearing them for looks. They do finish off his hipster look nicely. "Why are you guys looking at me like that? Who freaking cares? We passed Latin club, and that's a dead language."

"Um, thanks, I appreciate it." He's not going to make a joke out of me just like he's making a joke out of the ASB. "But I'm not the only one who needs pep. This is for the whole school, and if you look at my mission statement, you'll see that it really is a necessary club. We don't have pep rallies anymore, except for homecoming, and I was thinking maybe we could, you know, cheer for other sports besides football and basketball, maybe even like academic activities? Or something?"

"What, like cheerleaders for mathletes?" Blake asks.

"Sure, well, not cheerleaders." So my mission statement was vague BS, but now that I'm actually talking about a club I was only forming so I could be the secretary, I start to think... hey. Why not make this club something worthwhile, something new and essential? Grandma didn't achieve everything in life by being passive. If she were here, either almost-seventy Grandma or sixteen-year-old Vivian, she'd go all out. I should push a little more than usual, make this something worthwhile. I'm here already, right?

Wow, so this is what follow-through feels like.

"We could organize the rallies!" I exclaim. "It's like your job and the cheerleaders combined. We can do fund-raisers too, help you guys out with homecoming—"

Blake stacks some papers in front of him like a news anchor trying to stretch during the last few seconds of airtime. "We don't need help. Homecoming is next week. We planned it forever ago. I'm going to say no. Sorry, Mallory. Seems like a bust. Thanks for trying."

As if on cue, ASB members look down at the sheets of paper in front of them. "So, next item of business," Chelsea says.

Just like that. They said no *just like that*. For no reason, because they could, because they have other items to get to, probably something essential to humanity like a bake sale.

I stand up and turn to leave, my knees wobbly. This isn't a big deal. So I don't have a club. It's one item on the list. And it's not like I'm peppy anyway.

But if I can't do one thing on The List, why try any of it? Why try to live in some bygone decade, when I can just go home and call Jeremy like nothing ever happened. I can try to fake that feeling of security that I used to have with him, with my life. Because without The List, I don't have a path to a fresh start; I only have my tainted past.

Without The List, I'm not a future Vivian. I'm just plain, old, *single* Mallory.

"Hey, wait. We didn't even take a vote." Oliver reaches over and pounds Blake's gavel. "Order, order."

"Hands off my gavel." Blake's voice is completely void of humor.

"Just following protocol," Oliver says. "Don't we have to do a motion to vote and get it seconded?"

"Since when do you care about that?" the commissioner of something special asks. "Have you ever talked in a meeting?"

Oliver points at me. "I just think it's rude that we dismissed this girl when she obviously put something together and cares enough about this cause, however stupid it may be—"

"Hey!" I say.

He holds up a hand. "—to go through all the necessary steps to form a club and show up at this, I'm sorry, *boring* meeting. So we're voting. Blake, pound the gavel or I will."

Blake cradles his great hammer of power, staring at Oliver with fascination. "'Kay, seriously, you haven't had an opinion since the bathing-suit debate for the back-to-school car wash. Where did that come from?"

"I'd like to motion a vote on whether... What's your name?" Oliver asks.

"It's still Mallory."

"Mallory can form a pep club."

I'm just as shocked as the rest of the council that Oliver is coming to my rescue here. The guy is usually his own faction, his own brand. He once wore the same T-shirt to school for forty-two days straight. Everyone speculated the reasoning behind the bright orange STAFF shirt—he was protesting unemployment, flipping off commercialization, going green. I think he just did it because he could. To say, "Hey, I'm Oliver Kimball, and when I wear a shirt every day, it's a statement, but with anyone else, it's a hygiene issue."

"I'll second that motion," Blake says. "So, fine. We vote. All in favor of forming a pep club, say aye."

"Aye," Oliver says.

"Aye," I say.

"You can't vote." Blake shakes his head. No one else says anything as they wait for their fearless leader to weigh in.

"All opposed say nay," the vice president starts.

"Wait." Blake rubs his thumb along the head of his gavel, like magical leadership powers will spring out and aid him in this life-changing political decision. I bite my tongue. Come on, mighty gavel. Make him say aye.

"Fine." Blake waves his hand dismissively. "I'm an aye."

"Aye!" everyone else chimes in unison. Freaking lemmings.

"Have your club, but I don't want this to be something you made up just to get your picture in the yearbook," Blake says.

Do people really do that? "Of course not."

"I want to see some of those things you talked about happen. Raise some money for a cause. Maybe you can help out with Spring Fling, once you're unified. I really hope you get more than five members."

I can't guarantee that, but I give a brave smile. "I promise, it's going to be a worthwhile club."

"And, Oliver, dude." Blake feigns a frown. "Don't touch my gavel again. This thing is sacred, got it?"

I hurry out of the meeting before they change their minds. Oh, blessed gavel! We did it! I have a pep club. I'll call the first meeting together, assign myself as secretary, and ... and ... do other official club things.

I'm halfway down the hall and a million mental miles away when someone calls my name.

"Mallory?"

I cringe at his voice. *Now* Oliver remembers who I am. Figures. I bet he was pretending to forget my name as some sort of statement about my breakup with Jeremy, like I'm not worth remembering now that I'm out of that couple. A freeze-out, a continuation of his rude comments Monday at lunch. And maybe what just happened in there was all a joke too. Oliver better not tell me that they've reversed their decision, that I don't deserve my club. I'll hit him. Nose, stomach, groin. I don't care. "Yeah?"

He covers the space between us slowly, like he could take this conversation or leave it. "Congrats on your club."

"Thank you?"

That slow smile creeps up on the right corner of his mouth, like he's trained his left side to stay cool but the other half keeps rebelling. "Is that a question or statement?"

"I'm not sure." I jiggle my leg. There's a punch line coming. I hope I'm not it. "Why did you help? Just then?"

"What, with your club? Why wouldn't I?" He sounds genuinely confused. "You obviously went through a lot of work to put it together."

"I did." I step back. Did Jeremy put him up to this? Is he

trying to lull me into a false sense of security? Is there a video camera in Oliver's glasses?

"Besides, you're my cousin's girlfriend. Figure he'd want you to have your way."

"I'm not…" I scrunch my eyes at Oliver. Is he really bringing up this stupid joke again? He has to know about the breakup. "Look, you know I'm not his girlfriend, and it's bothering me that you keep saying that."

"Ha-ha-ha. Okay, fine. Fiancée. Sorry, I didn't get the wedding announcement."

"We broke up." I intone the words slowly. "Please stop being stupid about it."

Oliver widens his eyes, and this time it's with shock. Real, legitimate shock. "Seriously?"

Now I'm the one confused. Maybe Oliver was being nice the other day at lunch, and really *did* want to help me in that meeting. But if Oliver isn't a tool, then that makes Jeremy a double tool. How did Jeremy sit through an entire lunchroom conversation with his cousin and not mention our breakup? The breakup that had just happened a few periods before, so it was raw and fresh. Here *I* am, still feeling like there's a knife slicing through my chest, and he forgets to mention that he lost the love of his life? If he respected me at all, he would have at least told his cousin.

Then again, Jeremy wasn't dealing with the shock of betrayal. He already knew that he was talking to another girl. Our breakup might have just been an inevitability, a formality to him. And it's not like he's hiding it. Half of the fight is broadcast on the World Wide Web. I haven't seen it, but the breakup news and the way it has played out...it's big. Or does it just feel big to me? "You didn't see anything on Friendspace? I swore the whole school saw what he wrote."

"I'm not on Friendspace. It's so...obvious." Oliver takes off his glasses and cleans the lenses. "I don't want to talk to people that much in real life—forget the cyberworld. Jeremy's on there all the time, though."

"I know." I don't mean for it to, but my voice comes out harsh. Yes, Jeremy is in the cyber world *plenty*.

Still, it's refreshing to meet someone who doesn't measure his worth based on how many friends he has on Friendspace. Refreshing and odd. And I'm starting to think this wasn't all a joke. Can I trust him? "Anyway, thanks for your help. I guess I'll see you around."

"Sooner than you think." Oliver's voice has taken on something close to warmth. Or pity. No, please don't let it be that. I've withstood enough lately. Oliver Kimball feeling bad for me might just break me. "I'm going to join."

"Join what?"

"Pep club."

"*You* want to join pep club."

Oliver punches his arm in the air like a cheerleader. "What, you don't think I have enough pep?"

"I would be surprised to learn that you're pro-pep."

"I'm going to take that as a compliment." He brushes his fingers across his lips, rubbing the half smile away. "But seriously. You're going to need people with experience in the spirit business."

"You don't need to campaign." I hoist up my backpack on my shoulder. "The club is open membership."

"And I'd like to be vice president, if that's okay," he says. "I won't lie—I need to pad my résumé if I'm going to get into Stanford. I'll help you with your presidential duties as much as I can. Here, why don't you give me your cell and we can figure out logistics?"

"I don't have a cell."

He gives me a sympathetic look. "Did your parents take it away?"

We've already gotten into the breakup. I don't need to explain my tech fast. It's a personal, private decision, like being a vegetarian, or joining some New Age Hollywood religion.

"No. I don't believe in them. Too obvious."

He laughs, a surprised, rich burst that feels earned. "That was really funny."

"That's usually the reason people laugh."

"No, it's not." Oliver leans against the wall in that effortless way that good-looking people do. He's not worried that his cardigan will snag on a nail, or he'll slide down, or that his thigh looks big smooshed against a flat surface. I would have to practice wall leaning in front of a full-length mirror for months to achieve his cool. "People laugh because they're nervous, or to cover up tension, or to flirt, or because there's some instant applause meter in their head telling them that it's the socially acceptable thing to do. Genuine laughter, I don't even think that happens daily."

I almost laugh at this, but I would just be proving his point, because it wouldn't be a laugh of humor, but a laugh to ward off his crazy. "Laughter is the most natural thing on Earth. Babies laugh."

"Because they're trained to."

"Because it's in our genetic makeup!"

"So then it's a reflex," Oliver says.

"Remind me not to make any more jokes around you." I see why he drives Jeremy bonkers. Jeremy invented the status quo, or the upper status quo, whatever it is everyone else wants to be. And Oliver's sitting in the back of the theater, dissecting the laugh tracks like an overthinking freak. "Look, Oliver. You're right. This group is going to need leadership and you have *leader* written all over you. So I'll do you one better. You can be the president, but I need to be secretary."

"Secretary?" He knits his eyebrows together. "Why secretary?"

"Why pep club? I'm full of mystery. Are you in?"

"President. I like it." He folds his arm over his chest and looks off in the distance, like he's striking a pose for a magazine announcing his new title. Then he breaks into that halfway grin and says, "Can you tell me one more thing?"

"What?"

"I know I'm not going to get the truth from him, so I'll ask you. Why did you break up with my cousin?"

My voice catches in my throat. It's not the question I expected. This whole conversation is not what I expected. I didn't even expect a conversation *period*. "How do you know I broke up with him?"

"Five minutes of talking to you is more entertaining than a lifetime knowing Jeremy. So either you came to your senses, or he did something stupid."

Door number two. "I'll see you at pep club, Oliver." I turn and walk down the hallway. Five minutes of what? That was just me being me. He's never noticed me, never talked to me. You can't just go around laughing a special laugh and complimenting people like you know them. I turn around to tell him that, to get a few things straight, but Oliver is already gone, back to Blake, the ASB, and the gavel of truth.

Chapter 9

Favorite beach destinations of Orange County:

1. Tide pools at Corona del Mar
2. Bonfires on Huntington
3. Surfers at Laguna
4. Balboa Pier at Newport

On Wednesday at 6:20 a.m., Dad drops me off at the parking lot by Balboa Pier. Grandma is already sitting on a bench, the fourth one down on the right. I slide in next to her as she wordlessly offers me a beignet out of the paper sack she picked up from our favorite bakery in Newport. It's a healthy eating day for me, but this is a tradition. Her top lip has a dusty mustache of powdered sugar. "Do you have your Rumination?" Grandma whispers.

I nod and we turn our faces to the promise of morning. Grandma always said that you can find the answer to any question in a sunrise, and so she calls these meditative sessions Ruminations. During our weekend sleepovers, she used to kick me out of bed and drag me to the back porch of her town house near the top of Telegraph Hill in San Francisco, her home before San Luis Opispo. At first she'd give me a Rumination, like *Who do you want to be, Mallory?* Or *If you could fly anywhere, where would you go?* But as I got older, she made me pick my own thoughts, and in those moments I would ask myself things I never had the courage to consider during regular life.

But I can't settle on a clear Rumination today. I have to comb through all the doubt and whining, the *Why would Jeremy do that?* and *Will I ever find love again?* to The List and what it means. I'm two beignets in when I finally settle my mind on what I really want from The List: understanding. I don't know if I'll figure out what happened with Jeremy, or who I really am, or who my grandma was. But if only one of these questions is answered, it will be a win.

The sun awakens and the clouds stretch their dusky pink arms into the morning. A sunrise is one of those frequent snapshots that you take for granted because it's on a million dollar-store calendars. But here, next to my grandma, with sugar on my lips and so many thoughts in my heart, I know that this dewy moment matters.

A fisherman plops his bucket down on a weathered plank, perching his pole on his knee as he digs through his tackle box. Grandma wipes her hands on her bohemian-style skirt. "Thanks for meeting me here. I haven't had a good Rumination in a while."

As busy as my grandma was being a Very Important Person, she always made time to make Ginnie and me feel special. Well, I suppose that hasn't quite been the case for the past year or two, not since Grandpa's life ended and Grandma's dreams seemed to die with him. This retirement community must be her new dream, and although she hasn't seen us as much as usual, I can't blame her for the separation. "I really needed this today, Grandma. Thanks."

"Is there a reason you needed this?" Grandma asks. The sky is completely blue now, the sun illuminating the worried lines around her eyes. "When you were over with Ginnie the other day, it seemed like there was something wrong, something besides a homecoming dress. I'm here if you need to talk about it."

This is my opening to tell her about Jeremy. This is my chance to talk to someone who meditates during sunrises, who loved the same person for forty years, who never questions me like my mom does. But it's her compassion that stops me. She's been all around the world, seen children literally die from preventable diseases. How can I tell her I'm upset because my boyfriend fell in love with a computer avatar? No, she would think it's stupid and that I'm stupid by extension. I want to pretend that I'm as wonderful as she thinks I am.

"I'm fine. I've ... gotten into history some more, you know? It probably comes from digging through your stuff with Dad. Looking at your yearbook, it just seemed like ... like that was the perfect time to be a teenager, before the sixties got all crazy. I wish I could time-travel back to that." I can't help but get a little misty-eyed, like I'm the old one here, remembering my cherished youth. "You wore gowns to a dance, not skanky dresses. And you went on real dates, not the hang out and hookups that we do. And! You went steady and gave class rings and passed notes, not texts, and—"

"I think I'm going to barf." Grandma crumples the empty beignet bag into a ball. "I wasn't living in *Happy Days*."

"You weren't happy?" I ask.

"No, it was an old TV show. You know, the Fonz?" Grandma asks.

I shake my head. I would Wikipedia the Fonz right now if I could.

"My point is, we still had issues back then." Grandma folds her arms over her chest. "Communism, Cuban missile crisis, repression, segregation, race riots. But nothing catastrophic like broken cell phones, right?"

"I . . . it was just different. Being a teen is hard now, Grandma."

"Sweetie. Being a teen is *always* hard." She swallows, and it's clear she wants to say more but doesn't think she can. She starts to walk away with the expectation that I'll follow. I swear Grandma and Ginnie are twins, separated by a generation.

"Now," she says. "I need to get you to school by eight, so let me figure out what I'm working with here. What kind of experience do you have sewing?"

I gaze at a runner as he races past us. He's shirtless, and he has those weird hip muscles that are like arrows to a guy's goods. He's almost as glorious as the sunset. "Experience. I wouldn't say experience so much as . . . exposure."

"Fine. How much exposure do you have?"

"That would be . . . none."

Grandma stops walking and smacks my shoulder. "You expect to sew a homecoming dress in just over a week and you can't sew."

"That was my Rumination today. I ruminated really hard."

She laughs and veers me toward the parking lot. "Fine. I'll help you, but only if you help yourself. Take a sewing class, practice, do something proactive. You don't learn through *delegation*, you learn through *participation*."

Participation, not delegation. Once we're in the car, I scribble that last line down on my arm. Grandma wrote The List. Now she's given me a mantra how to finish it.

Chapter 10

Possible steadies for my sister, Ginnie:

1. Hector Cortez: aka the Sexy Mexi. He gave himself the nickname, just like Jeremy is the Amazing Asian, and so he might have some toolish tendencies. But he lives up to that nickname. As Spanish club would say, Ay, caramba!

2. Garth Nowak: He plays soccer and I know he's already in awe of Ginnie. He's shorter than her, but he has the confidence to pull it off. And, um, he's also a rumored drug dealer, but love could change him.

> No, Mallory. No future criminals.
> You're not that desperate yet.
> YET.

3. Oliver Kimball: president of pep club, and I'm making Ginnie join, so there's an opportunity. He's cute enough. I mean forget _enough_, he's hipster hot. I don't know how they would mesh, though. He's a senior while she's a freshman. And he still might be a jerk. I haven't decided yet.

4. Bennett Williams: because he's there.

I have to stay after school so I can finalize all the pep club paperwork in the office. I miss the bus and all my usual rides, so I beg a sophomore band kid named Bennett to take me home. I hesitate because Bennett is young, and California law says something about teens not driving other teens until they've had a license for a year, but obviously no one follows that.

Bennett's the nerdy/skater guy who may or may not be handsome one day. It's hard to see past the Dickies and hole-riddled T-shirts. He's in love with Ginnie, and spends the ten-minute ride peppering me with questions about her. He pulls up to my house and cranes his neck, like Ginnie might be sitting in a window, pining for her dream boy to drive up at any minute.

I throw my backpack over my shoulder and open the door. I'm about to tell Bennett to exit Dreamville when I remember that Ginnie needs a steady. I decide that yes, someday he *will* be hot, once his future girlfriend takes him shopping and talks him out of parting his hair in the middle. He showers regularly and even has a car. Ginnie and I only have so much time to complete this list, so why not Bennett? He's already smitten. She'll just need a touch of . . . *persuasion.*

My sister is totally clueless about guys. She also annoyingly but endearingly has no idea how gorgeous she is, and that when a guy says, "Want to go out?" they usually do, in fact, want to go out. So we go for direct.

"The only way you're going to get Ginnie's attention is with a grand romantic gesture."

Bennett leans forward in his seat. "Yeah? Like what?"

"Giving her sister a ride is a good start."

"Do you think she'll go to homecoming with me?" His voice is borderline whiny.

"Not if you ask her in that voice."

He drops his voice an octave. "Any other pointers?"

"Yes. Be firm. Persistent."

"Got it." Bennett scratches the side of his nose a bit too close to the nostril that it's almost a pick. Okay. So . . . we'll work on that too. "Thanks, Mallory. You know what? I don't care what everyone says. You're nice."

'What everyone says'? So what rumors did Bennett hear now? Do I want to know? Probably not. "Thanks. Tell all your friends."

I run into the house and throw on a T-shirt and old jeans. Back in the early sixties, girls never wore jeans to school, only for the most casual of events, and you can't get more casual then a storage sweep.

My friends think I have the worst job ever, but I honestly love it. I travel with my dad down to San Diego or up to San Francisco to talk with dealers, or to watch him in action at storage or estate auctions. But usually what he pays me to do is to comb through recent acquisitions. I don't have the same eye as him, so it's his job to decide if an old video game is a collectors' item or if an oil painting is an original. I just shift the potential from the obvious trash. And you'd be surprised what trash people hold on to.

My first instinct is to text my mom and tell her I'm home and ready to leave, but with that convenience gone, I walk down to her office to ask for a ride to Dad's main storage unit. Dad's been backed up lately, and the unit is jammed with mysterious boxes and trash bags.

Mom doesn't look up from her computer at first. Her heavily highlighted brown hair is in a ponytail, but still styled, curled, and teased. She has on her standard work uniform—bejeweled designer jeans and a fitted T-shirt, this one with roses curling around a large cross. When we walk into a store, guys always check out my mom first, taking in her tight body and large chest before noticing that she's in her forties, not twenties. If Ginnie's around, they usually shift their leering to her. I'm a cute girl—I can say that about myself—but sometimes I feel like a piece of old bologna between two slices of finely crafted artisan bread. Maybe not bologna, but pimento loaf at best.

Mom's bright pink-and-lime office is all order and cheerfulness. Afternoon sunshine spills through the window onto the leather chair and ottoman she bought on clearance at HomeGoods. Smaller cataloged items are on one white shelf while the larger items are kept in the garage so she doesn't have to look at them. Her one weekly splurge is the fresh bouquet of flowers she gets at the farmers' market every Tuesday.

"Mom?"

She jumps and clutches her chest. "Mallory! You scared me."

"Sorry. Are you cataloging?" I move over to Mom's desk.

She clicks on something and shifts her body so it's covering the computer screen. Which doesn't seem suspicious *at all*. "A little. Just catching up on e-mails and things. You ready to go? Why didn't you text me?"

I know I can only put off technology for so long before another school assignment comes up or I go to the dentist and they want to do some 3-D X-ray on my cavity. So I need a deadline. Homecoming is next week, and since it was such a highlight in Grandma's high school existence, the dance seems like a good end point. And once The List is done, well, I don't really know what happens then. It's a day-by-day plan.

"I can't find my phone," I say.

"You didn't lose it, did you?" Mom grabs her designer knock-off purse and starts shooing me out of her office. "We can't afford to buy you a new one."

"I know. I'll find it. Besides, it's not a big deal to walk down the stairs and come get you."

Mom switches off her lights and closes her door. "I just value my privacy, honey. I like to have some warning first."

"I'll knock next time." Why is she acting so weird? It's not like I walked into her bedroom. She knew she had to drive me. Ha, maybe Mom has a secret Authentic Life too.

Scratch that. Not funny.

Mom smears on lip gloss in her rearview window, even though she's not getting out of the car. "I feel so bad that I haven't even asked you how school went. How are things with Jeremy?"

"Over. Awkward."

"That's got to be hard. Are you sure you two are done?" Mom manages to pull out of the driveway and check her phone at the same time. She does not, however, manage to avoid the trash can behind us. The bin clangs to the ground, but mom doesn't look back. "Wow, there's a sale at Kohl's this week and I just got an e-mail with another twenty percent off. I still have those bonus bucks I need to spend."

I reach over the console of her minivan and grab the phone. "Mom, don't text and drive. Watch the road."

She grabs the wheel with both hands. "I'm still paying attention."

"To answer your question, yes. I'm sure Jeremy and I are over."

"I won't ask what happened if you don't want me to."

"I don't," I say.

"But did you at least get closure? Closure can take the edge off the pain. Did I ever tell you about my first boyfriend, Michael? We had the worst breakup, happened at school..."

I look out the passenger window. I appreciate that Mom is asking me these things, because it shows she cares. Even though she's gone overboard more times than I can count, she also can be very sweet when it comes to life's little earthquakes. I just don't want to have this conversation now, if ever. No. I do not have closure. What I do have is a random list written fifty years ago by Grandma, which is as close as I'm going to get. "That's a good story, Mom. But everything is fine."

"It doesn't *sound* fine. Are you sure you don't want to talk?"

"No," I say flatly. "It's okay. I'm okay. Don't worry."

Mom pinches her glossed lips together. "If there's any way I can help—"

"You can't," I say.

"Maybe if you tell my why you broke up—"

"You just said you won't ask what happened."

She sits back in her seat and stares out at the road. "You're right. I did say I wouldn't ask."

We pull up to the storage place, and Mom inputs the code. I jingle Dad's key ring, finding the one with the red dot for this unit's lock.

"I can stay," Mom says when I open the car door. "Get some work done on my phone. Or help you unpack. We could talk more."

"Mom, you dry heave if you even look at an uncombed box. Remember that time we found that family of mice?"

Mom shudders. "You're right. I'll be back at six."

I wait until she drives away to open the unit. It's true, we did find mice in one garage, and dirty magazines in a travel trunk Dad found at a garage sale in Watts. But we've also found gold coins and an early-eighteenth-century Shaker-style table. You never know what treasures are found in someone's personal history.

Today starts with duds. Lots of worthless files, yellowed paperback novels, semibroken toys—old stuffed animals are the worst—and bags of clothes that are either too worn or the wrong style/era to net us much of anything. But then I find an old ring box in the bottom of one of the file boxes. Inside are blue jeweled cuff links and a tie pin. Whoa. If the stones are sapphires or something semiprecious, we're in business.

I stick the case into my pocket and start to bag up the donation pile. Dad sends the clothes that aren't valuable to a charity in Africa, which gets him a tax break and a feeling of goodwill. I'm folding the clothes when I see a large letter *O* in the pile. It's an old Orange Park High cardigan made of scratchy wool, orange and black. It's not sixties, I'd guess more early eighties, but it has a preppy importance that puts Blake's gavel to shame. This could get some money, especially since it's a sentimental piece in our geographical area, but I'll keep it and tell Dad to take it out of my check. Save it for a day that calls for loads of pep.

I see motion to my left and jump. A cockroach scurries out from a sagging box. I squish it with my sneaker and bag up the rest of the clothes. The unit is organized and mostly divided by five thirty, so I lock up and wait the last half hour for Mom. If I had a phone, I could text her and tell her to come early. Or I could call a friend, play a game, look up information on my history paper. I could do something besides sit on a curb with absolutely nothing to do. Freak, I don't even have music to listen to.

I open the box of paperbacks, pull out an old romance, all heaving bosoms and bare chests. The hero is the duke of Somewhereshire instead of Eduardo, but this will do. The sun is dipping below the horizon, there's an insect buzzing nearby, and the breeze holds the promise of fall. Sunrise this morning, sunset tonight. That's twice in one day that I'm outside like this, just sitting, breathing, waiting, watching, without my fingers tapping out something on my phone.

Now if only I had some soap or wood to whittle. Super-vintage.

I come home to a surprise in the kitchen. A message from Jeremy. Written on a note card. Attached to a bouquet of lilies.

Mallory,
I'm sorry about class Monday.
Got frustrated. Talk to me, babe.

"Please tell me those aren't from Jeremy." Ginnie tries to grab the card, but I shove it down my shirt.

"These aren't from Jeremy."

"Really? Who are they from, then?"

"Jeremy."

"Ha-ha. Of course he's trying to save face. He's super in love with his face." Ginnie readjusts her sweaty ponytail. Her

T-shirt is still wet from her league soccer practice, not to be confused with her school soccer practice, or off-season soccer practice, or camp soccer practice, or future Olympian soccer practice, all in older age brackets. Sometimes she comes home from athletically annihilating her elders and thinks that talent gives her a right to be a snark-face to her older sister. "You two better not have made up. I'll disown you."

"Of course not. Gross, I stink." I wash my hands in the sink. "I'll never understand why people pay money to keep a storage unit, but let the stuff in there get so dirty. And attics! All that filth just floating above you?"

"You're avoiding my question. Why did he send you flowers?"

"Peace treaty." I wipe my hands on a dish towel. "He wants to talk."

"Are you going to?"

"I don't know."

"That's a yes."

"No, it's an 'I don't know.' I just got the flowers two minutes ago. I need to figure out what this is about."

Ginnie opens the fridge and rummages around until she finds a half-empty orange Gatorade. She finishes it in one long gulp and wipes her mouth with the back of her hand. "Fine. We'll discuss the flowers later. So instead, can you tell me why Oliver Kimball called you?"

"What?" The hairs on my arm stand at army alert. "He did? When?"

"Right before I left for soccer. I left a Post-it note with his number on your desk." Ginnie hops onto the counter. "If you had a cell, you would know this by now."

"So he called our home phone number? *I* don't even know our home number."

"He must have asked Jeremy. You know, his cousin. The one you dated." Ginnie looks at me expectantly. "Details?"

"He wants to be president of pep club," I say.

"We are talking about the same Oliver Kimball here. Senior, too cool for school, pretty eyes."

Well. I haven't noticed his eyes. "The one and only."

"So he wants you." Ginnie pulls the cookie jar closer and shoves a gluten-free cookie into her mouth. "Wow. And so Jeremy sends flowers to mark his territory. Better than peeing in a circle around you. Looks like you're not going to have a problem finding a steady."

"Stop it. Oliver doesn't want me. He's joining because he needs another extracurricular for college."

"But maybe *you* are Oliver's next extracurricular." Ginnie glances down at her phone and scowls. "This is the fifth text today from Bennett Williams." Her frown deepens. "You don't think he's asking me to homecoming, do you? I don't want my first real date to be with him. Although, list-wise, I guess one of us should go to homecoming."

That's right. I no longer have a date. This is the first event in over a year where I will be boyfriendless at a time when having a boyfriend comes in handy. And now the chances of me finding a date, even with a guy friend, are minimal. I have to sew and wear a dress to the dance. Alone.

I find one of Ginnie's organic burritos in the freezer and stick it in the microwave. "This might be perfect. Now Bennett Williams can be your steady."

"You're kidding."

"Now, Ginnie. Give it a chance. He has nice hygiene and he's very passionate about...about life. And! He told me that he reads crime novels to his grandpa every Tuesday."

"*Why* were you talking to Bennett?"

Oh. Oops. "Hmmm? Oh, we just ran into each other after school. He's really a sweet guy. One shopping trip and he would be solid."

"Bennett Williams told everyone that he made out with Gina Fitzpatrick in middle school and it was a total lie. He's toolier than Jeremy." Her phone buzzes with another text. This time, her mouth goes from a frown to a snarl. "Wait, Bennett gave you a ride home today? And you talked to him about homecoming? What's *that* supposed to mean?"

I take a step back. "That's not the romantic gesture I told him to do."

"So you *did*?"

"He asked about you and I said you like guys who are persistent."

Ginnie slaps her hand on the countertop. "Mallory! This is my first high school dance. I don't want to go with Bennett! And I have to say yes because he's the only guy asking me. Late, by the way. Why didn't you talk to me about this first? What is wrong with you?"

"He asked me a question, I answered. And this isn't just

about you. Someone has to find a steady. Think about The List." I open the microwave and grab my burrito, ready to retreat to my bedroom.

"You want me to think about your list? Fine!" Ginnie steals my plate and holds it up in the air. "You just used a microwave. People didn't have microwaves in 1962."

"Stop being a brat."

"You wanted my help, you got it." She takes a big bite of my burrito. "How does it feel to be 'helped'? Maybe you could stop helping my love life too, *helper.*"

"Grow up."

She smiles and takes another bite of my burrito. My stomach growls. Did they have pizza delivery in 1962?

I grab my bouquet of flowers, resisting the urge to slap my sister. Sure enough, there's a bright pink Post-it note with Oliver's number in my room. I pick up the home phone and consider calling him. What would we talk about? I'm too exhausted to get into the logistics of pep club tonight. I need a shower, I need to do my homework, and I need ... I take a sniff of the flowers. Lilies. My favorite. Jeremy remembered.

If a guy messes up one time, one *epic* time, does that mean he'll always be that way, or can he change? Bennett Williams might have said something stupid in middle school, but that doesn't mean he's not right for Ginnie now, right? And Jeremy could possibly ...

I rub Grandma's necklace. No. Forget it.

Flowers or not, I'm staying strong.

Chapter 11

Top five favorite bobblehead dolls:

1. Willie Mays: legendary All-Star from the 1962 Giants. One of the first, the finest bobblehead ever.
2. Derek Jeter: even his bobblehead is good-looking.
3. Mike Schmidt: I used to get this Phillies' third baseman confused with the old actor Chuck Norris because they both have red beards.
4. Evan Longoria: found this at a thrift store. I know nothing about him, except that he's hot. Noticing a trend in my collection.

5. Brian Wilson: he wore a spandex tuxedo to the ESPY Awards one year. Now that I'm single, I think I shall marry him.

I wake up the next morning to a rainbow of Post-it notes splattered around my room. There's one on my bobblehead shelf. No, what *used* to be my bobblehead shelf, before my amicable athletes were bobblenapped. All that remains is Willie Mays and a note:

> Most of these guys weren't alive in the sixties, and if they were, they were in diapers. Willie Mays in the only exception. You're welcome. I know this isn't technology, but I'm seizing the opportunity since these guys always freaked me out.
> NOT AUTHENTIC.

And another Post-it note where my alarm clock used to be.

> LED digital alarm clocks weren't available until the mid-seventies, and they sure didn't have docking stations.
> NOT AUTHENTIC.

Ginnie's handwriting is on another note on my now computer-less desk.

Personal computer? Please.
NOT AUTHENTIC.

My sister, my insane sister, has removed every bit of technology not available fifty years ago, which basically is *all* technology in my room. Like my phone. Not my cell, but the cordless landline. Now I have no contact with the outside world.

I flip the light switch in my bathroom and see my blow dryer. Ginnie's note says:

> *Your model is obviously too modern, but*
> *there were home hair dryers as early as*
> *1920, so I'll give you a pass. Also, your hair*
> *frizzes when you air-dry. You could always*
> *ask a salon to give you a beehive. Ha!*
> *You're welcome.*
> *SEMIAUTHENTIC.*

"Ginnie!" I pad down the hallway and throw open the door to her bedroom. "What the crap is this?"

Ginnie rolls over in her bed and pries open one eye. "Bennett asked me to homecoming last night after you went to bed. So I decided to 'help' you some more with your stupid project. Don't pimp me out again."

"Where is all my stuff?"

"I'm selling it online. I need the money to buy a dress."

I yank her comforter. "Go take it offline. You're not selling my computer!"

"Oh, lighten up." Ginnie stretches her arms and yawns. "I'll give it back to you when you're done being retro."

"Ginnie, my alarm clock? How am I supposed to wake up? And what about my little LED reading light?"

"Get a flashlight."

"It's not enough light!" I cry out in despair.

Ginnie covers her mouth with her hand, but a giggle escapes.

I ball my hand into a fist and slap at my thigh. "Do you know how hard this is? I'm already completely isolated from my friends—I don't know what they're doing during the day, I have no clue what's happening online. My reputation is going up in flames and I can't even watch it play out. And now my room is prehistoric." I flop down on the bed.

"So basically I gave you exactly what you asked for."

"I hate you."

"You're welcome."

I wrap Ginnie's covers around my head. It was easy for Grandma to live like this because the technology wasn't there to miss. But there's all this networking and connecting floating around me, and I'm not a part of it. No one but Ginnie knows Jeremy sent those flowers or Oliver called my house. Normally I would spend hours dissecting those advancements with my friends.

Maybe the communication isn't all real, maybe those online personas are facades, but even if it's 30 percent truth, that's still more than the big fat *Zero* I was getting now. What was I supposed to do, bike over to my friend's house? Paige lives two miles away. No wonder all those small-town teens used to spend the weekends driving up and down Main Street—it was the only way they could find their friends.

The fact remains that I need to create a space that was as close to sixteen-year-old Vivian's as possible if I really want to know what her life was like. No one ever said The List would be easy. Probably because no one else knows The List exists.

"Fine. Thank you. No more helping, though," I say.

"Agreed. And no more helping me find a steady, either."

"You could tell Bennett no."

Ginnie swings her legs over the side of her bed. "I don't know. He gave me a basket filled with those organic peanut butter cups from Whole Foods that I love and wrote, *You butter go with me to homecoming.* Peanut butter, Mal. That's special."

"Wait, you *want* to go with him now?"

"The dance is next week. No one else is asking me. I think I was building up the first-date thing too much. Bennett will be good practice."

I clench my fist again, this time with the intent to punch Ginnie. "Then why did you go dark ages on my room?"

She reaches down and unclenches my hand. "Because I care. And if you're going to do this, you're going to do it right."

"You're evil." I rub my eyes. I need to get ready for school. My electronic toothbrush was probably confiscated too. "Even if you took my phone away, I'm still going to see Jeremy at school, you know."

"You can see him, just don't forgive him, all right?"

"Yeah, yeah."

I follow Ginnie to the kitchen, passing my room as we go. I do a double take. "Ginnie, the flowers."

She gives me a quick peck on my cheek. "In Mom's office. If you sit and stare at them all day, you'll give in."

I motor through my morning routine, grateful that showers made the authenticity cut. Ginnie's blow dryer is roaring, so I hurry down the hall to Mom's office. It's not like I need the flowers, but I need to assert some dominance over my little sister or else she's going to think she's the one running the show, whatever show this is.

My flowers are on Mom's desk. I grip the glass vase and pause when I see a flash of light on the computer screen.

If I checked Friendspace, or my e-mail, no one would ever know. I mean, what if the stuff on there isn't that bad? What if Jeremy wrote me this incredibly heartfelt e-mail that explains his devastating split-personality disorder? The screen flashes again. There's a page open with a blinking font. "COUPON ALERT! COUPON ALERT!"

I click off the site, obviously a pop-up. The mouse is smooth and yielding in my hand. I'm about to open another window when I hear Ginnie yell down the hallway. "Just because you're living in the sixties doesn't mean you need to move like you're sixty!"

No, I can't. My skin prickles and I rush out with the

flowers. No one will know, but I will, and if I give in to the technology temptation now, all this work is for nothing. No, insert older word.

All for naught.

Oliver Kimball is waiting at my locker before first period. I see him and stop walking. Do I really need my trig book? Can I get by without it? No. Too late. He's spotted me.

"Hey." I rush through my locker combination and shove a textbook inside. I don't know why I'm in such a hurry. So the kid wants to talk about something administrative. It's all business. He didn't even remember my name yesterday. "What's going on?"

"Why didn't you call me back last night?"

I don't look at him, just keep arranging books and binders with feigned purpose. "Did you call?"

"First I e-mailed you, but you never wrote back."

"Sorry, no e-mail."

"Figures. Then I had to go Sherlock and find a phone book, text Jeremy, ask what your dad's name is so I could find the listing, and call your home phone number."

"You asked Jeremy?" I slam my locker shut.

"Uh, yeah. He should know since you two were make-out buddies for the past year."

"He was my boyfriend, not my—"

"Right, whatever." Oliver leans against the locker. His hands are shoved into his pockets, and his right bicep flexes. I never thought of Oliver having biceps, but yep. He does. Nice ones, if you care about that stuff. Which I don't, because muscles are just a bunch of mass and . . . sinews under his skin. And I'm not thinking about his skin or sinews, or any guy's skin and sinews for a very long time, because I'm still trying to get over Jeremy's . . . sinews.

That's an awful word, isn't it?

"Not whatever. He *was* my boyfriend. Past tense."

"So. Present tense. I'm getting really geared up for pep club. It's so traditionally conformist that it's uncomformist, you know?"

"Oh no, you aren't joining to make a statement, are you?" I ask.

"Everything I do makes a statement." Half grin. Another casual bicep flex.

"Can we hurry up with this statement?"

"I was just saying that although I joined with ulterior motives, I do appreciate an institution that's so true to what it is, you know? No hidden agendas. They want pep, we deliver."

I can't help it. I laugh—he would consider it a nonlaugh, because it drips with scorn. Oliver has on a short-sleeved button-down plaid shirt, slim jeans, and . . . a loosened tie. The kid is wearing a tie. To school. Biceps are canceled out by his transparency. "Nice tie."

"What?"

"Nothing." It's not his orange STAFF shirt, but the tie is just as obvious. Jeremy always said his cousin wanted everyone to know how different he was from the rest of the school, how unique, brilliant, and above us all. "It's just…it must be exhausting to look like you're not trying."

"What's that supposed to mean?" He's befuddled, like no one has ever questioned his style or air.

"Never mind. That was rude. Sorry."

He gives me a once-over. "You're not one of those snobby girls who puts everyone down to lift yourself up, are you? You can't be in my club if you are."

"It's *my* club."

"Still. There are limitations." He looks down at his outfit. "I was going for presidential. What was your inspiration? Funeral procession?"

He's not far off. I'm wearing Ginnie's black shift dress that she got for our great-aunt Wendy's funeral last spring, along with a gray cardigan. I know it's not totally 1962, but until I go shopping, I only have so many choices. I change my voice so I sound like a forties gangster. "What do you say you and I blow this joint and hit up a job interview? Sunday school? Or the symphony, see?"

Oliver grins. It's the first full smile I've seen on him. "God, you're funny. Lacking in pep, of course, but Jeremy never told me how funny you are."

"Maybe we shouldn't say anything about Jeremy." I feel a misplaced loyalty to my ex. He's always had such a strong opinion about Oliver, and although I realize it's just that—an opinion—it's weird discussing Jeremy so openly, so quickly. Especially to his blood relation. The five-minute bell rings. "I have to hurry. First period is across school."

"Then let's get to business. Do you think we could have an unofficial pep club meeting today?" Oliver readjusts his black frames. The lenses are thick, so they must be prescription after all. And he wears them almost every day. "I might try to recruit a few more people if you could get the four you have signed up to show. Then we can vote on officers or whatever. And we really need to start planning if we're going to do something for homecoming."

"Homecoming?"

"Yeah, every club has to do a float."

The float was my idea. How'd he know? "A float?"

"Man, you're echoey." Oliver starts backpedaling across the hallway. "After school, at the outdoor theater. See you then."

So the first meeting is Oliver's idea. I might have to get him his own gavel, because he is taking this presidential thing way too... presidentially.

Paige and Yvonne can't make the meeting, because they have an SAT prep class at the same time. Ginnie has a half an hour until she has to leave for soccer. I'm most excited that Cardin joined my club, since she's my most popular friend. Once word gets out that she's joined, we'll have five instant sign-ups. Male sign-ups. Yes, Cardin's *that* kind of popular.

She meets me in the cafeteria after school and links arms with me. "I feel so behind with you. It's like you've disappeared off the face of the earth since you broke up with Jeremy."

"Cardin, that was only six days ago."

"Really? Seems like forever."

"Feels new to me."

"Well, I'm sorry it wasn't sooner. I've been calling you, but Paige just told me that you've sworn off technology."

"Only for a while." Until I finish The List.

"I don't know how you're doing that."

"Neither do I."

"I guess we'll plan ahead and set a date to hang out. Put it on the calendar, all official." She squeezes my elbow. "But I want you to know I'm here for you, 'kay? Breakups blow."

"Like a hurricane."

"Is that a song? If not, we need to write it."

My empty heart feels fuller, like when the Grinch unstole Christmas. "Thanks for joining pep club."

"Girl, there aren't a lot of clubs I can get into, but pep?" Cardin readjusts her bra. There's plenty to readjust. "Pep I got."

Cardin has this magnetic pleasantness that nets her a steady stream of boys and a slightly scandalous reputation. We became friends sophomore year when we both tried out for soccer (upon my mother's urging) and were the only girls who got cut. Cardin just laughed and made me walk with her to Baskin-Robbins to buy "we suck" ice-cream cones.

Pep club needs Cardin.

We push open the cafeteria doors. Our school has an open layout, meaning there aren't interior hallways, just blocks of buildings with wide spaces in between. The quad, with its picnic tables and benches, is the hub of the school. The tree next to the outdoor theater is nicknamed "The Tree of Life." The folklore goes that the tree was there first and they built the school around it. It's roped off because so many students carve into the poor plant, but it's still the best spot to sit in the quad on a sunny day. Which is most days in Orange.

Oliver's decorporate-ified his look with a blue-and-gray reindeer beanie. The large yarn ball on top bobs as he talks to Ginnie and another freshman named Vance. And that's it. First meeting and we have five people. A rousing start.

Oliver waves us over. "Hey, I was thinking we should trash being democratic and just let everyone pick the office they want."

"We don't have everyone here. Should we wait?" I ask.

"No way. I'm dressed for success. So, I want to be president. Are we cool with that?" Oliver lifts an expectant eyebrow.

Ginnie sips on a bottle of iced green tea. "Maybe Vance wants to be president."

"Oh, I just needed a ride home. Oliver lives on my street."

"Wow, Oliver. Heavy recruiting," I say.

"This school has insufficient pep," he says. "We'll build on that."

"I think you'll be a good president." Cardin beams at Oliver. She's not being flirty, just nice, but her niceness comes off as flirty. I should tell her not to bother. She's an obvious pick—Oliver won't go for her, because everyone else does. "So I give you my vote."

"Sounds like a landslide victory for me." Oliver glances down at a fresh spiral notebook. He already has a pen out and…oh wow. He's written an extensive list in tiny, slanted caps. No writing tablet or smartphone. He's a pen-and-paper lister, a beautiful and dying breed. "So first order as president… Wait, we need to introduce ourselves. I'm Oliver Kimball, pep club president. Oh, and Mallory wants to be secretary."

"I'm vice president!" Ginnie raises her hand. "I never get to be higher up than Mallory. Please?"

"I'm Cardin. I don't want to be anything," Cardin says. "Save the other titles for Paige. She loves that stuff."

"Wait, why don't you get to be higher than Mallory?" Oliver asks.

Ginnie's mouth falls open. "Because she's my big sister? I'm Ginnie? Hello, I talked to you on the phone yesterday."

"Oliver has a hard time remembering names," I say.

"Mal-lor-y." He sticks a hand on his hip. "Pretending to forget your name at ASB was part of my *strategy*. I couldn't have them thinking I was campaigning for the club just because I knew you."

"*You* got pep club approved?" Ginnie asks.

"No, I did!" I say. "Oliver thinks just because he's president, he can take all the credit."

Oliver waves his hand in the air, no apologies. "Lets stay focused. I can see why Blake uses a gavel."

"We can make a spirit stick and you have to hold it to talk," Ginnie offers.

"Uh, maybe." Oliver scratches his chin, covered with

stubble. Not prepubescent stubble. We're talking five o'clock manliness. "So, Mallory did a mission statement, but we really need to decide what we want this club to be. Let's brainstorm."

Chapter 12

What we decide at our first official pep club meeting:

1. We don't want to have too many meetings.
2. We need more members. We force Vance to join.
3. Oliver needs to chill (Ginnie's contribution).
4. We are going to do a float, or a trailer. We'll work at Oliver's house, since he lives near the Circle and has a detached garage in the back. We still need a theme. Decorations start early next

*week. We'll have five days to finish
before the parade.*

Pep club is wrapping up and I'm feeling good. Like maybe I actually would want to do an extracurricular activity, even if my boyfriend hadn't cheated on me, even if my grandma hadn't had the perfect adolescence, even if I could pull out my phone right now and pretend to be looking up something really important because . . . crap. I see Jeremy across the quad and he is COMING. OVER. HERE. NOW.

He looks marginally tortured. Before I can let pity creep in, I have to remind myself that his torture is self-inflicted and only 0.083 percent of what I feel.

"All righty, then. I think we're good until next week." Oliver glances up and sees Jeremy approaching. He shoots me a quick look before jumping up and giving Jeremy a fist bump.

"What up, cuz," Jeremy says. "What'd I miss?"

"The meeting," Ginnie says. "Good thing."

Cardin slides her hand over mine and squeezes. "You okay?" she whispers.

Jeremy gives me a nod. "Hey, Mallory."

"Hello."

I used to not mind the fact that Jeremy always nods in greeting, but when it's directed at me, the gesture feels forced. Also, what is he doing here? We broke up, he sent flowers, I ignored them. This is very cut-and-dry stuff, right?

Oliver doesn't look at me when he says to Jeremy, "I'll fill you in on the meeting later."

"Fill him in on what?" Ginnie stands up and brushes her jeans. "As VP, I say he can't join the club."

"I second that motion," Cardin says.

"I thought you needed more people?" Vance says.

"People. Not tools." Ginnie tries to yank me up. I've gone statue. "Come on, Mallory. I'll call Mom to pick us up."

"I can give you a ride," Jeremy says.

"So can I." Cardin pops up to my right, my sister and my friend a barrier on either side. "We're not going to leave you with him."

"*I* still need a ride," Vance whines.

"Vance, shut up. I told you that I'll take you." Oliver seems to be holding his breath too.

I wish I wasn't in this tight dress, regardless of how nice my legs look. I wish I was back in my sweatshirt phase so I could pull a hoodie over my head and hide. I squint up at Jeremy, who's standing right in front of the sun. "I don't need a ride."

"Can we talk for a second?" he asks.

"No, Toolerina." Ginnie sticks her hand on Jeremy's chest and pushes him away. "We don't have a second. I need to get home for soccer practice."

"I'll give Mallory a ride," Oliver offers. We all turn and stare at Oliver, curious why he's stepping into the Mallory tug-of-war. He holds his hands out in front of him, like he's blocking off a possible attack. "I mean, if you need to go, Ginnie. Then Mallory can talk to Jeremy but doesn't need to ride with him. We have a few more club things to talk about anyway."

"What about me?" Vance hops from one leg to the other.

Ginnie's so mature, sometimes I forget how clueless freshmen can be.

Cardin jingles her keys. "Okay, I'll give both of the freshmen a ride." She points at me. "I'll text you later."

"No texting. You'll *call* me later," I say. "At home."

"I hid the cordless phone," Ginnie reminds me.

"We'll figure it out." I exhale, trying to keep the edge out of my voice. A phone, at this moment, is not my biggest problem. "Go. You'll be late for practice."

Ginnie gives me a skeptical look and follows Vance and Cardin out of the quad, leaving me alone with my ex-boyfriend and the boy I'm pretty sure just ambushed me. Jeremy nods at Oliver. "Thanks, cuz. Can you give us a second alone?"

The *cuz*? Annoying. Did Jeremy use that before when he talked to Oliver? Wouldn't I remember if he did, or was I just blinded by love?

Oliver glances at me, checking that I'm okay, which is pretty chivalrous considering that he's the one who invited Jeremy here in the first place. "I'll get something from Blake's fancy vending machine."

Jeremy sticks an arm on each side of me, pinning me against The Tree of Life. "You look adorable in that dress."

I cover my face with my hands. "You don't get to say that."

"Mallory, I know you're upset, but it's nothing we can't work—"

"Don't."

Jeremy actually kneels down in front of me and grabs my hand. It's the kind of thing he would do in public, when everyone is around, to show how in love we are, how romantic and sweet he is. It's the kind of thing I used to crave, but now it's too much. Like he has to be all touchy-feely to prove that we're together, when really, we shouldn't be worried how other people look at our relationship, just how we both feel.

No one is watching now, except maybe Oliver, but I don't look over to check. I pull my hand away. "You don't go stick OVER IT on Friendspace and then try to hold my hand. And, by the way, OVER IT? Was that the best you could come up with?"

"I wasn't trying to be a douche; I just reacted to what you did to me," Jeremy says reasonably, or what he thinks is reasonably. "It's not cool to have your girlfriend hack into your account."

"'Hack'?" My voice echoes across the quad. "I did not hack. I clicked online to write your paper—on *moral* philosophy, by the way—and saw the Authentic Life page that you left up."

"I don't know what you saw, or thought you saw. But this is the truth." Jeremy is still kneeling, looking up at me. I can't see his eyes behind his sunglasses, which makes this a little easier. He's always had really earnest eyes, brown and soft. I wonder if they're as fake as the rest of him. Can you fake eyes? "I met Jenny online."

"Who is Jenny?"

"Oh, er, BubbleYum."

She has a name. He used her name. I hate that name. "Okay."

"And she's really advanced at Authentic Life, knew all these levels and stuff I didn't, so she offered to help me out. We started e-mailing as our different, you know, characters. You always talk like you're living in the Authentic Life world. That's part of the game."

"But you just called her…" I can't even say it. Jenny and Jeremy, it's practically the same name. They can paint it on their mailbox, all alliterate and cute. "You just said her name."

"Right." Jeremy stands, his knees creaking, and starts pacing instead. He's not facing me anymore. How can I know if someone who has lied to me is telling the truth now? "Well, obviously we, uh, blurred the boundaries a bit. But it was still just this fantasy, this alternate reality. She lives in Illinois, she's eighteen, and she's—"

"Not me."

"This had nothing to do with you. It's not like I talked to her because of anything you did or didn't do."

"Then why did you?"

"Because she wasn't, like, real. So it was easy."

"I'm easy!" I roll my eyes. "I mean, easy to talk to."

Jeremy rubs his neck. "Yeah? What if I told you I had a bad day or I was depressed or my parents are fighting again?"

"That's the reason you have a girlfriend, so you can share that kind of stuff!"

"But you're different. You're always happy, you don't get mad at people…"

"Ha, yeah. *You want to see mad?*" I am about to walk away because I am shaking again, physically shaking, and I can't keep that quiver out of my voice, can't stand how weak I feel in this moment, don't know why I can't just turn off my emotions and get out. It's almost like I *want* to hurt. Asking Jeremy these questions that I don't want answers to changes that vague, haunting ache into a piercing jab of truth.

The way he describes me, like I'm this vapid girl who doesn't care about deeper things . . . that's so off. I listened to all his problems when he shared, and he never even asked about my issues, because he never thought I had issues. *Everyone* has issues.

"Did you ever meet her?"

"No."

Relief. My next question is answered—nothing physical happened. But that's not what matters here. Jeremy got plenty of physical from me. BubbleYum was his emotional connection, the girl who knew his truths. In some ways, she was more real than me.

"How long have you been married to this girl?"

"Dude, we aren't married!"

"That's not what your profile said."

"I don't know why you're getting so mad about this. It's a stupid game!"

I look over at Oliver, who's leaning against the vending machine, his phone in one hand and a bag of popcorn in the other. He glances up, catches me staring, and looks down at his phone. I wonder how involved he was in orchestrating this little conversation, if he has any idea what Jeremy and I are even talking about.

"Okay, how long have you been in contact with her?" I ask.

"I don't know. Last spring. Maybe April."

Five months, give or take. Jeremy and I had been together for almost a whole school year by then. He'd already been to one of our family reunions. We'd already started talking in sentences like "Let's go snowboarding at Big Bear next winter," which shows that we were planning for a future together, maybe not forever, but at least for the immediate soon. "When did you start saying *I love you*?"

Jeremy freezes, which is my breaking point. I never actually read *I love you* in an e-mail, but his reaction tells me it's happened. How can someone say something like that to two different people at the same time? Not only did he *write* that to his cyberlove, but I believe he *felt* it. For her. And they weren't just words he said to get the girl to blur her physical boundaries. He said it because Jenny knew him—all of him.

And all I got was a piece.

"Mallory, look, I shouldn't have gotten pissed online, and in class I should have acted different. But what's past is past and—"

"No. The past isn't just the past. You don't get to use that as a cop-out. You have to learn from the past, or else it repeats." I turn away from him. I will not let him see me cry. I will not. I am just like my grandma—strong and independent and... peppy. Think pep. I march over to Oliver. "I need you to take me home now."

Oliver looks at his cousin. I don't know what expression or gesture Jeremy makes in response. "Are you two good?"

"Oliver, do I look good? Can you please take me home before I break down in front of him?"

"Mallory!" Jeremy calls. "Don't be dumb. Come back!"

"I'm parked in the senior parking lot. Let's go." Oliver doesn't say anything else as he hurries out to his battered maroon Nissan and opens my door for me. I slump into the passenger seat. He has three hula girls on the dash, three more in the back. I wonder what they think behind those vacant smiles, their plastic shells. These are women who will never wear a shirt, who must spend their existence dancing on demand. There's something so sad about that, about me, about this situation, that the tears come hot and fast.

Oliver gets into the car, glances over at me, and sticks the key into the ignition.

"What's with the hula girls?" I have to pause between words, I'm crying so hard. "Do you hate women...or something?"

"You know, I got one, and then everyone thought I had a collection and I started getting them as gifts. But it's pretty rock-and-roll, how they stay stationary and move at the same time. Like a bobblehead."

"I collect bobbleheads. Baseball players."

"Do you hate baseball players?"

"I don't care about baseball. I just like the bobbleheads."

"Then do you hate men?"

"That's not a good question...to ask me right now." I snort, and with it comes snot that I hide with my hand.

Oliver leans across me and opens his glove box. He smells like oranges. I mean, we do live in the city of Orange; citrus is not a rare scent, but they are my favorite fruit, and the smell is so strong, the kid must have showered in orange juice. He grabs a few wadded napkins and hands them to me. I wipe, trying to be discreet but not caring much.

"Um, where do you live?" he asks.

"I need...a few minutes...I don't want my family...to see this."

"Too close to rush hour to go to the beach. You want to go to El Modena for a few minutes so you can cool off?"

"What's El Modena?"

"It's called the Open Space too, you know, that big hill off of Cannon Street. We'll go there. I don't have anywhere I need to be yet."

I nod. Cooling off is what you do when you've had a little spat with someone. We both know I've moved beyond that to full-on hysterical.

He tunes the radio to something acoustic and soft, and lets the music continue the conversation. He's a careful driver, staring straight ahead so I can have the privacy to deconstruct in his passenger seat.

The only person I hate more right now than Jeremy, or Jenny, is myself. I hate that I am crying, hate that I still care about a boy who hurt me the way he did and that he's not acknowledging his mistake. I hate that I believed him to be one person, only to see this whole other person come out who must have always been there. And I hate girls like me. I have never been this girl before. If I were outside of this situation, if I were watching another girl go through this, I would shrug and say, "He's a tool. Get over it."

But I haven't. And I can't.

Jeremy was partially right about the relationships in my life. I've never gotten in cat fights with girls, never had problems with boys, never had huge tension with my family. Maybe I'm not solid enough to even manage the conflict. My only stability is mobility.

I rub the napkin against my eye. At least I'm trying to move on. It's a very small *at least*, but I hold on to it with everything. The List is my attempt to find reason in this unreasonable situation. It's all I really have to push me through to the moment when Jeremy becomes a two-dimensional memory and not the flesh-and-blood person haunting me now.

Oliver drives. Jeremy would try to fill the silence with talk, would try to fix my problems, or tell me it's not that bad, or even try to top my story with something worse. But Oliver doesn't. He just drives.

He parks at Cannon Street, at the base of a hill, which I guess is Open Space. You have to love a park that's so straightforward with its name. There's not much to it—it's a patch of undeveloped land sandwiched between a sea of subdivisions. I've driven by here, but I've never actually hiked up. Hiking seems very, I don't know, laborious.

I flip the visor down and try to get all the mascara and snot off my face. It's a failed effort. Oliver made that funeral crack earlier about my black dress, and right now it doesn't feel too far off.

"Let's go." Oliver slips out of his car and starts up the trail.

I scramble after him, tears still spilling down my cheek. It's sunny, warm, breezy…one of those days you hope tourists don't experience because they'll inevitably sell everything and move out for the weather. "We're not hiking this whole mountain, are we?"

He looks behind his shoulder. "It's a hill. Something to do until you're ready to go home. Besides, it's hard to cry and hike."

He's very right. It's also hard to hike and think, hike and breathe, hike and wear questionable ballet flats. I follow him for a good ten minutes, watching the ball on the top of his beanie bounce, Oliver's long gait stretching from step to step.

I know he's giving me space, and I appreciate the solitude, but I also wouldn't mind him next to me, if anything so he can catch me if I keel over. Pretty soon I'm going to accidentally accomplish Do Something Dangerous when I fall over and twist my ankle. "Oliver . . . I can't go any farther."

It's all dry sage and prickly pear cactus and dirt. Nowhere to sit, except back at the car, which is half a mile away.

He bounds down the trail and stops just in front of me, his tie loosened like a lawyer at the end of a long day. "Having fun?"

"You didn't tell me that you're so athletic," I say.

"I *am* point guard on the Mötley Crüe basketball team. Besides, walking up a straight line doesn't require advanced skill."

"But you're so fast."

He shrugs off the compliment. "You stopped crying."

"I could have stopped crying in the car."

"No. My hula girls were mocking you. Besides, check the view."

It's not like there's this grand view of the ocean or even Los Angeles. We're not that high up and we can't see that far out. But there are some housing developments, and more important, a relatively smog-free blue sky.

"I've never been here," I say.

"Really? I thought Jeremy would've taken you. We used to hike this all the time in middle school."

"No more use of the *J* word."

"Just for a second." He cracks his neck. "I want you to know I didn't mean to invite Jeremy. He overheard me telling someone else about the meeting, knew you were trying to get a club together, and said he wanted to come. I didn't know he was going to propose to you."

"Jeremy wasn't proposing to me." I give a hollow laugh, thinking how ridiculous a proposal would be. I hadn't planned on forever with Jeremy. I don't really know what I'd planned on. Maybe when we went away to college things would fizzle, but whatever happened, it would be mutual, friendly. That I would always look back on my first love as something real and right. Now I can't decide if I was ever really in love with Jeremy, or just in love with love. Did I want a boyfriend so badly that I accepted the warm body, just like he did with me? Or is it Jeremy specifically who I want? Wanted. Past tense. Mostly. "He was apologizing. Although, actually, he never said *I'm sorry*. Or admitted that he was wrong."

"So he *was* wrong." Oliver said.

The breeze picks up to a gust and an old water bottle bounces past us. I get a faint whiff of Oliver's orange musk again, unless there's a tree somewhere close. "Have you ever heard Jeremy talk about a girl named Jenny?"

A look of understanding crosses Oliver's face. I wish I'd phrased that question in a different way or at a different time. I don't want him to understand what happened. I don't want anyone to know what an idiot I was. "No. But we aren't kissing cousins."

"Um, I'd be worried if you were."

"That's an expression, Mallory. Jeremy's not really my type."

"No?" I smile, relieved by the shift in focus. I can't believe I just said Jenny's name out loud. "Why not?"

"I try to stay away from blood relations. And I like girls. So that's two strikes. I'm sure you could help me find a third."

Try thirty.

"Oh, and here's another." Oliver gives a theatric grimace. "He used to tease me when we were kids. The scars still run deep."

I hesitate. Jeremy is always a nice guy to his friends, but he has a temper with people who make him mad, and Oliver could certainly be on that list. "What for?"

"Really awful things. Smarty-pants, weirdo." Oliver fakes a sniff.

"Kids can be cruel."

Oliver tugs his beanie off and starts playing with the fountain of yarn on top. "I don't know what he did, Mallory, but I'm sorry. For him. I don't think he tries to be a jerk, if that helps. You know my uncle isn't the best relationship role model."

I do. Jeremy's parents are still married, but his dad has high expectations and a sharp tongue. Jeremy always swore he would never say the things to a woman that his dad says to his mom. And he never did, to me. That wasn't his problem. He just said nice things to two girls at once.

"And I do know he really was... really is into you. You're the only girl I've ever heard him talk about, and it was always good."

"Yeah?"

"Yeah." He twists off a piece of yarn. "So whatever happened, it's probably not you. Just him. And it's not even him, not completely."

"That's good of you to defend his honor."

"I don't know about that." Oliver dangles the string in the wind. "Give me your finger."

I hold out my left ring finger, my wedding finger, and he shakes his head. Seriously, Mallory? No. This is not your second fake proposal of the day. He grabs the pointer finger on my right hand and ties the string around it. "This is a reminder."

"What am I remembering?" The Open Space suddenly feels very small, and now that he's closer, I smell apples with the oranges, apple shampoo. Jeremy always used a pine shampoo.

Why am I thinking about Jeremy?

I'm not.

Why am I thinking about Oliver?

I'm not.

"Remember that you don't have to forget what happened, but you can forget the pain." Oliver's eyes darken. "I promise.

Sometimes you think there is no way anyone has ever hurt like you have, that you'll never stop hurting, and then little by little you do, until it doesn't. Hurt. Not like it does now."

"How do you know that?"

Oliver holds out his right hand and there's a braided twine ring. "I made this when my parents got divorced. It was bad. Like choose-her-or-me bad, and my dad doesn't exactly want to play catch with me since I went with Mom. It'd be a long throw, anyway—he's in Toronto."

"I'm sorry."

"Don't be. *They* should be sorry. And I still hate them, a little, at times, and there are moments that are big and painful, but it's not like...how do I say it...like—"

"Someone singeing the entire surface of your skin with a curling iron, one limb at a time?"

"That would be the overdramatic version, but sure. The memory stays. The agony fades."

I knew that, about Oliver. He's Jeremy's cousin through their moms, and that's why Oliver moved to Orange in middle school, so his mom could be close to her three siblings. It's funny how something that is just a random fact that you hear about someone—parents divorced, Dad far away—is really that person's life, something they deal with every day. He must think I'm such an idiot, crying over a high school breakup, but he isn't looking at me like I'm an idiot. He has a gentle smile on his lips, not his half smile, and I almost want to clink our rings together in solidarity. I don't know this kid at all, but in this little way, I feel like he knows me completely.

I turn my face to the sun so I'll be too blinded to cry. Why is he being so nice to me? I don't know how to respond to it. Jeremy always asked if I was on my period when I got weepy. "Okay. Well, thanks. Smarty-pants."

Oliver grabs at his chest like he's been stabbed. "Not you too!" He slumps onto his knees and gasps for air. "Can't... breathe."

"The weirdo line was probably right too."

"Well, now you're taking it too far. Beat you back."

I trudge behind him down the trail and within fifteen minutes he's driving me home, hula girls swaying to his acoustic music. He keeps his eyes on the road, but every few minutes he casts me a quick glance, a reassuring smile. It's not lost on me that the string is on the same finger I used to wear Jeremy's ruby ring.

Oliver Kimball. Huh.

Chapter 13

1960s items I spend all my savings on at thrift stores and antique shops:

1. A teal rotary phone that works, but with lots of static.
2. Analog clock radio with peeling fake wood exterior.
3. A gray high-waisted skirt with two Peter Pan collar shirts I can tuck in, a knee-length plaid skirt that looks like it's half of an old Catholic school uniform, and an ugly brown housedress that's at least true to era. Maybe I can get Grandma to spruce it up with some stitching or buttons.

4. Saddle shoes that smell like roast beef.
5. A satchel. Backpacks don't jive.
6. Vinyl records. Two singles from poppy, hair-sprayed girl groups I've never heard of and *Help!* by the Beatles. Okay, so *Help!* came out a couple years later, but I am in grave need of a breakup song to repeatedly play on Dad's record player. "Yesterday" fits the bill.

Jeremy doesn't try to talk to me for the rest of the week. I'm almost happy that I have no default person to hang out with that weekend, that I can do anything I want with whomever I want. I can do something dangerous.

Or I can take a sewing class at the community center.

Ginnie agrees to take the seven o'clock class with me. She'll go to a party or something afterward, while I shall "research" early sixties cereals like Cap'n Crunch. And by research, I mean eat. Alone, in my bed, without even a good rom com to keep me company.

Ginnie has afternoon practice, so I go an hour early to the library by the community center. The library, with the books and articles and Dewey decimals, is admirably vintage. I want to check out some books for my history paper, but they're harder to find that I thought. The City of Orange's library card catalog has, naturally, gone online. When I ask a librarian for help, she points to the computer. Telling her I can't use it makes me feel like a little kid whispering that I have to go to the bathroom. But I finally end up with a stack of books, half about the Industrial Revolution, the other half a mix of novels, etiquette books, another cookbook—anything that can achieve time travel with a flip of the pages.

I write two pages of notes about the Industrial Revolution. The virtual project took less time. The historical information is all on one site—each time the user adds an element, a lesson is attached. So if I have a dress factory, and click on a seamstress, five pages of facts appear. With books, I have to read a lot to get to the words I want. Then I need to quote those words, combine the quotes, and add my own arguments and thoughts to that.

This crusade would have been a lot easier in the summer, when school projects weren't involved. Too bad I didn't see into Jeremy's cheating soul three months earlier. I would have saved money on his birthday present too.

"Being at the library on a Friday night is geeky enough, but you're reading books about the Industrial Revolution on top of it?" Ginnie slides into the chair next to me.

"Homework." I check my watch, which I've taken to wearing again now that I don't have a cell phone. "Our sewing class starts in ten minutes."

"Homework *and* sewing on a Friday night? What a social calendar."

I stack up three books, hoping I can find more information later. I'm starting to form a thesis, but in no way do I know enough to write five pages. "You're also at the library on a Friday night. What does that say about you?"

"That I'm a nice sister." Ginnie picks up *The Busy Girl's Guide to Etiquette*, published in 1959, and starts thumbing through. She stops at a passage and snorts. "'Wake up two hours before your husband so you can have time to bathe, do your hair, powder you nose, and make a healthy breakfast. No man wants to see a sleep-tousled wife!' Oh, Mallory. This is awful."

I reach for the book. "That's one passage."

Ginnie holds the book up higher. "Really? What about this? 'Don't whine to your spouse about your daily troubles. He's had a harder day providing for you and your children.' *This* is what you're aspiring to? To be some guy's house slave?"

She thumps the book down and I slide it across the table so I can read for myself. Ginnie was reading a chapter called "The Happy Husband." There is not a "Happy Wife" chapter.

"It's not that bad. Besides, you even said that it would be nice if Mom cooked dinner every night," I reason.

"What, and miss out on pizza night? Thai night? Sushi night—"

"The point is, I'm not trying to be a housewife. I'm a teenager; Grandma was a teenager. That's what The List is about."

Ginnie hops out of her seat. "I hope you're not romanticizing this too much. That prefeminist movement crap is scary."

"What do you know about the feminist movement?" Um, what did I know? I'd meant to read some books on that too, but when I thought of old feminists, I thought of armpit hair and bra burning and lots of angry, political yelling, which is not nearly as fun as party dresses and school clubs. "So what if women cared about their families and cleaned a lot? That's probably why Grandma ended up so great."

"Grandma ended up great because she worked her butt off, not because she went to the soda shop with her steady. I've read up on the sixties too. They didn't have hardly any sports for woman, or jobs, and they made less money for doing the same work." Her voice has taken on that matter-of-fact edge. I hate when she thinks she knows more than me. *Younger* sister, remember? "It's not like today, where you can say you want to be a doctor and work hard and it happens. You have better opportunities now than she did then."

"You're totally missing the point."

"Am I?"

I blow out an exasperated breath. "Let's just go to sewing class."

I check out the Industrial Revolution books, but don't bother with the sixties stuff. I'm worried history will only discredit my sunshiny hypothesis.

The classroom on the first floor of the community center is packed with wannabe sewers. No, that's not what you call them, right? Seamstresses? But that's girls, so what are the guys? Oh, tailors. We are a robust group of future seamstresses and tailors.

Except it turns out everyone already has basic sewing skills and they're here to learn more. Even Ginnie nods along as the teacher explains we'll be working on cross-stitching and hemming and fusing, whatever that means.

"How do you know what she's talking about?" I whisper to Ginnie.

"From when I used to sew with Grandma during our weekend vacations. Didn't you?"

No, I got early-morning wake-up calls and shopping trips. Which I would normally prefer, but it's not fair that Grandma's tutelage means Ginnie is better than me at something else.

I spend twenty minutes trying to thread a needle, tie that little knot at the end, and stitch two pieces of fabric together in a straight line. My hands shake as I poke, poke, pull, all the while trying to ignore the hum of sewing machines run by professional sewers...seamstresses masquerading as beginners.

Meanwhile, my sister has already rummaged through the fabric scraps and is designing a quilt. Swell. She can make my dress. Make it, wear it with her steady, cook a fabulous dinner, and finish the whole stupid list.

No. Delegation is not as worthwhile as participation. I will do this, even if my homecoming dress ends up looking like a pillowcase. I stick my needle into the fabric again and prick my finger on the side.

Ugh. I'm trying to abandon the present, but I don't even have the skills to master the past.

Grandma picks me up Saturday for an afternoon of fabric and pattern shopping. Orange County is famous for its big retail centers like Fashion Island and South Coast Plaza, but the very best shopping in all of Southern California is ten minutes from my house at the boutiques at Orange Circle. One of the stores also sells vintage fabrics, and I'm hoping we'll find something perfect for my dress.

We find a spot on the street and Grandma effortlessly

parallels her Mini Cooper, all without interrupting her Ode to the Fancy Senior Community. "We're reading *The Awakening* for book club. It's amazing how progressive Chopin's views were for the time, and how relatable the text can be over a hundred years later. Oh, and tennis is better, I can overhand serve now. Not over the net, but it's progress. But my favorite friends so far are the ladies in the Slot Group."

I'm pulled away from my daydreaming about pale blue satins to ask about that last one. "Slot Group?"

Grandma feeds the meter and slings her purse over her shoulder. "The ladies and I carpool to Las Vegas once a month. It's only a four-hour drive, fun chance to gab. We eat at the buffet, play poker... I won a thousand bucks in fifteen minutes, so my new nickname is Cool Hand Luke."

"Who is Luke?"

"Never mind. It's an old movie."

"Grandma, you gamble?" I'm scandalized. For how world-weary she is, my grandma is straight-edged. She rarely drinks (and only wine), doesn't smoke, and saves unhealthy food for special occasions like sunrises. She always says she got her wildness out in her twenties, that stability looks better on her.

"Yes, I gamble and play tennis. I'm not dead yet, Mallory."

"It just doesn't seem like you," I say.

"Who does it seem like?"

"No one. You just, I mean, you're usually at charity galas or hobnobbing with another ambassador."

"I've only met three ambassadors."

"Only?"

Grandma's wearing a cropped Indian sari, pink leggings, and glitter flats with her hair knotted in a loose bun. She marches down the street, a one-person parade, each passerby stopping to stare. It's just so evident that she's seen and understands the world in ways the guy in the Dodgers T-shirt doesn't.

"You sound like your sister," Grandma says.

"What did Ginnie say?"

"That I'm forgetting who I am." Grandma stops at a rack of sale clothes outside an overpriced maternity store. "That's not what I'm trying to do. But I spent almost forty years with your grandpa. You know sometimes I still wake up, roll over to tell him about my dream, and I have that realization that he's not there? You can't know what that feels like."

"Of course not."

"So I got a new bed. And a new home. And maybe a new life. He still haunts me, but at least I'm not tripping over his shoes and finding old notes he left me in the drawer."

Or old spiral notebooks with teenage lists.

Grandma blows out a breath and dabs at the corner of her eye. I reach across the rack of clothes and hug her. She gives me a curt pat and pulls away. "Anyway. There is one old thing I'm good at, and that's shopping. Here's your store."

She pushes open the blue painted door of Worn Again Vintage. I stand outside for a minute, trying to come up with the right thing to say. I don't know if I should ask her more questions about her two-year loss, which is really no time when you consider their decades together. Do I bring it up again or make a joke about something else? Stay quiet? I have no idea how to touch someone else's pain, and it makes my own, again, seem so trivial. What Jeremy and I had was a speed date next to my grandparents' relationship.

The bell clangs as I enter the funky store. Chinese lanterns and old Tiffany lamps offer warm lighting, and vintage gowns hang from the exposed ceiling beams. A line of mannequin heads sport hats from different eras, many of which I've tried on but never had the confidence to purchase. The girl at the counter, Kimmy, looks up from the antique cash register and flashes me a bright red lipsticked smile. "Mallory! Are you here to sell or buy?"

"Kimmy, this is my grandma, and she's going to help me sew a homecoming dress. Late fifties, early sixties cocktail. We're looking for patterns, fabric if you have it."

Kimmy peers down at me over cat-eye reading glasses. "Isn't homecoming soon?"

"Next week," I say. "But I don't need anything fancy."

"It's homecoming. Of course you need something fancy." Grandma leans against the counter and says in a conspiring whisper, "The labor is going to be an eighty-twenty split. This girl can't even thread a bobbin yet."

"What's a bobbin?" I ask.

They both laugh.

What?

Kimmy points us to the back of the store, where bolts of fabric are shoved into shelves. Most of the fabric is thirties or forties replica cotton prints with sailboats or ducks, but there are a few shelves of "new fabric to create that old look." We came here last year when I wanted Grandma to make me a flapper costume for Halloween. Chiffon, pleather, muslin, calicos, and silk. I try not to look at the price tags—vintage isn't cheap. Grandma plops a bolt of purple velvet onto the small table in the corner. "Velvet's formal, but the stretch is forgiving."

I make a face. "Grandma. When I said I wanted vintage, I didn't mean eighties rocker. I want something that you would have worn when you were my age." I spot some soft peach chiffon and reach up on my tiptoes. "Like this."

Grandma purses her lips. "I don't understand this blast-from-the-past thing. There are plenty of beautiful on-the-rack dresses. We looked like big powder puffs back then."

"No, you were *perfection*." I grab a male mannequin wearing a tux and wheel him over to Grandma. "Come on. Tell me about your junior homecoming. Was it different from prom?"

"I didn't go to prom," Grandma mumbles.

"Okay, but did you go out to dinner at all? Or did everyone just stay at the dance the whole time?"

"I can't remember."

"I wish they still did that. Sometimes people just come to take their picture and leave for an after-party. No one really dances. Oh, did you go to the drive-in after? Was there a bonfire?"

"Honey, you've been watching way too many movies. Let's find you a fabric, already. I'm getting a headache."

"But I'm just trying to *visualize*." My voice has gone a little whiny. I can't help it. There's this poem we read last year in

English from *Spoon River Anthology*, which is a collection of voices from everyone who died in a small town a hundred years ago. It's not like I memorized the whole thing, but there was one poem, a short one, that talks about how, when the guy was young, his wings were strong, but he didn't know the mountains well. When he was old, he knew the mountains, but he didn't have the energy to fly them. And the last line says, "Genius is wisdom and youth."

Look, I'm not asking for genius. But I could sure use some perspective, and I don't get why Grandma is being so stingy with the shares. I thought she would whisper all her list pointers, the secret to a happy and clean adolescence, some tidbit that would take away all the pain. Isn't that why we have grandparents, anyway? So they can get all misty-eyed about the days of yore? Grandma Vivian, I need to know about yore.

"So. Peach chiffon." Her reading glasses are perched on her nose, a notebook out, all business. "It'll look pretty with the red in your hair, but what do you think Jeremy will think about it?"

I rub my hand along the fabric. So she's not giving up the Secret of Life, but she is offering up her time and talents. And in return, I'm giving her a very limited slice of the truth. She thinks I'm just doing this because I need a dress. She has no idea about The List or the event that inspired its significance. And if I only tell her what happened and not the particulars (ahem, BubbleYum), then maybe she won't think I'm completely moronic. "Jeremy and I broke up, Grandma."

She reaches for another fabric, this one a bedazzled pale

blue. "A week before the dance? I would have stretched it out a bit. At least get another date out of him."

"I think he wants to get back together, but...I can't. It isn't worth it."

"Did he do something wrong?" she asks, her voice much more tender. It's similar to my mother's questions, but Grandma's inquiry feels more heartfelt. She doesn't ask questions unless she wants to know the answer.

"He did. Nothing horrendous, but...I don't trust him anymore."

"Betrayal." She clucks her tongue. "Been there. Not easy to come back from that."

The store bell jingles again, followed by girls laughing. I step back against the wall, in case it's someone I know. If anyone sees what kind of fabric I'm buying, they might assume it's for a formal and then they'll want to know who I'm going with and...

Yvonne squeals when she sees me. "Mallory! Did you disappear off the face of the earth? I haven't seen you in a week! Why weren't you at the party last night? Paige, look! It's Mallory!"

Paige rolls her eyes and smiles. "Hey. Are you buying fabric for your Industrial Revolution project too? Yvonne and I are getting muslin to make a true-to-era dress. Big sleeves, high neck. Extra credit."

"No. I'm just here with my grandma. She's making a quilt." I squeeze Grandma's arm, a silent prompt not to mention homecoming.

Grandma smiles. "You know grandmas. Always quilting, baking cookies, threading bobbins..."

I squeeze her harder. Gambling and sassiness. Seems I don't know Grandma at all.

Yvonne's eyes widen, like she suddenly remembered something. "Did you get my text? Paige, did you text her?"

"She's doing a social experiment, Yvonne. No cell phones. It's very cutting-edge."

"Why did you text me?" I ask Yvonne.

She bites at her thumbnail. "Um, you should read the text. I like texting bad news instead of saying it to the person's face. It makes it less awkward."

"Saying things are awkward is what makes them awkward." Paige shakes her head and takes a step closer to me. "Um, Lincoln Gleason had a beach bonfire for his birthday last night. Totally unplanned, I just saw an e-vite on Friendspace. I stopped by your house to see if you wanted to come, but no one was there, and I couldn't call—"

"What happened?" It's crazy how unplugging has made me so invisible.

Paige glances at Grandma, who takes her cue and starts to rummage through her purse. "Oh, I think I left my measuring tape in the car. I always prefer using my own. Be back in a minute, girls."

Paige waits for the store bell to ring until she speaks. "Jeremy was there. And, apparently..."

"He asked some other girl to homecoming!" Yvonne jumps in. "She doesn't even go to our school! He met her at camp or something. She's from Indiana."

"Illinois," I say faintly. BubbleYum. I can't believe him.

Paige slips her arm around my shoulder. "Well, the good

news is that everyone thinks he's a jerk for not having a mourning period. I don't know if he had this girl on the side or what."

"It doesn't matter." I pull back from Paige, not giving away any information. "I don't care."

"Is this why you guys broke up, then?" Yvonne asks. "Because that would totally make sense. I knew all those Internet rumors weren't true. You don't really have a chat-room college boyfriend, do you?"

I expect to feel that cutting, sharp pain, that out-of-body surrealism that's been like an old sweatshirt since my discovery. But my body isn't reacting at all. No butterflies, no shaking, no sweats. I don't feel one pinprick of tears. It's almost like I've been expecting this, almost like knowing there is a flesh-and-blood girl traveling here makes it easier. And it helps me make up my mind about something.

Grandma clangs back into the store and pretends to search through a rack of leather jackets. When I make eye contact, she mouths, "Are you all right?"

I stick the bolt of peach chiffon under my arm. "Well, good seeing you girls. We have to go. I'm sewing my own dress for homecoming."

"I'm going to write an editorial on you. Strength in the face of adversity." Paige nods with pride. The fact that she likes me for traits that I'm just now discovering, and liking about myself, makes me think we should hang out more often. Actually, I should have more friends in general. Like, in-person, spend-time-together friends.

"Wait, so you're going?" Yvonne asks. "With who? Everyone already has a date. It's only leftovers now."

Yvonne, however, is not high on my get-to-know list.

The goal was to sew a dress for homecoming. And I'll do that, at least with Grandma as a very involved party. So I could get by without attending the dance, maybe give the dress to Ginnie. But the strong move would be to go, to see Jeremy and BubbleYum, to prove something even The List can't. That I am going to be okay. Eventually.

"I don't know who I'm going *with*," I say. "But you can text everyone you know this. Mallory Bradshaw is going to homecoming."

Chapter 14

Things I have sewn in my life:

1. A button.
2. A tie quilt for a fourth-grade project. I quit midway and my mom finished it for me.
3. That piece of half-finished fabric in sewing class.
4. Um, wow. That's it.

I wake up Sunday morning to a weird burring sound. It takes a few minutes before I realize it's my new/old rotary phone. I glance at my new (old) alarm clock. It's 9:12. "Hello?"

"May I please speak to Mallory?"

"Oliver?" I sit up in bed. "What's with the formal greeting?"

"You don't have a cell—I didn't know who would answer. I had to use proper phone etiquette."

I cradle the phone on my shoulder. "Oh. I didn't know there was proper phone etiquette."

"Of course. We learned it in Scouts."

"Scouts? Like Boy Scouts?" I giggle. Genuine giggle.

"Don't laugh. I just earned my Eagle Scout. That also looks good on college résumés."

"Sorry, but practicing phone calls doesn't sound like scouting. Aren't you supposed to make a bear trap out of a lunchbox?"

"Ah, yes. The bear-in-the-lunch-box merit badge. Took me weeks to get that. No, we had to take an etiquette class. I also know all my dinner forks, so you know who to call in case of an emergency."

"I'll remember that." I rub the yarn that's still on my finger.

"Sorry, so proper phone etiquette is introduction, small talk, and now I'm going to move on to my point."

Honestly. I can't even hear irony in his voice. I think the boy is so wry that he probably doesn't recognize his own sarcasm. "Another merit badge? Make me a booby trap with dental floss and a quarter. Go."

"So I was thinking." No laughs at that one. I'll have to try the joke on Ginnie later. Just the expression "booby trap" should have earned me something. "About the float. Since we're not going to be able to go full throttle, we can make up for lack of size with good costumes. Now, the theme this year is ToonTown. Blake's idiot idea, but whatever. SpongeBob is out, the sophomores are doing some Disney homage, so we need to think of a cartoon no one has used."

"Oh my gosh, you're a closet spirit freak!" I laugh.

"What?" Oliver sounds wounded. "No, I'm not."

"This college application thing is all a cover-up, huh?"

"I just think if we're going to do something, we should do it right."

I slide out of bed and start walking toward the bathroom, but forget the phone has a cord and get yanked back. My neck snaps and I cry out.

"What happened?"

"Nothing." I sit down on the bed and massage my neck. What happened? I gave up my cell phone, had my sister confiscate my cordless phone, and am now injuring myself with a rotary dial. As you do. "So you obviously have a plan for this float. What's my part?"

"Are you and Ginnie doing anything today? I was hoping the VP and secretary could come with me to buy supplies."

I feel an unexplained flicker of annoyance that he asks about Ginnie, even if I did initially have him on her steady list. "Ginnie has soccer and I have to work on a paper."

"One hour. Two, tops. If we get everything together today, we'll be able to start the float right away."

I rub the sleep out of my eyes. I wouldn't mind hanging out with Oliver again—maybe this time I could even manage to not break into tears—but I seriously have to get going on that history paper, and Ginnie wanted to do a big Sunday dinner to help prepare for our soiree. "Look, I really want to do a float, but I'm not sure today is good for me."

"We only have until Friday." Oliver coughs. "I can't believe I'm the one begging to do this."

"I can't, either."

"Your school needs you, Mallory."

I smile. Ginnie's the only one who ever jokes like this with me. Maybe I'm not losing my touch. Maybe I just need to be around the right people. "Fine. I will make a sacrifice for spirit."

"And I promise I won't ambush you with my cousin this time."

My smile fades. Oliver is always going to have that asterisk by his name when I think about him—Jeremy's cousin. Being around him isn't going to make the grieving process happen any faster, but completing The List will. If I want to call myself a real pep club secretary, I have to go secretarial on that float.

Oliver offers to drive, but I go legit and ride my bike instead. Because in the sixties, a lot of teens still didn't have cars, so they had to ride bikes, see? Also, in the sixties, Orange was half the size it is now, so they didn't have to ride so *far*. The cracked banana seat of the old beach cruiser I found in the garage keeps pinching the thin material of my vintage 501 Levi's.

In Southern California, it's easier to *feel* fall than see it. There isn't an autumn blitz of golden colors and the weather only dips a few degrees. But there's still something in the gray sky that whispers change. I button my jacket against the chill. A cardigan or pea coat would have been more authentic, but I didn't think to get winter clothes for my project. I just need my clothes to last until I finish The List.

I pretend I'm biking because of the cooler weather, pretend like I wasn't nervous to have my parents accidentally meet Oliver and ask who he is and find out he's related to Jeremy. I don't want Ginnie to point out that Oliver and I are going alone and he could have asked Cardin or Paige or even freshman Vance to come too. I want this little shopping excursion to be simple and mine—not something to be dissected by anyone else, especially since there isn't anything to dissect.

Oliver's Nissan chugs up to the craft store and I watch him from behind the glass. His door is jammed shut, so he slides out the driver's window like a dancer in some hipster ballet. He zips up his hoodie with one quick flick, his fingers long and strong, just like Jeremy's.

But he's not Jeremy. I need to remind myself that. Oliver's ears poke out and his eyes are a hypnotic blue. He's unkempt and charming, while Jeremy is ridiculously handsome and has perfect lips... Oh. I still miss those lips.

If I try hard enough, I can almost pretend Oliver is just another boy who happens to have the same set of grandparents as the boy I'm trying to forget. Besides. We're only buying crepe paper together.

Oliver strides across the parking lot, not bothering to look both ways, just assuming the cars will stop. Which they do. His face breaks into his sideways grin when he sees me through the window. I hop back and scramble for a shopping cart. There's no reason to feel guilty for watching him. We were supposed to meet here and I just made it first. It's not like I was checking him out.

It's not.

"I realized something driving here." Oliver eases the cart away from me and strolls down the arts-and-crafts aisle. "I have no idea what decoration things we need."

"Decoration things?"

"For the float." He pulls out a little notebook and pen from his back pocket. He tries to flip to a clean page, but I notice the cover first. It's purple and pink with tweeny peace signs. I don't comment, just flick the paper.

"What? It's my sister's. I couldn't find mine. And we need to make a list. Lists help."

Truer words were never spoken.

He starts jotting things down, his long fingers gliding across the page. "So we probably need streamers and balloons. Where do you get that paper that's thick and on the rolls? The ASB always uses it for signs?"

"Butcher paper?" I ask. "I'm sure the school has some available. If not, an art store will."

He writes down "butcher paper" in slanted, all-caps print. "See, I knew you'd be good at this."

"Why, because I'm a girl?" My tone turns to steel. I hope I haven't given Oliver too much credit.

"What?" Oliver glances around the store. "No, because you're sharp. Your mission statement was well-written. Criminy, you're on edge."

"Criminy?"

"Can I say something without you turning it into a question? Yes. Criminy. It's a legitimate word and this is a perfectly fine notebook and we are on a mission. So let's focus." He spins around the store, utterly lost. "Uh, so what else do we need?"

I grab Oliver's notebook and add to the list. Masking tape, tissue paper, balloons, paint, fringe, glitter garland. That should be good—we're only decorating a little trailer and standing inside, not doing a whole float. "That's a start," I say. "We should go to a party store for this other stuff."

He beams at me like I've just written a world peace treaty. "I am so glad you're here."

I can't help it. I smile back. "I am too."

For the record, I'm glad because I want pep club to be a success, not because my ex-boyfriend's cousin just made me feel more important and useful than I've felt in forever. "Although this should be natural for you. You're the one in ASB. I've never been in a school club in my life."

"Seriously?" Oliver throws a pack of blue glitter into the cart, which wasn't on the list, but maybe he has a vision I don't. "What do you do, then? Sports?"

"No. My résumé has zero padding. Blank and free."

"You've never done a school activity? What's your thing, then?" He sounds genuinely interested, like he can't imagine a life not filled with responsibilities and activities and lofty college goals.

What do I do? Before last week, I hung out with my boyfriend 24/7. Well, obviously not 24/7. Maybe 20/6. The rest of his time went to basketball or BubbleYum.

I lean against the shopping cart. The neon lights are despairingly bright in here. They radiate my dim realization.

I don't have a thing.

How can I not have a thing? I've tried a million things, but nothing that I can claim. Nothing that I'm good at, nothing that's mine. I am a thingless chunk of tofu. This is why Jeremy went elsewhere. BubbleYum plays lacrosse and probably owns an extensive corset collection. I have a bedroom filled with bobblehead dolls and thirteen months spent devoted to Jeremy's hobbies, Jeremy's schedule . . .

Crap. I'm *that* girl. Miss No Thing. *Crap.*

"I work for my dad," I finally get out.

"At his office?" Oliver chews his pen. He doesn't know—can't see—how deep his question pierced me.

"Not really. He's sort of an antiques dealer. I help him sift through his . . . acquisitions, figure out what has potential value." I like how highbrow this sounds, like I'm tagging up priceless art and not sweeping up cockroaches.

"So you *do* have a thing. You're a . . . sorter of the past."

I don't know how he knows that these are the most perfect words to say. I'm not a loser; I'm an eclectic. I am something and someone outside of Jeremy, and every day that becomes more and more clear. "Thank you."

Oliver finally looks at me, sees that this conversation is more than chitchat for some reason. He doesn't question it. "You're welcome."

I stick my bike in Oliver's backseat and together we drive to Walmart. Our cartoon theme comes to us in the middle of the checkout aisle when Oliver sees this light-up, futuristic spinning toy.

"That's it!" Oliver holds the toy above his head like a guide down on Hollywood Boulevard directing a pack of tourists. "*The Jetsons!* It's an old cartoon, from the sixties."

The sixties view of the future? Oh, that is rich. "I haven't seen it, but I've heard of it."

"We can do dangling balls, make the trailer a *spaceship*, dress up all futurey!" His face glows with assurance, and he jumps into the shopping cart and pumps his fist, overcome with pure pep.

I step back from the cart, both embarrassed and enthralled. I thought Oliver was trying hard before, but now I realize it's quite the opposite—he doesn't *try*, he just *is*, makes up his mind and doesn't check if it's going to work for his image or come off wrong. Since the rest of us are being so self-aware, his presence seems calculated. No one can possibly be that breezy, saying what he thinks, feeling what he feels. I can see why people *don't* like him for this very reason—it's so much easier to call him a poser.

Because if he's the real deal, then that makes the rest of us fakes.

It's noon by the time we're done. Oliver vaguely mentions another stop and drives to Curry in a Hurry, an Indian buffet in a nondescript shopping center. Oliver gives me a grin and without saying a word, rushes inside. What does Indian food have to do with *The Jetsons*?

Oliver's paying the cashier when I get in. He sticks the change in his turquoise money clip. "I couldn't risk you saying no to such a fine dining experience, so I already paid."

"We're eating here?"

"Uh, yeah. That's how buffets work. You pay. Make a plate of food. Sit down. Eat."

"I've never had Indian food."

"Then you, Mallory Bradshaw, have not lived."

Oliver describes the different dishes, which helps, since everything looks like it's already been digested. Usually, I order something very specific, something I know I'll like, and now I'm scooping sauces that could be laced with fish heads for all I know. We get a separate plate of some flat bread called naan and Oliver comes up with puns ("Whatcha eating?" "Naan-ya business") as we look for a table.

I can't decide if it's right that I'm having fun. I tug at my finger string. I'm going vintage, but not so vintage that I need to dress in black and mourn the loss of my past life. I've seen people laugh at funerals, so why not be giddy postbreakup? Especially around a guy who makes life feel so effortless, like a meteor could crash into his car and we would just shrug and take the bus.

We slide into a booth and begin the steady work of consumption. I dip the naan into a yellow chicken curry, loving the flavor explosion. Within two more bites, I've already curried my shirt, but Oliver doesn't seem to notice. He's inhaling his green lamb stuff. He finally comes up for air and swallows. "I come here with my grandma a lot. She still takes us out to eat when we get good report cards. I think about the rice dessert during every test."

I pick at my paper napkin. "Yeah, Jeremy said he loved grade dates with Grandma."

"Look." Oliver sets down his fork and wipes his face. "Can we just state how awkward this is? I mean, if Jeremy knew I was hanging out with you today, he'd punch me."

"No, he wouldn't."

"Well, he would do *something*." Oliver takes a sip of his Dr Pepper. "I'll tell him, of course. It's not a secret. We'd be doing this stuff whether or not you two were still together, right?"

No. We wouldn't. If I were still together with Jeremy, we'd be at the park on Sunday, feeding the ducks because I love it, then finding a spot under a tree and making out, because I thought Jeremy loved me. "Sure."

"Or I could go back to the buffet and spoon some of that nasty-looking brown lentil stuff onto a plate. We have to take a bite if either of us says Jeremy's name."

"I like that game." I poke at my basmati rice. "I mean, I'm okay talking about him, but I'd rather not."

"Then it's agreed." Oliver raises his glass. "He is impeding your pep, and I need your A game."

"Only if I get a merit badge."

"I will make some calls."

Then Oliver starts telling me about his Eagle Scout project, how he collected lap blankets for nursing homes, then stitched a little note in the corner of each quilt to personalize it. He worked on the project for six months, much longer than he needed to, but he wanted to do it right.

"I can't believe you're really an Eagle Scout."

"Lying about being a Scout is a double lie, Mallory. Scout's honor."

"Then this college application thing is a crock. You like service. And I don't care how you act at school; you like people too."

He leans across the table, the string of his hoodie narrowly missing his food. "You tell anyone, I'll secretly nominate you for student body president, got that?"

"See? Even your threats are filled with spirit."

Oliver startles, like he realizes how far off course we've gone, whatever course he had in mind. "Spirit. Hey, we're not going to have much time to work on this float. The homecoming game is Friday."

"We'll get it done," I say. "It's really not that much effort— I promise. Class floats are the ones that go all out."

"I just mean, I'm glad joining this club gave me a reason to hang out with you." He takes a bite of chicken on a kebab, chews slowly. Too slowly. He needs to finish this thought. "Hang out with you alone. You're different from who I thought you were."

My back goes straight. "And who was that?"

He shakes his head. "I don't know. Not you. Not"—he gestures around the table—"this."

This? *This?* That's all he gives me? Is *this* good or bad?

Maybe he means the same thing that I was thinking. That he was the product of someone else's skewed point of view, and we tend to take that as fact, when really there's so much more to us beyond the scope of one person's opinion. Especially when the character reference is courtesy of Jeremy.

"Should I say thank you? I'm going to say thank you. Then it has to be a compliment."

Oliver laughs. "See? This. That. You're funny."

I cover my smile with my torn napkin. So I don't need to save my jokes for Ginnie. Oliver appreciates my humor. Maybe funny is one of my things too. "It's for Girl Scouts. Comedian badge. I've been working on it for months."

"If you're not a Girl Scout, you shouldn't joke that you are. Double lie, remember?"

"I'm underground. So high up in the organization, I shouldn't even mention it."

"Badge achieved." Oliver looks out the window, his face serious again. "So. After this float. We'll still have a pep club meeting here or there, and you'll either get back together with my cousin or stay broken up."

"I'm not going to—"

"Either way, we can say hi in the hallways and it's going to get less weird, right?"

"I didn't think this *was* weird." Of course this is weird. But we're not supposed to point that out. Brown lentil platter for you, Mr. Kimball.

"Because I like being around you." He's still looking out the window, and I wonder if he's focusing on one object when he says this and what that object is. "I probably shouldn't, but I do. And I can't say why. I mean, I can think of a bunch of reasons why."

Like? *Like?*

"But given … the obvious roadblock, I'm not sure how much we can get to know each other." He rushes on. "As people, because you're an interesting person and I value that in friendship. That's seriously what I'm after, not that I'm *after* you and I'm not talking about, you know, 'knowing' each other. Like in a biblical way or anything, although you're obviously pretty, I mean, *very* pretty and totally worth knowing *both* ways … Okay, shut it, Oliver. Shut it."

I try my hardest to act cool, like when you're on an airplane, and there's turbulence, and you know everyone's stomach is dropping, you know everyone is just a teensy bit freaked out that you're all in a metal tube hurtling through the air, but seasoned travelers don't grip their armrests or make that instinctive "oh" that happens when the plane drops. Cool people just keep flipping through their copy of *Us Weekly* like crashing to a fiery death is the last thing on their mind.

Oliver wants to get to know me. Oliver thinks I'm pretty. This is Oliver Kimball we're talking about, a guy so far out of my social sphere he's not even in my solar system. He's, like, Pluto. No, Pluto isn't a planet anymore, but it is still in the solar system … Wait. He's far out, okay? And I'm not talking in a groovy kind of way.

"Say something," he says, almost under his breath.

"Sorry. I like knowing you too."

He finally tears his gaze away from the window, but he can't quite meet my eyes. "Yeah?"

"Yeah." I am hyperaware of everything in this little restaurant. The Bollywood movie playing on the TV in the corner. The Buddha statue smiling from the entrance. The squeak of the vinyl when I shift in the booth. The red on the top of Oliver's ears. The goose bumps on my arms because I don't know what this conversation is really about, how it started, or where it's going. "But why did you act so indifferent to me before, when we first talked?"

"I don't know. Seemed safe."

"Safe?"

"You're doing that question-echo thing again."

Safe. I get what he means. The safest thing for me to do would be to dig out my cell phone and call Jeremy. Despite his change in homecoming dates, I know he'd take me back. He likes safe too. BubbleYum was safe to share his feelings with because he had the buffer of a computer screen. And I was safe to share his kisses because I was there, and willing.

And part of what feels so exhilarating about talking to Oliver now is he is the *least* safe option. Not necessarily in a romantic context—in any context. Except for that Jeremy's cousin asterisk, I don't really know anything about him. I'd have to go back to all those bumps that happen when forming a new friendship or . . . not-friendship. I could get especially hurt from this because of what people would think, because he could tell Jeremy, because I'm doing things I've never done before, or at least not since I moved to Orange.

It's a truth free fall when I erase that J-shaped question mark and let the words slip out. "If we're going to be, you know, friends, then you should know what happened. Jeremy cheated on me. Sort of. He had this online girlfriend and I accidentally found all their e-mails, really serious and loving and . . . real e-mails." I squeeze my eyes shut. "I used to think there was something wrong with him, you know, that he never got my jokes and we never talked. That maybe he was just closed off. But it was us. Or me. I was just a cardboard cutout girlfriend, the one who was geographically convenient." I open my eyes and Oliver's are so, so wide. "She's flying out for homecoming, so I guess they worked out the geography problem."

"So that's why you wrote that tool thing on his Friend-space page."

"Not my strongest moment." I pause. "I thought you didn't have Friendspace."

"I don't. Okay, fine." A whisper of a smile touches the right side of his mouth. "I created a profile so I could look up your pages. There should be laws against the stuff people posted."

"I'll take your word for it. I'm completely off-line." I hesitate a moment. I've already told Oliver something I haven't told anyone but Ginnie and Paige. Why not go full throttle?

No. A girl can only let out so much crazy at a time. Besides, The List is more than a secret. It's sacred, something not to be discussed with just anyone. I wouldn't want my fragile resolve to be stepped on with one flippant remark. "Anyway, yeah. That's what safe got me."

"Mallory, I'm so sorry—"

"Oh, no. Please. Don't do that." I grip the sides of the booth. "I didn't tell you that so you would feel bad. I just wanted you to understand."

He punches his straw into his soda, jiggling the ice. "I don't understand, not what he did, but I get where you're coming from now. I'd probably throw my computer out the window."

That would just be crazy. No, my sister is holding it hostage. Far more sane.

He scoops up rice with his fork. "I was going to say sorry, though, because I told Jeremy to come after our pep club meeting so you two could talk and get back together."

"You said you didn't!"

"I like to lie sometimes. You should know that about me." He shrugs. "It's fine as long as I'm not under Scout's honor. But the good news is, the awkwardness is *completely* erased now."

"Oh, yeah." I laugh. "Nothing weird about hanging out with your cousin's damaged ex."

He scoots out of the booth and offers me his hand. "You're not damaged. And I sure don't feel bad hanging out now that I know how stupid Jeremy was. Now come on. I'm going to introduce you to gulab jamun."

"Who is he?"

"He's the rice-pudding dessert."

I take his hand. We wander around the buffet tables. Neither of us gets more food, but we still browse, holding hands. My skin doesn't tingle like it always did with Jeremy. This isn't that kind of hand-holding; this is like when I was little and my mom would guide me across the street, although, obviously I don't think of Oliver as a parent, because, you know, gross.

It's... There's something achingly familiar about this contact.

I feel safe.

Chapter 15

Possible ways Mallory can live dangerously:

1. Drag racing. Except I don't have a car. Or someone to race against. Or a place to race. Or any desire to put my life in mortal danger.
2. Slash Jeremy's tires. Still considering this one.
3. Drugs. Drugs are abundant at our school, but I have this thing about obeying the law. Plus, marijuana was bigger later in the '60s, so not authentic.
4. Jump into the ocean naked. Too clichéd. Also, see above: obey law.

5. Tell Oliver what I'm really feeling in this moment.

Oliver drops me off a couple of miles away from my house, despite insisting that he take me home. The buffet was too perfect, and I don't want to risk an entire car ride of me saying the wrong things. Plus, I need some time alone to digest our conversation. And that Indian food.

"So I'll schedule a couple of days to decorate the float," Oliver says. "How does your week look?"

"Remember? I don't have things. I'm open."

"Whatever. I bet you have more things than you think."

Oliver jumps out of the car and wedges my bike out of the back. He taps the seat for me and leans over, smelling like a sunshine smoothie. Freak, I think he's about to kiss me, but instead he gives my bell a quick ring.

No kiss. So there's another one of my things. Apparently, I'm a moron.

This is what happens to hormones when you're in a relationship and used to filling up the action tank all the time. I'm technologically famished and emotionally ravished, and I haven't kissed anyone in nine days. It was a physical feast, and now I'm in a famine, and any old boy comes along and I think we're going to make out. Like on Friday morning, Derik Doogleman held the library door open for me and I actually looked at his butt, and I never look at boys' butts, especially Doogleman, who has greasy hair and supposedly glued his hands together in fourth grade.

I roll the bike out of smelling distance of Oliver and smile. "Thanks for the ride. It's nice *knowing* you."

Oliver groans. "Way to leave on a high note."

He drives away, and finally I'm alone to think. Think about Oliver, think about Jeremy, but mostly think about myself and the gumbo of emotions bubbling in my stomach. I bike across the street to the entrance of the Villa Park subdivision, wondering what I'll say to Oliver the next time we talk, when the first drop of rain plops on my arm. It's not the steady drizzle we usually get. Once the rain starts falling, it's fast and furious, flooding the gutters and soaking my clothes. Our house is tucked deep in the sprawling master-planned community, still a ten-minute climb. Normally, I would call my mom to pick me up, but I don't have a freaking cell phone.

I don't know how people ever *lived* like this.

It's a long fifteen minutes trudging through the rain. When I finally get home, all I want to do is take a hot bath before finishing up my history report and going to bed early. My weekend suddenly feels so open without the pull of texts and Friendspace and scouring the Internet for cute clothes and other assorted cyberstalking activities. Open, and a little lonely.

But the oddest sight is waiting for me in the dining room. My family is sitting. At the table. And there is food on top. Is this . . . is this an early Sunday dinner?

Ginnie glares at me as she walks in with a yellow Jell-O mold, a frilly pink apron tied around her waist. "I told you dinner was at three."

I am such a bad sister for forgetting this. Ginnie must have spent all day cooking. There's a roasted chicken, some sort of veggie casserole, the Jell-O mold, ready-made rolls, and a three-bean salad. The spread could be on the cover of one of Grandma's old cookbooks.

I'm still standing in the doorway, not wanting to drip inside the house. Mom retrieves a towel from the bathroom. I wrap myself in the warmth and wring out my hair. "I'm sorry. My phone—"

"Yeah, yeah," Ginnie grumbles. "We waited twenty minutes and now we're starving. So sit down and eat."

"Just let me change my clothes."

She grunts. I hurry into my bedroom and throw on a T-shirt and too-short pajama bottoms. Ginnie is just lighting the dinner candles (dinner candles?) when I take my seat.

She extends each arm, grabbing Dad's hand and mine. "We need to bless the food."

Dad blanches. "Like, pray?"

Ginnie already has her eyes closed, but she pries one open. "Dad. The family that prays together stays together."

Mom and Dad exchange a glance across the table and join hands. Ginnie looks at me. "Mallory?"

"Ginnie?"

"Say the prayer."

We don't pray. Not together. Not ever. There are the Ruminations I do with Grandma, and sometimes I try praying when I'm in my bed at night and sorting out my thoughts. I need to talk to someone, so I turn to God. But daily prayers, habitual prayers like blessing the food—no. I'm not sure where to start. "Dear God. Thank you for this food. Thank you for…the hands that prepared it. Thank you for this family…" I peek one eye open. Everyone's head is bowed. Everyone is holding hands. This…this is nice. Why don't we do this more? Not just praying, but the together thing. Being a family. Was Ginnie right? Did The List do this? "Thank you for the things that matter. Amen."

Mom raises her head and blinks at me. "That was a beautiful prayer, Mallory. Thank you."

No one reaches for the food. It's like we're waiting for a butler to come in and spoon-feed us. Ginnie finally lets out a giggle. "Mallory. Thank you so much for blessing my hands." She holds them up. "They are now sacred."

"Shut up." I survey the food. I'm so full that it all looks gross. I start with a little bit of the lemon Jell-O. "You don't mock prayers. That's just what people say."

"Where were you all day?" Dad asks me as he tears off a chicken leg. "And why were you outside?"

I poke my Jell-O with my fork. "I rode my bike. I had to get some decorations for our pep club float."

Mom and Ginnie say the same thing together, but they're actually asking different questions. "Pep club?"

"Yeah, I helped start a pep club. And I went with Oliver Kimball, Ginnie. He needed help and you were at soccer."

"Just you and Oliver Kimball?" Ginnie asks, her voice smug.

"Who's Oliver Kimball?" Dad asks.

"Can you pass the casserole?" I say to Mom.

Mom's chewing on something, and it's not the food. "You went out? With another boy? So soon after your breakup?"

"It's not even like that. He's Jeremy's cousin, actually." I don't know why I say this. To show that this is a purely business relationship *because* Oliver and Jeremy are related, when really, I feel like everything between Oliver and me is in *spite* of that relation. And obviously, that *everything* is *nothing*. "We bought streamers."

"But imagine how that looks, honey." Mom sticks her elbows on the table. "I'm sure this was just a school thing and I'm sure nothing happened. But you don't want anyone getting the wrong idea, right? What if people think you're rebounding with his cousin?"

"But that's *not* what is happening, Mom. *I* know buying decorations was innocent, Oliver knows it." In theory. Mostly. Probably. "So what should I care what anyone thinks? And no offense, but it's not your business."

"Not my business?" Mom asks. "You're my daughter. Of course it's my business."

"Just . . . drop it, okay? It doesn't matter. My reputation sucks anyway."

"What do you mean, your reputation sucks?" Mom sets down her glass of soy milk. She has that This Is an Important Moment look on her face, like she needs to whip out a camera and snapshot this discussion, document its relativity to her role as a mother and my mark as a person. "Mallory, did you give a piece of yourself to this boy? It only takes one bad act to ruin a girl's reputation."

"Dad, do you remember this casserole recipe?" Ginnie asks

loudly. She's trying, God bless her. "It was your grandma's. Over seventy years old. The recipe, not the casserole. This whole meal is food that could be served in the early sixties."

"Tastes like home," Dad says.

I am not in the conversation. I am not in this room. I am sinking, sliding, shrinking. My pieces? Mom thinks this all happened because I gave up my *pieces*? Why can't she get over herself enough to see what I'm dealing with here?

"Mother." Have I ever called her *Mother*? The word slices through the air, nearly extinguishes the long, skinny candles. "Jeremy cheated on me with a girl he met on an online computer game, and now he's flying her out to be his homecoming date. My reputation should be the least of your worries."

Dad sets down his roll. Mom's mouth forms a silent *O*. Ginnie reaches under the table and squeezes my knee. And I hate that I told Mom. Hate that I exposed this part of me and now she can run with the revelation in any direction she wants.

What should happen in this moment: my mom should hug me, smooth my hair while I sob into her designer T-shirt, this one with angel wings. She should say it's fine, I'm enough, that boys aren't important, and what other people think really doesn't matter.

What does happen: Mom's face floods with relief. "Thank God. I take back every nice thing I've said about that Jeremy, but trust me, it's better to be the victim than the instigator. Just as long as you stay away from his cousin." She pats my hand. "It'll get better, I promise."

I slide my hand away and stare down at Oliver's ring so the

tears won't fall. Sometimes I feel like a cardboard cutout to my mom, like I'm playing the role of her daughter, but I'm not an actual person in her eyes. Like our whole family is a part of this image that all reflects back to her. And she's so blind to it, I could never even call it out. In her eyes, she really is the perfect mother, caring and involved. It's just…the things she cares about aren't the *right* things.

"Conference call!" Ginnie sticks her head under the table, and I follow so we are almost nose-to-nose. "I know Mom is being an idiot, but can you please, please keep the peace right now? I'll tell you why later."

"I want to throw up on her."

"Forget her. Forget Jeremy Mui. What everyone else thinks doesn't matter. I think you're wonderful, okay? And if I think it, it must be true because I'm always right."

My mother makes up for all shortcomings because she birthed Ginnie. I might not have loads of friends, but Ginnie is enough. More than enough.

"Thanks. And you make good Jell-O."

Ginnie rolls her eyes. "That is the worst comeback compliment ever."

We sit up and get to task eating food I have no appetite for. It's one of those awkward moments that everyone knows is awkward, but no one can think of anything to say to break the tension, so we all just sip our drinks and clank our silverware and pretend this is the dinner Ginnie planned it to be.

Blessedly, mercifully, Mom finally claps her hands together and exclaims, "I almost forgot! This is so perfect that we're all together and Ginnie made this dinner today because I. Have. News."

Dad's rubs his forearm, just above his tattoo of a wave, but below the Ferris wheel. "If you're pregnant, I'm worried, since I got that fixed five years ago."

"Ew," Ginnie says.

Mom ignores them and points at me. "Remember those cuff links you found cleaning the other day?"

"What? Where was I?" Dad asks. "You didn't tell me about this. Were they good quality?"

"We wanted to surprise you." Mom is now glowing. She's shifted her role from concerned parent to antiques dealer. And as much as I want to hold on to my anger, I'm a sucker for a good find.

"They're real?" I scream.

"Mallory. Chill." Ginnie isn't in the family business; she has no idea what this means. If this means what I think it means, we can toss the chicken and eat lobster every night for a month.

Dad grabs Mom into a squeeze. "You are Wonder Woman. Did you appraise them?"

"Vintage. Early twenties. Real sapphire, platinum. *Tiffany's.*"

I grab at my chest. All this jubilation after Indian food is heartburn city. "You're killing us. How much?"

"How much?" Dad whispers.

"Fourteen *thousand* dollars!"

Our mouths hit the floor in one collective thud. Then Dad grabs Mom into a kiss so passionate that Ginnie and I have to look away. Money makes them giddy. Money means kissing.

Money means a happy feeling in this house and a couple months of breathing room for Dad to really get his business going. When my parents finally pull away, they're shiny-eyed. Dad holds up his glass of water. "A toast! To my daughter Ginnie, for working so hard on this dinner, and setting the perfect backdrop for our good news."

Ginnie slides down in her seat. She's trying her hardest to swallow her proud smile and totally failing. "It was nothing."

"And to Mallory!" Dad holds his glass out to me. "For her talents. You have a collector's eye. Now. Huzzah!"

Mom and Dad clink their glasses together and kiss again. My cheeks and ears warm. *Talents*. It's the second time I've heard that today, and I like the sound of it. I like the feeling that I'm vital, that I matter on my own and not because of what others think, despite what my mom believes. I cast a glance at Ginnie and we grin. The List is the best idea I've had in my entire life.

Ginnie and I sleep in my double bed that night. We stay up late talking and staring at the disco ball hanging from my ceiling. Which, I guess, technically is a decade off, but Ginnie didn't attack my funkadelic decoration with a Post-it, so I'm okay leaving it. Ginnie could give Oliver a run for his money tonight, what with all the peppiness pouring out of her like a hyperactive fountain. Maybe there was more than just sugar in that Jell-O mold.

"Isn't that *great* about Mom selling those cuff links?" she asks me. "It's going to make such a *big* difference for them. Money helps. And now Mom will *see* how important this job is, how important the family is, and she'll stay focused and happy."

"Gin, what are you talking about? She's a stay-at-home mom—she's completely focused on the family. Too focused, if you ask me. And of course she's happy. Why wouldn't she be happy?"

Ginnie goes silent, scary silent. "Haven't you noticed how she locks herself up in her office all the time, and how Dad is out of town for work so much? They're hardly ever together."

I have, but so what? Mom and Dad are starting a new business. There's a lot of work to do, and Mom is the only one who knows how to do anything website related. Not only is Dad a Luddite, but Mom never had the time or patience to teach us how to work things. It's all on her. "I know you don't know how businesses are run, but that's normal. It's a lot of work to get off the ground."

"That's the thing. I don't think she's working. I think she says she's working, but she's doing something else."

"Like what?" I ask, exasperated. "Playing Authentic Life?"

"Mallory. I think Mom is having an affair."

It's like Ginnie reached under the covers and punched me in the gut. Because if Mom is having an affair, then that is the worst news ever, but if she isn't, which she isn't, then it's the worst *accusation* ever. My sister's only fourteen; what does she know about affairs? She can't be right. It's almost funny. Not almost. It's ridiculously hilarious. "Oh yeah? Maybe it's BubbleYum's dad. Bazooka Joe." I giggle, but Ginnie kicks my knee.

"Mom locks the door to her office when she's working," she says. "She has a computer password. If I walk into her office, she gets all flustered like she's hiding something. Our parents fight a lot. She gets flowers all the time."

"That she buys herself," I say.

"So she says. Look, all I'm saying, I think she has a secret, and I think that secret is another man."

I flash back to the last time I was in Mom's office, when I almost cracked and went all twenty-first century. Mom's computer wasn't locked then; all she had were some coupon pop-ups, no scandalous love letters. And even though I know firsthand that cheating can happen to anyone, I still don't buy it with Mom. "That's a big accusation to throw out without facts. You could be right, but I hope you're wrong."

"So do I." Ginnie moves her feet and nestles deeper under the comforter. "That's why I'm doing dinners. To bring everyone together. And I'm going to make the dinner soiree super-romantic for Mom and Dad."

"Wait, we haven't planned that yet."

"I have."

"We're supposed to do it together," I say.

"Fine. Then plan."

I honestly hadn't thought about the soiree too much. I'd been so involved with pep club and my dress. "I was thinking we should do it before the dance."

"So was I. We'll do a cocktail hour with sixties canapés, invite all our friends, take pictures. Mom and Dad will remember their youth and deep love." Ginnie yawns. "Everything is going to be great. The List works."

The moonlight catches on my disco ball, spilling dull rays of purple onto the ceiling. Ginnie's asleep within moments, probably exhausted from her relief. But I stay up for a good hour, listening to my sister sleep, replaying the day with Oliver and the issues with my parents. If Ginnie is right about Mom, really right, then there might be some things that are impossible, even for The List.

Chapter 16

Top 5 hints that your guy or gal is cheating on you:

1. They act secretive.
2. They spend more time alone, especially online.
3. There seems to be a lack of communication and emotional connection.
4. You find unexplainable gifts, like flowers or jewelry.
5. They invite their cyberwife to homecoming.

I'm getting so good at looking past Jeremy, even looking *through* Jeremy, that I should probably add *ignoring tools* to my list of things. Although he may be ignoring me too, now that word is out that he's rebounded with a mysterious out-of-state girl. Best news, he's had a social fall from grace, and although I'm not online to cement this prediction, the student body as a whole seems a lot more friendly Monday. I leave school with something resembling a skip in my step. I don't know why I'm happy—my mom is an accused adulteress, my ex has a date to the dance while I don't, and the only boy I'm remotely interested in spending time with lately is his cousin.

And I have to get going on my Industrial Revolution project. I only have one page done and three days to write the other four. Books need a search engine. This is fact.

Grandma told me to stop by sometime after school, so I borrow Dad's car and book it to Newport. Grandma wants to make sure the dress pattern she found works and has set out some basic tasks for me. I hope *basic* means "BASIC." I haven't told her yet about the epically failed sewing class. She's elderly. Why worry her?

Since Grandma finally added the family to the Special Person List, I don't have to give my social security number or firstborn child to get into the building. I had hoped security would take a while, so I could watch the flat-screen in the lobby "by accident."

At Grandma's condo, I knock two times and ring the doorbell once. Her mind is sharp, but her hearing not so much, so I turn the doorknob. It's locked.

Without my cell, I can't call Grandma and tell her I'm

here. I pound on the door this time. "Grandma? It's Mallory," Pound, pound, pound. "Grandma?"

I'll have to go back to the lobby and see if they can page her. What a pain. I've just turned to leave when the door clicks open. Grandma blinks in the sunlight. She's wearing a cardigan set and dressy slacks, totally different from her usual bohemian style. Her hair is blown straight, but her eyes are bloodshot and she looks pale underneath the excessive makeup. "Oh, I forgot you were coming. I was just freshening up. Come in."

Grandma's apartment is dark, and she doesn't do much to fix that. I want to pull the curtains back, but this is her house, so I wait for my eyes to adjust in the dim light.

Her living room is on the messy side—dishes left out, newspaper scattered on the coffee table. Nothing big, but certainly nothing Grandma. Keys and change are on the counter, along with her monthly calendar, filled with the swanky comings and goings of hip senior living. Today has the name Candace circled with a phone number. I wonder if Candace is her new tennis partner or some lady from the Slot Group.

"Have a seat," Grandma says. "No sense standing around."

Her sewing center is an explosion of chiffon. I pull out a chair at the table. "So, it, uh, looks like you already got to work."

Grandma perches her reading glasses on her nose and paws through the stack of patterns. "Just figuring things out. I'm going to need to take your measurements since dress sizing was different then." She finds the pattern she's looking for and holds it out to me. "What do you think about this?"

The illustrated girls on the browned envelope are just what I want. Poised, cute cupcakes of poofy perfection. I'll do my hair in a chignon, find some white gloves. Um, find a date?

"I love it, Grandma. Yes, yes, yes. Let's do this one! Where did you find it?"

"Online pattern store."

"Oh, online." Uh . . . I'll pretend that I didn't hear that.

Grandma grabs a measuring tape and starts wrapping it around my waist. "So I'll just get your measurements and then you can go."

"Go?" I look around the room. I have a lot of things I need to do, but this item is at the top of my list. Well, figuratively. And I have Grandma all to myself. Sewing a dress takes a long time, especially for someone who doesn't know how to sew. I know it's not going to be easy, that the dress might not turn out perfectly, but I'm here to try. And . . . I was kind of hoping we actually could bake cookies and even talk about the breakup. That's what grandmothers are supposed to do, be all grandmotherly. "I'm not in a rush. I want to help. Don't delegate; participate, remember?"

Grandma writes down my waist size on the pattern envelope and sticks the tape around my chest. "Sewing's not something you learn overnight. I think it's best if I do this dress myself. Don't worry, it's simple enough. It's sort of like the dress I made when I was your age."

A window. "I saw that. Your junior princess dress? It's beautiful."

"Still have it." Grandma chews at the end of her pen, considering my bust size.

"Really? I didn't see it when I cleaned out your house."

She waves vaguely to her bedroom. "It's in my hope chest."

"What's a hope chest?" And where can I get one of these? A box that holds hope sounds essential.

"Are you kidding?" Grandma pulls the pen out of her mouth and points it to me. "Your mother will get you one, when you graduate, I'm sure. You put all your important keepsakes in there. I have my wedding dress, some quilts my granny made, pictures—"

I clap my hands together. "Can I see it, Grandma? I want to know about everything in there—"

"Can we cut the trip-down-memory-lane crap?" Grandma's voice is harsh yet tired. "I told you I'll make this dress, and I will, but I really have to get going. I'm meeting someone."

Candace with the circle and the number. Some stranger who is apparently more important than me. Grandma looks so corporate, maybe it's business. "Can't you reschedule?"

She snorts softly. "Don't I wish."

I'm starting to understand Ginnie's issues. It's true. Grandma doesn't have time for us anymore. What's so big in this new life of hers that she needs to push the rest of us out? "I was just...Look, Grandma. This isn't only about a dress."

"I know. You broke up with your boyfriend and you want him to eat his heart out. Don't worry, he will." She rubs her eyebrow. "We can spend time together later, after this week, okay?"

Her tone is kinder, but I still need her to know how important this all is. She's the reason I started all these goals. Grandma wrote The List; if anyone can understand my need for a better, simpler life, it's her.

I step back from her hurried measurements and let out a deep breath. "I found this list, when Dad and I were cleaning your house. You wrote it when you were sixteen. One of the items was to sew your homecoming dress. Do you remember?"

Grandma's expression is blank. "A list?"

"Yeah, of what you wanted to have happen during junior year. Find a steady, become pep club secretary. You did it, Grandma, and I can tell when I look in your yearbook how happy you were. The things that mattered back then aren't the same things that matter now."

"Mallory. I don't remember a list. I've blocked out a lot from high school. It's kept me sane." She glances at the clock above her sewing center. "And I really do have to go. Come by Thursday, and we'll do final alterations then. Maybe talk a bit, if I have time?"

If she has time? Doesn't she get what I'm telling her? I don't care about homecoming or even pep club. How can she not remember, how can she not see how important this is? Ginnie's right, she has changed, and not for the better. I know she's still dealing with the loss of Grandpa, but we're all dealing with something, and she should be more aware of that. More aware of *me*.

What I'm getting: a begrudged seamstress.

What I want: my grandma back.

Seriously, I'm going to work on my paper tonight, but first I need to *not* work on the paper. Maybe that's one of my things— not working on tasks I said I would: My dress. My homework. My life.

I have a date in my bedroom with a block of cheddar cheese and some Ritz crackers. It's going rather well when my rotary phone rings. I pick up and mumble, "Hello?"

"Hello. This is Oliver Kimball. Is Mallory home?"

"Oliver. Your formality gives me hives."

"Hey, it earned me a merit badge." He pauses. "What else should I say, 'Yo yo yo, I needs to get my talk on with Mall-Dawg'?"

I swallow my Ritz. "No. Never. Ever ever ever. Wow, aren't there some hipster police that are going to come after you now?"

"What are you doing?"

I consider my half block of cheese that was a full block when the evening began. "Homework. History."

"Oh, sorry. Do you need me to let you go?"

"No, I need a break." I stick the cheese in a plastic bag and roll up the tube of Ritz. "So, what's up? Did you want to discuss pep strategy? Go over float blueprints?"

"I hope it's okay, but I already designed everything. I'm in pep overdrive lately. So I thought Wednesday we could order pizza and have everyone come over. Does that sound good?"

Nope. Wednesday is the worst. I have a paper due Thursday. "Works for me." There's another pause. "Is that it?"

"Actually, I was just kind of calling . . . I was just calling to talk," Oliver says. "If you have time."

This is weird. No one just calls to talk. My friends and I don't even talk on the phone much anymore, not unless it's something that can't be addressed by text.

"So who do you have for history?" Oliver asks. I think it's his way to start an official conversation. I wonder if his etiquette merit badge included a list of twenty conversation starters.

"Mr. Hanover. Our Industrial Revolution projects are due Thursday."

"I wanted him last year but didn't get him. I'm taking AP this year—if I take the test early, I can test out of the class and get college credit."

"Oh. Wow." I feel like we should be leading up to something here, an item of business. Boys don't just call on the phone unless they have a motive. Homework help, for example. Or if they want to ask you out.

Oh, criminy. Is he going to ask me out? Is this about homecoming? It can't be about homecoming. Too soon, too soon. Avoid the question.

"Are you going to homecoming?" I ask. Or, you know, just ask the question first.

"Yeah, I am. With Carmen Berg? Do you know her?"

I don't know Carmen, but I know *of* her. Pixie blond hair,

nose ring—plays in a mediocre rock band, but she's smart like Oliver. They're a nice fit. So...good for him. Oliver deserves a deserving girl. I'm totally happy for them and not jealous at all because less than two weeks ago I had a date, and I can't expect the universe to realign just to suit my personal needs. I can hope for it, but not expect. Besides, I'm not even sure what my needs are. "Kind of. She seems like a great girl."

Great girl? Sounds like I'm a parent patting Oliver on the back. Of course he has a date. Why wouldn't he have a date? He's Oliver Kimball—I'm sure lots of girls have a crush on him. So naturally he has a date with an actual person and not a bubble gum brand. Good for him. Really.

"She *is* a great girl," Oliver says. "We made a deal freshman year that if we both were single when we were seniors, we'd go to homecoming together. So it'll be fun."

"Oh, I bet."

"No stressing about hooking up," Oliver adds.

"Well, cool." I pause. Why did he add that detail? "I'm going too."

"Yeah? Who with?"

"Myself." I thought that would sound lame, but it doesn't. There's nothing wrong with being alone. I've been alone for, what, ten days? And I've learned more about myself than in months with Jeremy.

"That's great, Mallory. Save me a dance, okay?"

"Sure." I could save him every dance. It wouldn't be hard. Well, I'll probably have to go to the bathroom at some point.

"So what else should we discuss? This talking on the phone without a set topic is kind of new to me."

"I don't know. I don't talk much to people on the phone or in real life. I was just sitting here in my room, listening to music, and this song came on that, don't laugh, kind of reminded me of you. So I called."

My stomach dips. And it's not dipping because a certain someone shared a similar moment with a certain other girl. This is a genuine, girly moment all by myself. Oliver was thinking of me. Song-on-the-radio thinking of me. "What song?"

"It's called 'Like She'll Always Be.' Have you heard it?"

"No, who sings it?"

"Great band called Jimmy Eat World. They broke out in the late nineties, now they're a little more under-the-radar. Look them up on your iPod."

"I don't have an iPod."

"Dude, no phone, no computer. Are you a Luddite?"

"I've sworn off modern technology. I got a little burned after, um, you know."

Oliver curses under his breath. "That's right. Sorry."

"How does the song go? Can you sing it to me?"

"What, right now?"

"Or during our next pep club meeting. You choose."

I expect him to say no, or get embarrassed, to maybe say a line or two of lyrics. But instead his voice comes out pure and strong through my crackling connection. The song talks about an awkward car ride, and I laugh, and the rest is sort of sad, about a guy who's trying to be enough for a girl. I wonder what he means about that. Is he talking about himself, or was it just that first line that led to the connection?

He stops after a verse. "Here, found it on my computer. Listen."

It's a fast song, not a love song, more bittersweet. The words pour over me and into me. It feels like he's trying to tell me something with the lyrics, but it's also a song with a distinct mood. Maybe that's why he thought of me?

It's only three minutes, but by the end I've driven myself crazy with questions. He clears his throat. "Anyway, that's the song."

"Your voice... That was amazing."

"Hardly."

Now, instead of his voice, it's silence, but not a bad silence. More like we're both absorbing something before moving on. I don't know what Oliver is thinking or feeling, but I still have goose bumps. A song made *him* think of *me*. And he wasn't saying something nice like that just so I'd make out with him. He might not want to make out with me at all, ever, which would probably be good, but then again, maybe not.

"So, um... now I feel stupid," he says. "Didn't you say you had homework?"

I push aside the cheese. Oliver trumps the cheese. "Nope. Do you have a singing merit badge?"

"Three."

"Sing some more."

"Good night, folks."

"Okay, talk more. For a second."

But we don't talk a second. We end up talking three hours. Don't even ask me what about. Everything? Nothing? Our favorite fruits and TV shows and bad middle school experiences and how Oliver reads the news every day and I have no clue what's happening in the world. Oliver talks about all the pressure he feels with college looming before him, and I confess that I'm not even sure I'll go to college, don't know where I'd go and what I'd do once I made it in. He's jealous of my breeziness; I envy his ambition.

His voice is soft and gravelly toward the end, when my mom pokes her head in my room and tells me I should get to bed. I untwist the cord of my old phone, thinking my grandma probably did that gesture too, when she was young and talking to her steady. It's weird how fast I can get to know a person when the conversation is so focused on . . . getting to know a person. I could probably be best friends with anyone at school if we had a few hours to open up like this.

"Hey, Oliver? I better go."

"Right. Of course." He clears his throat. "So, I'll see you Wednesday? Pep club?"

"Yep. I'm all yours." I stumble. "I mean, to work on the float, all yours. Not all yours, all yours."

Oliver laughs, deep and warm. I wish I could record it and keep it under my pillow to play in the middle of the night when I have bad dreams. It's that rich. "Sweet dreams, Mallory."

I don't need the recording. My dreams are all about Oliver. Oliver at my house playing board games, Oliver in his clunker car, Oliver leaning against my locker. Oliver under a tree, giving me a kiss.

That's when I wake up and the sweetness sours, because it's the first time I've let my mind, even my subconscious, go to that place with Oliver. The place we can never go, for reasons that are so obvious but somehow become less clear every time we talk.

Chapter 17

Other merit badges Oliver Kimball could earn:

1. Charm.
2. Wit.
3. Delicious laugh.
4. Asking the right question at the right time.
5. Grace. <u>Manly</u> grace.
6. More Charm. We're talking Charm School. We're talking earning ten charm O.W.L.s at Hogwarts.

On Wednesday morning, Jeremy is waiting for me outside first period. When he sees me, he jumps like a startled bunny, even though I've never seen a startled bunny, and maybe they don't jump when they're scared, only hop when they're happy? Regardless, Jeremy rushes over to me, starts to reach for my arm, then realizes that my body is now out of bounds, and awkwardly sticks his hand on top of his head, like that was his intent all along.

"Hey. I wanted to talk to you about something. School-related. Real quick."

I step back, away from the doorway, farther into the hall-way so our classmates don't have to pass us directly. I don't act annoyed or hurried. I'm not earnest or sweet. I am the Switzerland of conversationalists. Neutral and cold—with a deep appreciation for chocolate. "Sure, Jeremy. What is it?"

Jeremy steps back, that's how awesome my impartiality is. I've hit him with the force of my nothingness. "Look. I know it's been a crazy couple of weeks. And I know you asked to not be my partner anymore, and you did an alternative assign-ment, but I feel bad..."

He feels bad? *Bad* is not a bad-enough word for how he should feel. "About what?"

"How things worked out. So I already did the assignment—entire virtual factory, all ready to turn in. And I'm offering... if you want to tell Mr. Hanover that you're my partner again, I'm okay with that. We'd be even, with all the work you've, uh, helped me with in the past."

"Okay." I draw out the word, cocking my head to the side. "So what's in it for you?"

"Making you happy?" He rocks back from his toes to his

heels. He can't stay still. He never can, but especially when he's uncomfortable. I know this about him, I probably know things about him that he's not even aware of himself. "The thing is, if you don't want me"—he rocks forward. Back—"fine. Well, not fine, but I'll live."

"You'll *live*?" Nuh-uh. There is one victim in this situation, and it is not you, Amazing Asian. "Jeremy, this is your doing."

"I know!" Jeremy yells. His body stops jittering, but his voice shakes. "You think I don't know? You never mess up, you never make anyone upset, you're perfect and fearless."

"No, I'm not! See? You don't even know me."

"Then let me!" He spits when he shouts. "I'm trying to fix things. You're not letting me."

Moving away from the door hasn't stopped us from making a scene. But the bell is about to ring, there are only a few people around, and honestly, at this point, I don't care. About anyone. About any of this.

There's nothing that Jeremy can say that will *fix* anything. Our story isn't a new one. He fell for another girl. If I went back to him, that other girl wouldn't just stop existing, even if, technically, she never really did. If there was something substantive there to begin with, a relationship worth salvaging, maybe… maybe I could work on forgetting the exact wording of those e-mails.

"Mallory," Jeremy whispers. "Please."

"I already did my paper," I say quietly.

"I don't care about the paper. I only care about you."

I bite back the words, because I am Switzerland. Switzerland, remember? But my thoughts cross the national boundaries into Germany or whatever country touches Switzerland, and they're out. "Then why are you taking Jenny to the dance?"

He looks stricken. "I'm not. Why is everyone saying that? I would rather not go than go with anyone but you." This time Jeremy does reach out and cross that invisible barrier, and now that he's in that zone, I don't know how to push him away. I let him touch me as five long seconds tick by. He even rubs my skin with his thumb and, yeah, I tingle. You can't just turn off tingles.

His eyes are the same eyes that they always were, and he's looking at me the same way he always did, but I see *him* differently now, and tingles or not, this isn't good.

"So, what are you saying?"

"That I want to take you to homecoming."

I close my eyes. Last year, Jeremy lined the hallway leading to my bedroom with rose petals and Sour Patch candy. Sweet and sour. And he had a plate of Chinese food—sweet and sour pork—with a fortune cookie asking me to the dance. And it was one of the best days of my life.

This year, we can still go to the dance. We'll be hesitant at first, he will respect my space, and then we'll share a kiss that will remind each other what we have. What we had.

Or I could go by myself. All awkward and alone, watching the other couples feel awkward together. I could tuck away this chapter in my life and open myself up to the possibility of someone else. That new something might not be any better.

But it might.

And, right now, that *might* feels more honest than the sure thing.

"I can't."

"Sure. Sure." His body slumps forward, so different from his confident, strong posture. He looks like he's going to cry. Real cry, not I-want-to-show-you-how-sensitive-I-am-so-we-can-hook-up cry. "I'm so sorry. About all of it."

There's the apology. There's my victory. But there is nothing sweet about his words. *Sorry* doesn't make things better. It doesn't mean I forgive him.

"Can we go out to lunch at least?" he asks. "So we can talk?"

"I think we've talked enough. But thank you for the offer." I don't say which offer—the assignment, the dance, the reconciliation. "See you in class."

And then I am the Alps, chilly and unfeeling. I am not just going to melt and take him in, go back to us.

Us is over.

Us never really was.

Chapter 18

Tidbits about the Industrial Revolution:

1. Society used to be divided between poor and nobility, but this period saw the beginnings of the working middle class.
2. Steam was power back then. Being full of hot air was a good thing.
3. The nastiest storage unit in existence doesn't compare to the working conditions in many factories.
4. The word "Luddite", which I always thought was a person who hated computers, actually refers to a group of people who opposed the period's

industrial changes so much that they destroyed looms and, like, factory machines.

5.   *Are you as bored as I am?*

I'm supposed to meet at Oliver's to work on the float, but I have to do that stupid assignment and I don't want to be around anyone. I don't call, because I don't want him to try to change my mind. I'll help Oliver extra hard tomorrow. He'll understand.

I hole up with my library books, and by ten at night, I have nothing. I don't even know what my thesis should be—I don't even remember what a thesis *is*. I answer the phone when it rings, not because I want to talk to anyone, but because I need an excuse to stop staring at a blank sheet of paper.

"Yeah?"

"Mallory? Where were you today?"

Oliver. Oliver is probably the only person I want to talk to now, because he won't make me talk about anything I don't want to, which is close to everything. "Oh, sorry. I have this paper to write—"

"What, and you couldn't call?"

"Wow, what happened to your formal salutations?"

"Because I'm mad, if you didn't pick up on that. You flaked and I'm doing all the work on the club that *you* wanted to start."

"I know, and I appreciate all that you're doing." I pause, my heart prickling at his tone. Does this kid really care about pep club *that* much? "I was totally wrong and I'm sorry. I should have come or called. Did anyone else come?"

"Oh yeah," he grumbles. "We had plenty of people show."

"So, that's good."

"Look, I have to go. I'll do this float myself. It's not hard."

"No, I want to help. I just have to turn this in tomorrow."

"No, it's fine. Do your assignment."

He emphasizes *assignment* like I'm not really doing an assignment, like I'm sitting here painting my toenails and singing along with music and laughing at all those fools working on the float. What the crap? Oliver is the most easygoing guy on earth. Yes, it was flaky of me to miss the float thing, but:

1. I am flaky.

2. I don't think his reaction quite matches the crime.

All that Switzerland work from earlier in the day lingers, because I don't cry or ask what is going on. "Okay. I'll do my assignment. And I'll be there to work on the float."

"Yeah, we'll see."

"I'm hanging up now, Oliver." It's not technically hanging up on someone if you tell them you're hanging up on them. Proper phone etiquette and all.

Merit badge that.

I throw my book across the room. Trying to go simple is proving to be very difficult. I'm accomplishing things on The List, but I don't feel like I'm accomplishing much in *life*. Like this paper. Especially this paper. With the Internet, I could have been done hours ago, freeing me up to work on the float, or listen to music, or erase all of Jeremy's pictures still up on my Friendspace profile.

I check that everyone is asleep before I creep down the hallway. I have to keep moving so I don't have time to talk myself out of what I'm about to do.

I slip into Mom's office and log on to her computer. It's password protected, but what I didn't tell Ginnie is that I know the code—I had to use Mom's computer a few months ago when my space bar broke, and I watched as she logged on. GINMALL. Creative.

I type *Industrial Revolution* right onto the main page search engine, and instantly a million possibilities pop up. Thank you. *Thank you*. Ask and you shall receive. I could probably type in *Completed Industrial Revolution Paper* and find five reports to combine into one.

My blood is rushing, like I'm in the middle of some bank robbery. The thing is, I don't really care about the Industrial Revolution or this report. There's plenty of time to get that done. Now that I've given in, gone this far, I might as well do what I've wanted to do since The List started.

Check Friendspace.

A flood of random facts about all my friends and acquaintances assaults me on the home page. I go into sensory overdrive, scrolling through the last two weeks of my 623 closest friends' random thoughts. Cole wants a ham sandwich. Kyle is cheering for the Giants to win the pennant. Emma needs a hug. This is what everyone is thinking or feeling while they are thinking or feeling it. Even if it's just the surface and no one is posting their innermost fears and dreams, it's a sliver of that person, right? And a way for me to connect with people without having to actually talk to them, here, hidden in my mom's office.

I'm not ready to look at my profile just yet. Right now I'm

spying on other people, I don't want to reflect on my own corner of the Internet. Instead, I swallow, click, and ... I'm there. Jeremy's page.

He's written other posts since The Post. Today he quoted a song lyric. Three days ago he completed the What Simpsons Character Are You? quiz. And then I find the switch in relationship status that netted eighty-two comments.

I know that reading this string of words isn't going to bring me answers. I won't find happiness here, either. But it's just so ... there. I skim down to the very bottom, to comments that were posted only yesterday. Between Oliver and Jeremy, actually. How Ginnie could forget to mention this is beyond me.

Jeremy Mui's status: OVER IT!

Oliver Kimball says: Who posts something like this? It's disrespectful of Mallory and just makes you look stupid. Take it down.

Jeremy Mui says: Why don't you stop creeping on my girl and get my back instead? Bros before hos

Jillian Hefter says: Oooh, looks like a family fight!!

Peter Unger says: Gloves are out!

Oliver Kimball says: Creeping on your girl? Do people really talk like that? How are we even related?

Jeremy Mui says: That's what I want to know. And welcome to Friendspace

Oliver Kimball says: Why, thank you! It's such a fascinating study on people's characters or lack thereof.

Jeremy Mui says: I was being sarcastic, freaking doosh face

Oliver Kimball says: I think you mean douche.

Jeremy Mui says: Shut up

Oliver Kimball says: Seriously. FASCINATING study.

I have no idea what to think about this conversation. I thought Oliver didn't believe in Friendspace. And although it's flattering that he's defending my honor, I don't need a new guy to try to fix something my old guy said. I'm a big girl. Usually.

Oliver doesn't have a picture, just the default shadowy outline. He has four friends, and there is a friend request in my in-box from him too. I know I shouldn't click, because it will be obvious that I was on here, but so what? I want to see his full profile.

All his interests are obscure bands, independent movies, sports that aren't really even sports (disc golf?), and a long list of Orange Park High School groups. He's the moderator for another group, and I laugh at the name.

ANYONE WHO WOULD BREAK UP WITH HIS GIRLFRIEND ON A SOCIAL NETWORKING SITE IS A TOOL, AND I'M NOT AFRAID TO SAY IT.

He is the only member. I join right away. As a thank-you, I send him a virtual gift, a little icon of a dove with an olive branch—olive, Oliver—and write: *Please pardon my lack of pep today.*

A chat message dings on the screen. Jeremy. One word.

Mallory?

I close the window like hot lava is about to pour out of my screen. Why did I do that? Why did I get on there? Everyone can see that I logged on. Ginnie will be so mad. That wasn't worth it. I've come so far with this list and my goals.

I've binged, and now I feel dirty, like I need to purge. I go back to my report search, find a few articles, and cut and paste bits into a Word document. I do a quick read-through and rewrite the sentence structure so the words are my own. I'd been so worried about using the computer to type the report, but there's no point in finding a typewriter now when I'm already cheating The List. So I print out my less-than-average paper, feeling less than average myself.

I stand and stretch. Something on Mom's shelf catches my eye, hidden behind a small seascape oil painting. It's the jewelry box I found in the storage unit. The cuff links are still inside. The cuff links she said she sold for thousands of dollars and shipped out *yesterday*.

She could have just forgotten to ship this, sure. But I have that same sick feeling I had when I learned Jeremy's secret. I don't know how unsold cuff links would have anything to do with an affair, but there might be an answer on her computer.

I'm just not sure I want to know what that answer is.

I pace the office. No, an affair is just a far-fetched idea from Ginnie's overly imaginative mind. I'm sure there are plenty of men out there attracted to her, but my parents are happy, mostly. Just because Jeremy cheated on me doesn't mean everyone out there is a liar, especially not my parents, who are old enough to know better.

I go into Mom's browser and click on her history section. It's on default setting, meaning I can see the last week of websites she's visited. And it's a lot. And Ginnie was right—my mom does have a secret. But it's not an affair.

Unless my mom has a severe virus, those were not pop-up ads I saw on her computer that day. There are over two hundred hits on online coupon websites and blogs. For how much money she's "saving" from all these sites, she could get a full-time job. The site with the most hits is a blog called *Totally Hot! Totally Thrifty!* There's an illustration of a skinny lady with a shopping cart, and each post has a deal of the week. There are also posts about her two daughters, and antiques for sale and sapphire Tiffany cuff links that just sold for six thousand dollars, not fourteen...

This is Mom's blog. My mom has a blog. Advertisements scroll down the left column, and each post has hundreds of comments. She has over seven thousand followers. There's even a link to *Totally Hot! Totally Thrifty!* T-shirts.

This isn't an extramarital indiscretion. It's a business, but a business completely separate from the website she's running for Dad. And actually, this is an empire. There're, like, five posts a day, and one post has...

No. No.

One post openly discusses my private breakup, the one I didn't want to talk to her about because I didn't want her to get up in my business. But oh, my business? *It is all up on.*

Dear Thrifters,

I know you've gotten to know my daughters, Mallory and Ginnie, as I talk about our shopping adventures, antique finds, and family outings. Many of you have written and said that they feel like your own daughters, which is so wonderful to hear. They're great girls.

So today, instead of offering *you* advice, I'm hoping you can impart some wisdom. Last weekend, Mallory's adorable boyfriend broke up with her. I just now heard about it from Ginnie. Mallory won't tell me why, and the fact that she's holding back so much makes me thinks he dumped her hard. Ginnie's so active with soccer and school, but Mallory doesn't seem to care much about anything except the antiques business and this boyfriend. Now she doesn't even have him, and I worry she's going to get into trouble with all her free time. She needs a hobby, something to increase her low self-esteem.

I try so hard to be a good mom, I even took her to Disneyland today! But she's still not opening up. My own mother was completely uninvolved in my life, so of course I want to be there for my girls as much as I can. It hurts to have my daughter shutting me out. What should I do for her, and how can I deal with this motherly angst?

Also, tomorrow we'll have Carting Cathy on the blog to talk about her couponing secrets! Comment on this post and enter to win Cathy's latest book, FULL PRICE IS THE F WORD.

Hugs,

Tammi

Three hundred and forty-seven comments. Three hundred and forty-seven people weighing in on my personal life. The Friendspace debacle seems like a dust storm next to this online tornado. Here I am taking a break from the Internet and my mother is asking *complete strangers* how to fix me. Okay, yes, I could participate more in…things, but that doesn't mean I have low self-esteem! My own mother made me sound like a loser.

And she somehow manages to make my hurt and drama about her. All these commenters think they know me, think they have any right to speculate why I am "closed off" and why I have a "failure to commit," like I'm some actress who's been married five times and not a sixteen-year-old suffering her first high school breakup.

And she's using this "personal" post as a means to advertise Carting Cathy's book. Which means she has to be getting a kickback. Plus, there're all those advertisements and sponsors. I don't know how much money she's making off of this, but enough that she can lie and tell Dad that she sold those cuff links for fourteen thousand dollars. Is she even selling anything on his website, or is that just a blog cover? She always tells me we can't afford this or that, but maybe my parents have more money than I thought and Mom just has to live thrifty to keep up with her blog persona.

My mom has a persona.

I stare at the picture she added of Ginnie and me at Disneyland the other day, a whole post about how much our family loves to go there with, of course, no mention of my parents' fight in Adventureland.

I close out the windows and shut down her computer. I didn't think anyone could make me feel as bad as Jeremy did, but *Totally Hot! Totally Thrifty!* just proved that wrong.

Chapter 19

People I want to see today:

1.

I do not want to get out of bed Thursday morning. I do not want to face my dad, my sister, and, most especially, my famous mother. Ginnie, however, is still drunk from the family bonding on Sunday, and decides it's a swell day to wake up early and make us all this lumberjack breakfast. I'll have to check my facts, but I'm pretty sure a combined cholesterol level in the thousands was not a homemaker's goal back when women called themselves homemakers.

Actually, I'll have to check what cholesterol levels run—is thousands high?

Ginnie mans the kitchen like a short-order cook and

waitress in one. Dad's reading the paper—I didn't know we even *subscribed* to the paper—and Mom is flipping through an antiques magazine, like this is just another fine Thursday morning. Like she didn't write a blog last week about Dad's obsession with old junk and how sometimes she fantasizes about marrying Mr. Clean because he'd smell better.

"Mallory!" Ginnie chirps. She has on a frilly throwback apron Mom bought her at a mall kiosk. "We need to discuss the soiree. Do you have your list of things you need to buy?"

Do I have a list? *Please.* "Yep."

"Did everyone on your guest list RSVP?"

"They did." Everyone being The Stars, Cardin, and maybe Oliver if I can muster the courage to ask him. Ginnie has invited twenty-five of her friends to our soiree. The upperclassmen won't come; they'll want to go out to eat somewhere more fancy, but freshmen stay in their own flock. Plus, free food.

"Can I get you some orange juice?"

If she tells me it's fresh-squeezed, I'll go manic.

"I'll just eat some dry toast." I sit down and drum my fingers on the table. Is it tattling if I tell Ginnie about Mom? Does Dad know? Would he care? He would have to. She's not telling us the full truth.

There's a confrontation brewing, but I'm not ready for it yet. I still need to figure out what I saw, how I feel, and who my mom really is. "Mom, can I take your car today? I have a lot of errands I need to run for pep club."

"Actually . . . yeah, you probably can." Mom smiles benevolently. "I'm working from home today anyway."

Sure you are, Totally Thrifty. I still haven't made eye

contact with her. Maybe she'll consider eye contact a break-through and write a mother/daughter poem about it.

"I'm headed up to Burbank today to talk to a medical-history guy," Dad says. "Think I'll comb through some thrift stores while I'm up there. Want me to stop at Chervil's and buy those chocolate raspberries you love?"

Mom beams. "That'd be good. Come home early. If I get all my work done, I can have the afternoon off."

Ginnie swallows a smile at this. Her pancakes have saved this family.

I thought I felt nauseous when Jeremy tooled out, but this is so much worse. It's a gnawing *knowing* in my stomach. Dad doesn't look up from his paper to reach over and squeeze Mom's hand. There's something so simple and true about the gesture.

This scene is what I dreamed of when I began to seek out a bygone era. Our family together, for breakfast nonetheless. Who cooks breakfast anymore? If we ever did sit at the table before, Mom and I would be texting and Ginnie would be watching TV and slurping cereal, and Dad would be MIA. But this new, cheery version feels like a facade, like we're a family in a 1960s magazine, advertising syrup and wholesome values. I want to tear out of the glossy pages, jump away from this image.

I shoot out of my seat. "I have to go to school early."

Ginnie flips a pancake. "Meeting Jeremy behind the bleachers?"

"Ha-ha, Ginnie. Not in the mood."

"If you're with him again, fine." She flips again, the batter sticking to the skillet. "I mean, he's a V-necked loser and you're a complete idiot. I just wish you'd have told me first."

Mom turns around in her seat, excited. "You're back together?" Yay! Another blog post!

"What? No, of course not." The way Ginnie is frowning and not looking at me tells me she is not joking. I really should have stayed in bed. "If I was back together with Jeremy, don't you think you would be the first person I would tell? Where did you hear that, anyway?"

"Where didn't I hear that? Everyone saw you touching in the hallway—"

"No, we were talking. And he touched me! I didn't touch him back."

"*And* he took down that whole Friendspace thread late last night, probably because you're getting back together."

"Whatever. Friendspace also says I'm a freelance prostitute. Glad you're taking that as the gospel truth."

"Oh, yeah, saw you logged on last night. Way to be authentic," Ginnie says.

"Why does your Friendspace say you're a prostitute, Mallory?" Mom asks. A prostitute daughter would provide *weeks* of blog posts, probably net her a new sponsor. "What happened now?"

"You're mad at me for no reason," I say to Ginnie. "You're supposed to be on my side."

"I was on your side," Ginnie says. "I'm so on your side, I woke up early to practice cooking for a soiree. I joined pep club. So when I see you sneaking online and talking to your ex, it pisses me off. Typical Mallory follow-through. You came, you saw, you quit. You're soft."

"*Soft*? I am not soft. You don't even know what happened." Crap, I don't know what happened. But I deserve more credit than this. So I have one relapse. Look at all the other changes I've made. And it's not like I forced her to do all this. She got a homecoming date as a result of The List.

"I can guess what happened. You're going back to him." Ginnie sets down the spatula. Good. I'm worried she's going to flip me after those pancakes. "That's why you're hanging out with his cousin, trying to get insider tips. Did you know they got in a fight last night? Oliver told Jeremy to leave you alone, then Jeremy told Oliver he was taking you to the dance again."

"No, he's not."

"You could have cleared things up if you'd been there."

"I had a paper to write!" I yell.

"His cousin?" Mom's eyes are wide. "No, honey, remember, I said stay away from the cousin."

Dad merely cocks an eyebrow behind his newspaper. This is as present as he gets during female disputes.

I smack Ginnie's arm. How can she just turn on a dime because of something Jeremy posted online, a boy who *clearly* cannot be trusted? Because she heard some rumors and saw a fight that probably had more to do with Oliver and Jeremy's cousin issues than with me? Those two always fight. Believing Internet hearsay is exactly part of what we're supposed to be protesting here. And…freak. She's picked up the spatula again. Who cares about pancakes? PANCAKES ARE NOT GOING TO SAVE OUR PARENTS' MARRIAGE.

"So when I have a boy cheat on me, you get mad, but when you think other people are having affairs, you warm up the griddle."

I wish I could take back the words as soon as I say them. Ginnie's face drains of color. She's helping me, she cares, she's just mad because she thought I was giving up, like I always give up, but still. *Still.* She's my sister. She should believe in me when no one else does.

"Who's having an affair?" Mom asks, giddy with potential scandal.

"Get out of my kitchen," Ginnie whispers.

Under another circumstance, this line, with Ginnie dressed up in an apron, wielding a spatula, would be hilarious. Now the bite behind her whisper leaves me raw. I might be the one jumping in and out of things, but she's Miss Hot and Cold.

I grab my backpack and Mom's keys and hurry out of the house. Ginnie doesn't try to stop me, even though I'm her ride. I wish she would. I want to say sorry. I want to erase that horrified look in her eyes and the coldness behind her words. I'm Mallory. I'm the same. Just because someone thought they saw something and someone else said something online, that doesn't make it real.

It doesn't.

Does it?

Chapter 20

Times I have ditched school:

1. April—freshman year: Mom let Ginnie
    and me stay home one day, and we got
    manicures, read celebrity gossip
    magazines, and ordered Chinese food in
    the middle of the day. Mom took thirty
    million pictures. I'm guessing the bonding
    is all documented on her blog—she
    probably made good money on us too.
2. September—sophomore year: right
    when Jeremy and I started hanging
    out. We went to a corn maze, but it
    was the middle of the day Wednesday,

so the maze wasn't open and we ended up just wandering around a field. We were in a group, too big of a group, got caught, and I was grounded for a week, but Jeremy held my hand and asked me out, so it was worth it. Then.

3. February—sophomore year: Jeremy's house. We watched movies and made out. Don't want to talk about it.

4. October—junior year: today.

I get to school early. Mr. Hanover is alone at his desk, sipping tea and shuffling through tests. I hand him my paper and explain that I am deathly ill but wanted to turn in my assignment.

Mr. Hanover holds the paper in midair. "But... why are you turning this in?"

"Remember? Alternative assignment due today?" No need to explain that I used the very resource I was avoiding to complete the alternative assignment. Teachers are busy people—they don't need the details.

"But you don't need this." He scratches his beard. "Jeremy turned in your virtual factory yesterday."

"He... he what? But I told you I can't use the Internet."

Mr. Hanover flips through the report. "Did you use the Internet for this? You didn't cite your sources. Where's your bibliography?"

Oh, right. My bibliography.

If I go along with Jeremy, I owe him. If I do my bibliography, I have to name the Internet sources, which makes the whole reason for doing the report void. Or I lie and say I only used books, which I did, but not in the cut-and-paste job I'm turning in.

I cannot win.

"I'll . . . I'll talk to you about it tomorrow, 'kay?" I glance up at the clock. School starts in fifteen minutes. "I think I'm going to throw up. Sorry!"

"Bring in your bibliography tomorrow!" Mr. Hanover calls after me. "Stop by the nurse! You need to check out!"

No need to check out if I never check in. I don't have anywhere to go. Not school—with school assignments I didn't do. Not home, where Mom is probably blogging about a sale on condensed soups, or posting the picture she took this morning of Ginnie being all domestic, captioned "Like mother, like daughter!"

The rest of the school is pulling into the parking lot as I drive away. Oliver's Nissan turns left just as I make a right. He stops in the middle of the intersection and honks at me. I smile apologetically, sort of an I-would-love-to-talk-but-we-are-driving-cars-in-opposite-directions smile. But Oliver takes it as let's-stop-all-traffic-and-have-a-conversation time.

He rolls down his window. "Where are you going?"

"Taking a sick day."

"Are you sick?" he asks.

"No. Senioritis."

"You're a junior."

"Then juniorea. No, that sounds like an STD."

For that, Oliver gives a barking laugh. Cars honk. I want to freeze this, freeze us. It's never felt this good to make some-one laugh, especially after the morning I've had. "I'm fine. Just need a break."

"Go take something for that juniorea. I'll call you after school, okay?" He taps his horn once in good-bye and turns. So...I guess he's not mad at me anymore. That was signifi-cantly drama-free.

I have no set destination and half a tank of Mom's gas at my disposal. A free day like this is the perfect chance to finish up everything on The List, mainly my homecoming dress. Also, I'm ditching. That's dangerous, right? No? More cowbell?

It's still too early to randomly drop by Grandma's, so I pick up decorations for the soiree. Target has a vintage party line, and I know it's probably as authentic as a McDonald's salad, but even women in 1962 knew that party planning involves give and take. I also stop at the drugstore for some sixties-approved makeup: fake eyelashes, liquid eyeliner, and dramatic lipstick. By ten, I'm pulling into Grandma's community. I try to remem-ber what the Miss Etiquette library book said about drop-bys. The proper approach seems a phone call, so I stop to use the house phone in the main lobby.

When I get there, I find a tray of cookies and lemonade set out next to the flat-screen TV. I miss thirty-minute sitcom problems and fake reality with fake people, and since I want a cookie and it's rude to get crumbs everywhere, I take a seat and watch a reality show about an interior decorator who's dating a soap star. The room she's doing is sixties modern—all orange and brown and clean lines. So really, this is research.

A woman in a gray suit clicks into the lobby. She's in her late forties, maybe fifties, with short curly hair. Still too young to be a resident. She fidgets with the pamphlets while waiting for the front-desk girl to appear. I look back to my scripted reality show, which is far more interesting than someone checking in at a retirement community.

"I'm here to see Vivian Bradshaw?" the woman says.

And I take that statement back. Who is this? I switch my seat, pretending it's so I can be closer to the cookies, but this is really about Gray Suit and her mysterious involvement with my grandma.

"Are you on her list?" the receptionist asks.

"I don't know." Her accent is thick and distinctly Southern. "I was here last week, but y'all had to call her up. She might have added me."

"I can check," the receptionist says. "What's your name?"

"Candace Vintner."

"You're not on the list, but I do remember you, so let me call her and see if that's an oversight."

Gray Suit, Candace, continues to fidget while the receptionist calls my grandma. "Candace Vintner here to see you?" She hangs up the phone. "She said she'll meet you in the lobby."

Candace nods and wanders over to an armchair in the corner. The etiquette book would not approve of Grandma making this woman wait here. Then again, I have no idea who Candace is and what she wants with my grandma. If this were a reality show, she'd probably be Grandma's therapist, or life coach, or stylist, here to guide her through the backstabbing scandals of *Real Grandmas of Newport Beach*. That woman Grandma played tennis with is her archenemy, and they're both vying for the affections of the tennis pro, Eduardo.

Wow. Three minutes back to reality TV and I'm already going there.

I eye Candace, who pours herself a lemonade and pretends to sip. Surely they have a sedative around here they can give this woman—her legs are crossed and she's kicking the top one hard. Then she's motionless, stiff, and I hear Grandma's voice. "Mallory, what are you doing here? Shouldn't you be in school?"

Grandma's wearing khakis and a white button-down shirt, her former save-the-children-of-the-world uniform. She shoots a look to Candace but doesn't say anything else.

"It's homecoming week, so we got school off . . . No, that's a lie. I ditched. I had a tough day. So I thought I'd come over a little early and we could do dress stuff."

"Dress stuff," Grandma mumbles. Maybe I get the echo thing from her. She rubs her lips, glancing between the two of us. Candace stares at me with an open mouth. Her teeth aren't that great—she'll need to get them fixed if she's going to be a regular on Grandma's reality show.

Grandma doesn't say anything for a minute. Then: "I haven't had as much time as I'd hoped to work on the dress. But can we talk about that later?"

"Oh. Okay." What, is she too busy doing arts and crafts? This is a retirement community. Their whole day is supposed to be about having time. This is like the other day, when she rushed me out.

Except it isn't. I can feel that now. The tension in the room chokes back my snarky reply. Candace looks like she's going to blow over from shock, telling me that no, this woman is not Grandma's consultant or stylist. And the homecoming dress... the dress really doesn't matter right now.

"Mallory, this is Candace."

I hold my hand out to Gray Suit. "I'm Mallory. Vivian's granddaughter."

Candace takes my hand. Hers is cold and sweaty, and when I look into her eyes, they're watery and warm.

"It's fabulous to meet you, Mallory."

"And how do you two know each other?" I ask.

Candace looks to Grandma for help. Grandma appears stumped. This pause is longer. This pause is minutes. This is a decision-making pause, heavy and life-changing. "I suppose we don't really know each other. The name I gave her is Francesca. But they named her Candace."

"'They'?"

"She was adopted, honey. Candace is my biological daughter. Meet your aunt."

Remember that time when my grandma ditched her awesome, charitable career and tried to start this new life and never wanted to talk about the past, especially high school? And remember when I took it personally and thought it was because she didn't want to hang out with her family anymore and kept pushing her to make me a dress that reminded her of the very thing she didn't want to be reminded of?

Yeah, well. I suck.

Grandma gives me the quick version, the one she'd already explained to Candace, who'd tracked Grandma down online and is here for a week visiting. They'd met for the first time a few days before, the day that I'd come to visit Grandma and she'd been so out of it. Meeting the daughter you gave up for adoption fifty years earlier will do that to a person.

Bottom line—Grandma had a steady. That steady knocked her up spring of her junior year and broke up with her when he heard the happy news. So seventeen-year-old Vivian left town—her friends, her family, her church, her life—to live with an aunt in Baltimore and have the baby. She graduated high school, miraculously, and then went to college at Berkeley. Which explained why Grandma didn't have a senior yearbook. And why she didn't want to talk about high school, no matter how much her granddaughter insisted.

Did I mention that I suck?

They'd planned on brunch, but we end up back in Grandma's condo instead. I don't ask questions, don't need to. Most of the answers are in Grandma's hope chest.

"This is a quilt that my great-grandma made." Grandma lays out the threadbare patches of history on her bed. She's made some tea for Candace, which seems to calm her a bit. I haven't said much to my supposed aunt. Anything I say now, during our first encounter, will be memorable, and so I want to choose my words well. Also, I still don't know what the freak is going on.

Grandma unpacks a few scrapbooks and starts leafing through. She pauses on a yellow page and unsticks the vinyl holding the photos into place. "Here's what I was looking for. There you are." She holds a picture out to Candace, who takes it with tentative hands. She covers her mouth and shakes her head. Grandma doesn't touch Candace, but she closes her eyes tight, like she's practiced holding back the tears this long and she's not about to break down now.

"That's you at thirteen months. Your ... your mother sent me that. Adoptions, you know, were closed then. So seeing my little baby, not so little anymore ... it was a gift."

Candace shakes her head. "It means a lot to me that you kept this."

"What, you think I'd toss my one picture of my only daughter? Just because I gave you away didn't mean you left me." Grandma reaches across the bed and gives Candace's hand the tiniest pat. It's not even a squeeze or a hug, or a gushing recap of their time apart.

I have no clue what Candace is thinking, what she can possibly be thinking. What is it like meeting the woman who was just a name before, a name that probably popped up through a people-finder site on her computer?

Candace points at the hope chest. "What else do you have in there?"

Grandma sets out some baby blankets, an old doll, and bites her lip when she sees something toward the bottom. "Well, Mallory. How's this for vintage?"

It's her dress. Her snow-white, now slightly ivory, poof ball of a dress. And it's glorious. I feel a pang as I help Grandma smooth out the wrinkles, the Ruminations jumbled in my heart. Does this make Candace bitter? Her daughter isn't making dresses with Grandma, not like me. Does she like her adopted family? Is she happy with how things worked out? How different would they both be if Grandma had kept her—would Grandma have met Grandpa, had my dad, accomplished all she did? And either way, how does she feel now about her choice?

And this probably makes me a bad person, but my main thought is: Will Grandma let me try on the dress?

She does. Grandma had Ginnie's build then, that muscular/curvy/skinny combination, but the poof part is forgiving, and she could probably take the bust in a little. Okay, a lot. Not that I would ask her to do that.

Both women smile when I step out of the bathroom. "You're going to want me to take that bust in, aren't you?" Grandma asks.

"No, it's your dress. I couldn't ask—"

Candace is already pinching the side. "It should be easy, with the darts. I'm more worried about this cinching at the waist. I wouldn't want to mess with the bias hem facing. What do you think, Vivian?"

And it is this question that finally makes my grandma cry. The daughter she's never known is a seamstress and they're discussing alterations on the dress that was a small part of Candace ever even existing. Grandma doesn't acknowledge the tears slipping down her cheek; she just grabs a pushpin and the two get to work Mallorying up the dress. I guess sometimes participation is just standing there and letting someone do something for you because she needs to do that something for herself.

List item #3. Sew a homecoming dress. Almost done.

Chapter 21

Five hints that a boy likes you:

1. He sings to you, or tells you that certain songs remind him of you.
2. Thoughtful, homemade gifts, like string jewelry.
3. He picks up on your emotional cues.
4. Joins a club or activity so he can see more of you.
5. Kissing. No-brainer.

I leave two hours later. I invite Candace over for Sunday dinner so she can meet my dad. Her brother. She says she has a flight on Saturday, but maybe another time. Ginnie's going to have to cook a mother of a soy loaf to get us through that meal.

School hasn't gotten out when I get home, but I don't care if Mom sees me. The house still smells like syrup from Ginnie's breakfast.

Oliver's a senior, so he only has four periods and is home by one. He answers his phone on the third ring.

"Oliver Kimball speaking."

"That's seriously how you answer the phone?" I ask.

"Caller ID. I thought you'd like that." I hear his smile. "I'm sorry about last night."

"What?"

"On the phone. I completely broke all phone etiquette. I should be stripped of my Eagle Scout right now."

Right. Our first tiff. When I saw the online group, the rest was forgotten. I guess sometimes that happens, that you forgive someone without discussing it with them first, and just kind of assume they forgive you back. "Don't worry. I should have called. I sent you—"

"That dove. I saw that. It was my first virtual dove, you know. I don't think I'll ever be the same."

I want to mention the group he set up, but I don't want to mention it, because it's tinged with Jeremy's shadow. So I don't talk.

"Were you calling with a purpose or did you just want credit for the dove?" he asks.

"What are you doing?"

"Right now?"

"Yeah," I say.

"I just got home. I was going to finish the float—"

"Great, that's what I was calling about. I really want to work on it. Can I come over?"

"Are you doing okay?" he asks.

"Yeah, I needed a mental-health day." And nothing is better for your mental health than meeting your grandma's teenage love child. "What's your address?"

I spray some perfume on, brush my teeth, put on lip gloss, and am adding a coat of mascara when I realize this is my about-to-see-a-boy routine, and that's not what I'm doing. I'm going to work on a float. I grab the keys and I'm almost out the door when my mom pops her head out of the office.

"You left your sister this morning." She checks the clock on her cell phone. "And what are you doing home? School doesn't get out for two more hours."

"I didn't feel like going."

"That's it? *You didn't feel like going?* You think that's going to get you out of trouble?"

"I don't really care."

"Excuse me? What's with the attitude?" Mom's hand is on her hip and her lips are stretched into a thin, but not too thin, line. She's beautiful. Always. Angry, sad, happy. She works hard at keeping that image up too. It bleeds into the expectations for the rest of us—where we live, how we dress, our associations. But our beautifully decorated home isn't ours and Mom would die if I ever told anyone that we're squatting for practically free in Uncle Rodney's place, just like she makes a face whenever she sees my thrift-store outfits because old and dingy doesn't meet her high standards. Didn't I read on her blog that the goal is to pay less but look like you spent more?

"I'm tired because I was up all night working on a paper. I used your computer, by the way. Ginnie took mine as a joke. Hope that's okay."

"How'd you know my password?" Mom asks automatically, then tries to smile to cover up her worry.

"I remembered it from before. Really interesting stuff on your browser history, by the way."

"Why are you checking my browser history?"

"Just looking for some good deals. That *Totally Hot! Totally Thrifty!* site taught me a lot, especially about myself."

Mom blushes, and the face coloring is almost more incriminating than her Internet secret. I don't know why her blog makes me so mad. I should be grateful I have a mom, that we're not Grandma and Candace, that we have a place to live and Ginnie's home-cooked food to eat. I should be able to see all that, but right now all I can focus on is the blog post she wrote about me. I see the way she sees me and it hurts. And I don't know why she can't let her own family know who she really is when she's sharing all of our life dramas with the rest of the world.

I grip her car keys, resisting the urge to throw them. Instead, I say, "I'm taking your car. I don't know when I'll be back."

"Mallory, do you have a second to talk?"

"Not with you. I'd be too worried that you'd blog about it."

I hurry out the door. She'll change all her passwords now, I'm sure, try to cover up that piece of her. I don't know what

I'm going to do with that truth, if the blog would bother Dad like it does me, if this will compound their problems or if the fact that she's making money will solve everything. And I'll have to tell Ginnie. She'll be relieved it's not an affair, but maybe not that relieved when she reads the post Mom wrote about the first time Ginnie got her period.

Once I'm in the car, I realize I have Oliver's address, but no directions. Just my mom's navigational system, which is the only thing I've ever used to find a new location, besides, of course, my cell phone. I slam my hand against the steering wheel and see Oliver's string on my finger, blue and frayed. He wouldn't be reacting like this right now, all road-ragey.

I take a second to catch my breath. My mom's choices are my mom's choices. There is no use getting worked up about it right now, when I'm freshly glossed and perfumed and on my way...to a school function. Yes, a school function. So I do what any girl would have done in 1962. Drive to the gas station and ask for directions. Written directions.

Oliver's house is in the Old Towne District of Orange, which I think is one of the largest preserved historic districts in the country. The churches, library, post office all have the same look they did decades ago. Chapman University is nearby, so some of the homes are rented to students, but they're kept nice with shady trees and manicured lawns.

Oliver's house is gray with red shingles—Craftsman, my Realtor dad would call it. What it lacks in size it makes up for with charm. Our tract house is bigger, but it also looks like every other house on the block.

Oliver is sitting on his front porch in, I kid you not, a rocking chair. He's fiddling with something and my heart stops because I think it's wood and he must be whittling and I'm fixing to shuck some corn right now and join him in this old-fashioned, Main Street existence. Except it's not wood. It's string. And then I realize something else.

I'm at Oliver Kimball's house. Alone.

He's resurrected his orange STAFF shirt, except he's added PEP in black Sharpie above the peeling print. He's grinning at me, just waiting for me to ask about it. So of course I don't. "I didn't picture you living here," I say.

"It's a rental. My mom wanted small and quaint when my parents got divorced. I'm pretty sure there's a large rodent living under the house, but she's all about the neighborhood and her garden."

"Sometimes I drive by my own house because my neighborhood is so cookie-cutter."

"But you have a garage. We have a shed." Oliver leans against the top step. Even his slouch is confident. "Your cheeks are pink."

I touch my face. "It's from road rage. I had a tough time finding the place."

"Really? You've lived here for how long and you don't know this area?"

"I've always had directions," I say. "So I've never paid attention."

"Well, didn't it show up on your navigational thing?" He chuckles and shakes his head. "You don't use navigational things, do you?"

"Not presently."

"But Friendspace last night was okay."

My cheeks go from pink to red. "That was a momentary relapse."

"Are you sure you're not sick?" He actually sticks his hand over my forehead. It's surprisingly cool against my hot skin. Hot from embarrassment, hot from his touch. But not sick.

I push him away. Touching. Not a good idea. "I'm just having a long day."

"It's only one fifteen."

"I know. A lot can happen in a morning."

"Do you want to talk about it?"

I shake my head. Of course I do. I just found out my mom has an online coupon empire and I met my aunt I never knew existed. But that's not what he means, that's not what he wants. We are still new friends, and I've had enough meltdowns in front of him. I don't want him to know these problems.

I guess I can understand Jeremy's reasons for holding back. What I want Oliver to see is the normal girl underneath all these worries. I don't want my issues to define me.

"I made you something." Oliver opens the fist of his other hand to reveal a piece of string. Three strings, actually, orange, black, and white twisted into a braid. "It's, uh, a school-spirit string. For your finger. For you know, what we talked about in the car the other day. Remembering. Or forgetting. Whatever."

What do you say when someone gives you the one thing you need, even if you don't know it until you have it? How can I possibly communicate what my heart is doing right now, breaking and exploding at the same time? "Thank you."

He helps me tie the string around my finger. I bite off the other thread and stick it into my pocket. Oliver motions to the gate to the back. "Come on, then. I'll show you Bessie."

"Bessie"? I rub my hands together. "Is Bessie your pet rodent?"

"It's our float." Oliver shakes his head. "See what happens when you miss a meeting?"

He pushes open the wood gate. The backyard goes farther back than I'd thought. There's a humble vegetable garden on the left, a small blanket of grass, and a slab of concrete with a rusty, oversize storage shed. Oliver leads me into the shed, which really could be categorized as a garage if I weren't so worried about it falling down on me. He leaves the door propped open and clicks on the one lightbulb dangling from the ceiling.

And behold. There's our little trailer in all its peppy glory. The orange tinsel skirt covers the wheels, and he's painted the wood bottom black. There's a butcher-paper sign in girl's handwriting. "PEP CLUB! CHEERING FOR A BRIGHT FUTURE!" He's propped up a wood backdrop, which is painted with stars. Foam "planets" dangle from a wire mobile.

He folds his arms across his chest, appraising his creation like it really is a prized cow. "She's great, huh? Nothing fancy, but it'll be a good debut for the club. Vance's mom is making the costumes—your sister is the wife, Jane; Paige is the hot daughter, I don't remember her name. Sorry, maybe you can be Astro the dog."

"And take the honor away from you?"

"Oh, I'm George Jetson. Main guy. There's the robot maid."

"Only if there's a costume head to cover my face."

"Great idea. We wouldn't want that face of yours messing up this perfect float."

I give Oliver a quick punch on the shoulder. As much as I wanted to be a part of this float creation, I also love this grand reveal. Bessie isn't too elaborate or flashy. The float of a club that formed just a week ago. A float just like the one in Grandma's yearbook. This thing is so classically All-American, we could ride it over to Watson's ice-cream shop down the street and dance to a jukebox. It's like Oliver knew the reason I wanted to do all this and tried to channel that quest for wholesome simplicity into an eight-foot-long flatbed trailer. "Bessie is beautiful," I say.

Oliver kicks at the wheel, ducking his head to hide a smile. "She'll do. I never did all this school spirit stuff with ASB before, not with Blake running the show. It was actually fun." He points his finger at me. "Don't you dare tell anyone that."

I hold up my hand. "Your school spirit is safe with me."

Oliver digs through a bin of supplies and tosses me some glitter garland. "We still need to loop this around the handrail. Make yourself useful." We didn't buy this garland together, which means he went out and got it himself, or had someone else bring it, and it shows that he really put a lot of work and thought into this float. I like that he's the kind of guy who sees something through, even if it goes against his self-made brand.

We work for half an hour, making little jokes every once in a while, laughing—real laughing—but mostly concentrating on the final touches. Sometimes his shoulder brushes mine while we're hanging something up, and of course I'm aware that we're alone in this shed, and he's a boy and I'm a girl, and we're both, well, single. But that's not why we're here, and that's not what I want, not now, not really, not mostly, not … maybe a little.

And it's while I'm twisting the garland that I remember what my sister said. That she was here, working on the float, and that Jeremy and Oliver got into a fight. I'm not sure how to ask, or if I should, but I do want to know what happened. Obviously.

"So, who else came to work on the float?" I ask.

"I was waiting for that. Ginnie told you about the fight, huh?" Oliver rips off a piece of crepe paper. "It was nothing. Stupid family stuff. You know how it is."

I don't. I've never seen them fight. I almost never see them talk, only if they happened to be at the same place. This wasn't an accidental get-together. Jeremy didn't come to work on the float because of his pep. "We can talk about it if you want. But you don't have to."

"Jeremy came here so he could see you. And he was mad about what I wrote on Friendspace." Oliver's features are hard, and it's the first time I've seen anything close to a temper from him. "I mean, if you want to talk to him, you'll talk to him. But there were only five people here, and so no matter what, it's going to be awkward, and that's not fair to us, or to you."

"You're right," I say. "I already talked to him yesterday at school."

"Yeah, he told me. That you're going to homecoming together." Oliver's hands ball into fists. "Which, hey, isn't any of my business. Nothing between you two is. I mean, part of it is the challenge for him, I hope you know that. He wanted you back because he couldn't have you."

"He doesn't have me."

"...don't know why I got so mad, but it's like he was coming after me and he said..."

"What?" I whisper.

"He said I only joined this club so I could be with you." Oliver hops down from the float. "Which is...malarkey."

"'Malarkey'?"

"Yes, echo. Malarkey. Not true."

"I'm not going with him to homecoming," I say.

Oliver doesn't seem to hear me. "My mom can't even afford a junior college and I don't play school sports, so I *need* to be involved in all these stupid clubs and volunteer organizations. I don't even know what my future is, but I know I won't have one if I don't go star student every chance I can. So that's why I joined this club, and it wasn't because of you."

"I never said it was."

He pauses. "You're not going to homecoming?"

"I am. But not with Jeremy."

"That's the thing. It shouldn't matter. Nothing you do should matter to me. Not like it does." Oliver holds out his hand and yanks me off the float with surprising force. His grip is possessively tight. "Maybe this was a bad idea."

"What, finishing the float?"

"No. Yes. Just…being here." He starts to pull me toward the shed door. "We shouldn't be alone."

"It's not a big deal. We're just working." It's a boldface lie and we both know it. The tension between us is something I can smell, something I can taste. When did pep club become so *hot*? "Why are you freaking out?"

Oliver fixes me with a stare that pummels every other thought or worry in my head and heart until my whole universe is just that look. "I'm freaking out because every second I'm with you, all I can think about doing is this."

And he's pulling me again, but this time it's toward him, so our bodies are touching—arms and stomachs and shoulders and legs—and mouths. Mouths smashing into each other, nothing delicate about it, mouths that knew that this is what they wanted to do from the very first second he talked to me about pep club. It feels so good to have his body pushing against mine. Not just any body, but *Oliver's* body, who laughs for me when he doesn't laugh for anyone, who gave me a string so I'll remember to forget, who I like, who I *want*, and he wants me. I want so bad to be wanted, all of me, every piece.

He pulls back a bit and I grab his hair, crushing him closer, sucking his lips, tasting Oliver. If we don't talk, don't breathe, just keep our bodies close, then there won't be room for reality to slither in. We can just surrender and not think. Just feel.

But no. I might not have a thing, and I might not know what kind of girl I am, but I know who I'm not, and I'm not this. I can't give Oliver my pieces, literal, figurative, whatever. Being with him, this soon, this fast, would just be like hot-gluing my heart together—a quick fix. What I want, but not what I need.

I push away with as much force as we came together. I bend over, hands on knees, and Oliver swears. "No. No, forget that. I did that wrong."

"Felt pretty right to me." I laugh, cold and hollow, and realize Oliver is right. Very few laughs are in response to something funny.

Oliver kicks at the float. The tinsel swishes. "I even used a line. I swear I didn't rehearse that line."

I hold up a hand. "Oliver, dissecting kisses is fine, but not two seconds after it happened and not with the person you just kissed."

Oliver's head is in his hands as he paces. "That's not why I brought you here. I'm not like this. Seriously, Mallory, you're my cousin's girlfriend—"

"*Ex*-girlfriend."

"Not if you ask him." He stops pacing and lowers his voice, like he's talking to himself. "That was the stupidest thing I've ever done."

I stand, the bones in my spine rolling up one by one until I am a tower, a presence. I need to look in control, even if I don't feel it. Having a boy say that kissing me is his biggest mistake isn't the best confidence boost. "Look, you don't get to be the only one mad here. You think I'm like this, Oliver?"

"I'm sorry I kissed you."

"Don't apologize!

"All right. Sorry."

"You don't get all the blame. I was here too, you know. Do you think I just run around kissing any boy who drags me into a toolshed?"

"No." Oliver's mouth twitches. "Do you have a lot of boys dragging you into toolsheds?"

I try to glare at him. I try so hard. Anger's a great mask for the next layer of emotion, the questions and uncertainty that comes from kissing a boy I probably shouldn't kiss. But his hand is over his mouth now, and I can see the smile in his eyes.

"You're such a tool," I say.

"Hey, if the shed fits."

"I revoke my nomination to make you president."

He swallows back his laugh and nods. "I'll finish the float tonight. Don't worry about it."

"I was going to lose sleep." I widen my eyes in feigned terror. "We're talking float nightmares with flat tires and annihilated tinsel and severe loss of spirit. I can't even... Swear you'll make Bessie beautiful."

"I give you my word." His face goes serious again, and I would give my left pinkie to know what he's thinking. I wonder if he knows how adorable he looks in the dim shed light. And I wonder why I can't make myself stop thinking about how he looks or what *he's* thinking, because this is a crisis moment, subtle lighting or not.

He walks me to my car, and although the mood is lighter, it doesn't mean this isn't sticky. That kiss was perfect. Distressingly perfect. But there is nothing perfect about the events surrounding it. Although I'm free to kiss whomever I want, there should be a no-kiss zone after a long relationship, right? Random hookups are fine, but Oliver isn't random. I want to talk to him every day, kiss him again and again. I want Oliver longer than this messed-up moment.

Or do I? Do I want anyone? Things were wonderful when Jeremy and I first started, but who's to say things with Oliver wouldn't end badly as well? And maybe he only wants one thing, the thing all guys want. All this spending time together and talking on the phone and pretending like he feels bad kissing his cousin's recent ex is a clever disguise. That's why I should have waited with him, to finish grieving one relationship before diving into another. I should have made sure my feelings were real before acting on them.

Although they feel really real right now.

I don't know. I don't know what he's thinking. I don't want to know the answer unless I know the answer is what I want it to be, and I don't know what I want him to want.

I didn't even realize I was holding in my breath until I let out a shaky sigh. "So I'll see you at the parade tomorrow."

"Yeah. I got us all pom-poms for the float."

"You're kidding."

"Not about pep, Mallory. Never about pep."

He holds my door open for me. I roll down the window, thinking I should say some parting lines, because we only sort of talked about the kiss before we went back to joking around. We should probably make a final statement about where we are now, not that *we* are anything.

"So, I'm going."

He taps the hood of the car and steps back so I can drive away. So I do. He waves at me when I look in the rearview mirror.

And that's that.

It feels like I'm driving away from more than his house or the float. Maybe that's good.

And maybe it's not.

Chapter 22

Boys I've kissed:

1. Travis: behind the swings in fourth grade.
2. Sam: in front of the big slide in fifth grade.
3. James: by the handball courts in seventh grade. Yeah, I was a playground ho.
4. Nate: first time was at a bonfire freshman year. We dated for four weeks and kissed seven times.
5. Jeremy: on Disneyland rides, in his car, in his room, at the bank, in the Taco Bell

> bathroom…a lot of places. A lot of
> times.
> 6.   Oliver: storage shed.

Ginnie's in the kitchen when I get home, paging through a cookbook. She's wearing her soccer practice sweats with an apron over the top. I wish we didn't have the blowup this morning. There are so many things I need to tell her right now.

I slide onto the barstool. She gives me a quick glance before going back to her reading.

"We can do one of two things right now," I say. "We can rehash our fight this morning, which will probably just make us mad again, and we both know we said things we shouldn't and we're sorry, right?"

Ginnie turns the page of her cookbook.

"Or, we can call a truce and I can show you everything I bought for the party. We can cook and I can tell you all about the crazy day I've had." I don't know if I should tell her about Oliver first, or Grandma, because once she knows about Grandma she'll go batty. Or should I show her Mom's computer because the blog is self-explanatory?

"Oh, so we would talk about you again. That's new."

In my defense, it's not all about me. Today was the least *me* day in forever. Today was everyone else's problems becoming my problem. Plus a kiss. I'm not sure what to file the kiss under yet.

But as the older sister with a more dramatic life, the fact is that, yeah, we do talk more about me. Ginnie doesn't have boy problems, everyone is her friend, and she plays soccer every second beyond that. So maybe I should be more giving. Add it to the list.

The life list. Not Grandma's list. "Fair enough. We can talk all about the crazy day *you* had instead."

Ginnie closes the cookbook. "That's the best apology I'm going to get?"

"Hey, I didn't get one at all."

"Fine. Sorry." Ginnie pushes the book aside and leans across the counter. "So. I got my first real kiss today."

I don't react for a second, because although I knew we were switching gears to Ginnie, I didn't expect her to drop a bomb like that. "Wait, what?"

She squeals. "I know! Can you believe it?"

"Of course I can believe it, but … who? When? What?"

Ginnie rushes around the counter and perches herself on the stool next to me. Her arms are out, poised, ready to spring into animation as she recounts the details. "So I packed my lunch today, because you know how much I love cold wheat-germ pancakes wrapped around tofu sausage, with those little Carl's Junior syrup cups to dip them in."

"Disgusting. But yes."

"And I forgot my bag in my locker, so I raced back right before lunch, and I saw Bennett in the hallway—"

"You kissed *Bennett*?"

"Well, duh, who do you think I'd have kissed? Anyway, he was hanging on my locker and we started talking about the dance, and he asked if I needed help with the soiree. So sweet.

Then we figured out who is riding with us, and some parents want to come over to take pictures on the staircase now—"

"Ginnie."

"And *then* everyone was gone and the lunch bell rang and he said, 'I'm really glad you said yes.' And he grabbed my chin and kissed me. In the middle of school, Mallory. It was super-short, maybe five seconds, but isn't that the best thing a guy has ever said before a kiss?"

I swallow back my own kiss story. "Do you like him?"

"Sure. I let him kiss me, didn't I?"

"Then that's great, Ginnie. Wow, I can't believe Bennett had the balls to do that."

"I know! So do you think he'll kiss me again Saturday night? I mean, if he kissed me today, he'll want to do it again, right?"

It's logical reasoning, but nothing is logical in love. Bennett might break her heart tomorrow, or he could be the sweetest guy on earth. And that she might experience both heartbreak and new-love jitters within a two-week span, which is enough to confuse anyone. But that sounds jaded, and she's happy, and when you love someone like I love my sister, you say anything to keep her smiling. "Of course he'll kiss you again. He was just testing the waters."

"That's what Mom said."

"You told *Mom?*" I grab her arm. "Are you crazy? You know how she thrives on details. Trust me, she's going to be ravenous for information. Just wait until she gives you the sex talk."

"Was that what she meant when she talked about my pieces?" she asks.

"And so it begins." I squeeze her arm and let go.

"Well, I had to. I caught her crying in her office when I got home, so I wanted to cheer her up." Ginnie's face pales. "You don't think she was crying because something happened with Dad, do you?"

This is the portion of our sisterly bonding conversation where I tell her that no, it's not about Dad, it's all about Mom, and she quite possibly was crying because I know her big secret. It's what Ginnie deserves to hear, because this is the truth. But today is a big day for her, so I want to shield her from that truth right now. I lie out of love.

"No, I saw her after school. She's said she's menstrual, and she missed the Gap friends and family sale, and the website kept freezing, so it was probably just a combination. I'm sure she's fine."

The worry slips off Ginnie's face and she breaks out into a grin. "Bennett used a little tongue."

"Ah, he *is* your steady! He's your tongue steady!"

"I didn't know what to do, if I was supposed to use tongue back or just let him do his thing."

I grab a tub of strawberry frozen yogurt out of the freezer and stick two spoons into it. "Okay, little sister. You are of age. It's time I share the rules of tongue. Number one. Less is more."

School-wise, Friday is a joke. The classes are shortened to thirty minutes to allow time for the afternoon parade at two o'clock. Mr. Hanover returns my paper, and I get a C minus due to my lack of a bibliography, which I never did turn in because of my Internet sources. I kiss the paper because it could have been worse, much worse. Of everything I've given up during my tech sabbatical, this grade is going to be the longest repercussion. I'll be lucky to pull up my overall grade to a B now.

I'm one of the only juniors taking the school bus down to the parade. This is what I wanted, a little solitude before the onslaught of spirit. The homecoming parade is a huge tradition in Orange. The Circle and most of Chapman Street are barricaded off, and the elementary schools and junior highs are let out early so kids can come watch. Not only does every class have a float, as do the larger clubs, but there's the band, and cheerleaders, and a local Cadillac dealer drives the school administration. Now that I've started to take stock of things that are my "things," I'm going to say parades have not previously been on the list.

And probably won't be added to the list.

Everything certainly *looks* perfect. The seniors are the clear winners with their anime float, and one of the vintage stores made a float for the homecoming court that also has alumni from 1993 waving along. It's another clear California day, the kind that seems like it can never end and never should. And even though I've only been in a school organization for a little over a week, I feel like I belong to this big picture in a way I never did before. I have a piece of ownership in this school, instead of just feeling owned by one person. And I'm wearing my vintage letterman sweater. Forget the dirt smell I couldn't get rid of after three washings, I look fabulous.

The problem isn't the atmosphere; it's the number of people pushing past me, too many names and stories and situations. Normally I would be in the crowd with Jeremy, watching, not actively participating. This crush of involved students is overwhelming. There are girls who have T-shirts about their class, about their cliques, and there are boys in bejeweled Burger King crowns. I'm so isolated in my *O* sweater spirit, but it's my duty as pep club secretary to be here. And, like so many other things in my life lately, I want to do this to see if I can, even though being apart in a large group is the worst kind of lonely.

My Jeremy radar, which has yet to deactivate, signifies that he's near the JV cheerleaders' float, talking to Isaac Stevens and his sophomore girlfriend. The weird thing is, we're in the same general area and I'm not thinking about how good he smells or what a good kisser he was. Is. I'm not torturing myself with bittersweet memories and could-have-beens. Seeing him still isn't easy, but maybe I'm past the part where it's painfully hard. I rub the string on my finger. Oliver was right—you can remember to forget.

Oliver. I scan the crowd and find him leaning against our float, one leg up with a grip of pom-poms under his arm. Vance is next to him and they're scanning the crowd, looking for . . . me.

I push through the masses, sweat prickling underneath my sweater. "Hey! Bessie looks great!"

Oliver's in his George Jetson costume, a futuristic white shirt, blue pants, and a slick orange wig. Glasses are off. He's the hottest cartoon I've ever seen. "Seriously? I'm wearing this costume and *Bessie* gets the compliments?"

"You look great too." I clear my throat. "Or your costume does."

"Yeah, well, not me." Vance folds his arms over his furry gray chest. His mom makes the costumes and he still gets stuck with Astro the dog. "I wish we'd done some cool karate cartoon instead."

Oliver sticks the pom-poms into Vance's hand. "Karate cartoon over *The Jetsons?* Vance, no. Trust me, this is the best idea ever."

"It's your idea."

"Why, yes, it is. Now go find Judy and Jane. The parade is going to start soon."

Vance trudges away, his tail between his legs.

Oliver readjusts his wig. "Your costume is in the truck bed. Are you ready for this?"

"You might be the president, but don't forget that I was the originator of pep. I was born ready."

Oliver opens the door to the truck, courtesy of Vance's family. The kid ended up being a more vital pep club member than anticipated. Inside is a refrigerator-size box painted blue with a little white apron attached. A headband antenna and maid hat lie on top. "Here you go, Ruby the maid."

"Oh wow. This ... this is asking a lot."

"Just get in."

My sweater comes off, so I'm just in my gray T-shirt and jeans. I squat down, and Oliver sticks the box over my head. My arms go through the slightly uneven armholes, and I tug my head through the top. Oliver completes the look by adding the hat and antenna. He smooths down my hair (which doesn't give me goose bumps—nope, not one bit).

We analyze each other for a moment, both in our ridiculous cartoon replicas. Then Oliver scratches his ear and says, "Look, Mallory. About yesterday."

"Don't worry about it."

"No, I am." His forehead wrinkles. "I want to make something clear."

There's a buzz in the crowd, a frenzy of movement. Cars are starting, groups converging. The two of us stand still.

"What I wanted to say is ... look. I'm ... I'm *not* sorry."

"You're not sorry?" My voice comes out small and contained, like how my body feels in this huge box.

"Right." Oliver levels his gaze. Those eyes. "I'm not."

He's not.

Someone grabs my arm and whirls me around. It's Ginnie, in the Jane costume, looking futuristically frazzled. "Would you guys hurry? The trailers are starting to move."

It's pandemonium everywhere, with cheerleaders bouncing into a line and cartoon characters scrambling onto floats. But Oliver's still in front of me, waiting for some response I can't give.

He's not apologizing for the costume here, right? No, I'm buzzing down to my toes, and toes do not lie. Maybe that kiss wasn't the stupidest thing he's ever done after all. I break into a smile and look down.

Ginnie pushes me onto the float and I figure the moment is done, that Oliver and I can talk about this later, although I have no idea how *that* conversation will go down. But when I look back . . . when I look back, Oliver is still staring. The band starts up, the crowd stands and cheers, the cheerleaders erupt into a pom-pom frenzy, but Oliver doesn't budge.

"President Oliver, stop staring at my sister and get on the float before I assassinate your butt!" Ginnie yells.

Vance's dad starts the truck. Finally, that smile tugs on the right side of Oliver's mouth. He hops onto the float with effortless grace, and I wish I were Jane Jetson instead of the boxy robot. Then we'd be married, at least in an animated way.

And it would be so much better if we were going to the dance together. And how lame is it that I don't have a date . . .

Mallory. You don't need a date.

I turn around to see if that was Ginnie who just said that. But she's on the hitch side of the trailer, laughing with Cardin. No one else is near me, and I realize that the voice was in my head.

I don't need a date. A date wouldn't solve anything. The List is all I need for a boyfriend right now. Oliver might not be sorry that kiss happened, but I'm still not sure. About any of this.

Oliver shakes his pom-pom, and everyone else cheers and

jumps. And I am alone, in this crowd, on this float. I don't look at the passing faces. I don't find Jeremy, I don't look back at Oliver.

I close my eyes. Although there isn't an actual sunrise, I can feel something awakening in me, and so I drown out the sound and focus on finding a Rumination that isn't boy-centered.

I don't come up with anything. But at least I try.

Chapter 23

Menu for dinner soiree, compiled by Ginnie after meticulous early 1960s era research in cookbooks (hard core!) and the Internet (I'll forgive her):

1. Shrimp cocktail.
2. Cheese fondue with bread and green apples. (We've set up a little bar table for this, since you have to stay close to the cheese. Good rule for life, actually. STAY CLOSE TO THE CHEESE.)
3. Pigs in a blanket. Little cocktail weenies wrapped in Pillsbury crescent rolls. They're delish, but the name makes it

sound like I'm slaughtering a sleeping pig just so I can get my snack on. Which...might be the case.

4. Jell-O heaven. Pink Jell-O mixed with Cool Whip and topped with maraschino cherries, served in little cups.

5. Ritz crackers with sliced ham and a cheese ball.

6. Cream cheese in celery. That's it. I'm not making this stuff up.

7. Deviled eggs.

8. Stuffed mushrooms. Don't let the mushroom make you think we went all healthy. Sausage. Cream cheese. Combine. Stuff.

9. Rice Krispies treats. I didn't know that Rice Krispies existed back then, but I'm so glad we'll have something decent to erase the gross celery.

10. Sherbet punch.

Our team loses the football game that night. I don't know the rules of football, so I can't say how close the game was. They did have great Kettle Korn at the snack bar, though. Our family goes to Ginnie's soccer game Saturday morning, she scores two goals, and we're home by two to start soiree preparations. The good thing about early sixties cocktail food—there really isn't much cooking involved. It seems that the food item was deemed fancy as long as it was served on a frilly toothpick. Which really just proves I was born in the wrong era if there was ever a time when mini sausages equaled class.

Ginnie and I don't talk about any of the things I know we should talk about. I'm planning a huge information unload on Sunday, after the dinner and dance. There's no reason for her to worry about her long-lost aunt, blogging Mom, and her first date all in one day. Maybe I'll wait until I'm back in the technology world and text her the information. Like Yvonne said, it's less awkward that way.

Ginnie scowls at the mini sausages. "Next time you want to connect to another time, can you go with prerevolutionary France? Or can we do some hippie commune so there's food I can actually eat?"

"No one is stopping you from eating this," I say.

"The documentary I saw on the ingredients in a hot dog is stopping me." She wrinkles her nose. "But I guess Bennett loves meat, so he'll be happy."

"He'll be happy when you make out with him tonight."

"We'll see," Ginnie says mysteriously.

Today should be the day I finish The List. I've accomplished three out of five, and once Ginnie and Bennett cozy up tonight, the steady item will be done. I just need to figure out living dangerously, which might involve eating the cream cheese and sausage mixture Ginnie is presently concocting.

The doorbell rings a little after four. Ginnie is wrist-deep in trans fat, so I scoot down the hallway, whistling an old Beach Boys song. I stop midwhistle when I see who it is.

There is Grandma, holding a large hatbox that I assume contains my dress. It would be a glorious moment, the changing of the guards, were it not for my long-lost aunt standing next to Grandma. The aunt I have yet to tell Ginnie exists.

I should hide the frilly toothpicks now so they're not used as weapons.

"Oh, you're here! I thought you'd be out doing things for homecoming. I was just going to drop this off, maybe see if your parents were around?"

"They're out running some last-minute errands for the soiree. Ginnie is here, though."

Grandma shakes her head. "No, she's stressed. She doesn't need"—she glances at Candace—"to worry about us just now, before the dance. You understand."

Candace leans her hand on the doorframe, gingerly, like she needs the support but doesn't want to intrude. This is her brother's house, and she was about to meet him. But we aren't going to talk about that, or the fact that Grandma has always been involved in Dad's life, the child she kept. I still don't know if Candace is married and if she has kids and if those kids know that she is here meeting a grandma they don't know at all, and if Candace has anything in common with her birth mom besides sewing skills. She might not even like my grandma.

I don't want Ginnie to get upset by this, either, so I step out onto the porch and close the door behind me. Grandma opens the box and it's all poof and satin and glory. She shakes the dress, holding it out at arm's length. "Don't be mad, but I added some black underlay with embellishment around the waist. Candace had to help me. It's how I wanted the dress to look when I made it the first time."

I take the dress from her outstretched hand. Black crystal beads rain down the bodice, and she's added black tulle to the white poof. It's still true to period, but it's old-style glamour now instead of sugary sweet.

Candace holds out a pair of long black gloves to me too. "And we went ahead and found these too, since your grandma said you were going for sixties vintage."

They stand there, on the front porch, waiting for me to do or say something. But I'm at a total loss for words, because…

1. The dress is just that beautiful, and I'm going to wear it tonight, on my date with myself.

2. They are here, at the house, where no one else knows about Candace.

"Thank you," I say. "I can't believe you did this for me."

"Of course I did," Grandma says. "Although, for the amount of work we put into that today, we could have finished your original dress."

"No, this is better." I stroke the fabric. Tears spring to my eyes and I can't say why. It's like this dress is The List epitomized, everything I'd hoped to accomplish, everything I'd hoped to forget. "This means more."

Grandma doesn't notice the emotion in my voice, or if she does, doesn't acknowledge it. "I'm going to drop Candace off at the airport. She's flying out again in a couple of weeks. We'll have Rodney come down, set up a dinner or something with the whole family then."

"It's been a little overwhelming." Candace gives a timid smile. "But I'm glad I had the chance to meet you, Mallory. Have fun at the dance."

I should hug her, I know I should. She's my aunt and she just spent the last day with her birth mom sewing my dress. But I am like my grandma in that respect, not great at showing emotions. So I stand there like an idiot and say, "You too."

You too. That's all she gets. I suck.

The front door opens and Ginnie pops out her head. "Aren't you going to invite—Grandma! You're just who we need. Come inside—this Jell-O mold isn't setting up right."

I know I look as guilty as Grandma, and Candace is slack-faced, staring at Ginnie's hair—Candace's hair. I motion to Grandma, hoping for a signal or cue, but there's nothing there.

Ginnie isn't an idiot. She's going to ask who this woman is. So I do what I should have done earlier and link my arm into Candace's. "Ginnie. This is going to be a total shock and I just found this out too, but this is Candace. Grandma had her, like, uh, birthed her in high school and gave her up for adoption. So Candace is our aunt and she's here visiting and she sewed the beads onto my homecoming dress."

Yep. That covers it.

Ginnie sticks her hand over her mouth. "Seriously?" she asks Grandma.

"I wasn't perfect," Grandma says in a broken voice. There it is, her reason for keeping this a secret from us. She thought she'd lose our respect because she gave some stupid boy her pieces a long time ago. But really, seeing her in such a raw light, I respect her so much more.

My grandma has always seemed mythical, someone bigger than everyone else. But she's only a girl like me, a girl who once loved a boy who probably didn't deserve it. And the "proof" that her teen years didn't go as planned also helped redesign my homecoming dress. There's sweet serendipity in that.

My brain might come up with cozy thoughts in moments like this, but it sounds so stupid and cheesy when I try to say what I'm feeling. So although I don't have the voice to tell my aunt how much I appreciate her, or tell my grandma that she's the strongest woman I know, I grab my grandma's hand and give it a squeeze. Emotionally, it's all I can do right now, but she squeezes back. She doesn't need to say anything, either. The dress tells me plenty.

"Grandma, I've seen you play tennis. Of course you aren't perfect." Ginnie hurries down the front steps and gives Grandma a hug. "That must have been a hard secret to keep."

"It was," Grandma whispers. "But I'm very glad it's out now."

Ginnie hugs Candace next. No talking, she goes right for the hug. "It's good to meet you. We're having a party tonight. I hope you can stay."

Candace is frozen in the hug. "My flight leaves at eight."

"Great! That gives us two hours. Do you know my dad yet?"

Candace shakes her head.

"Oh, you'll like him. Well, he's your brother, so you'll have no choice. And we have all this retro food if you're hungry.

Or, if you're like me and prefer not to destroy your insides with animal flesh, I'll make you a smoothie."

She lets go of Candace and I'm ready for my squeeze when Ginnie punches my arm instead. "And that's for not telling me." She punches me again. "And for not inviting them inside." She pulls her arm back. "And this is for your stupid list."

I hold up my arms and block the blow. "I was going to tell you, but I didn't want to steal your first-kiss thunder!"

"First kiss?" Grandma grins.

Ginnie rolls her eyes. "Come inside. I'll tell you before my date gets here, but don't act weird around him! Aunt Candace, you're about to get to know me very well very fast."

Reason #40,345 I love my sister: see above.

Having never attended a soiree, I have no idea what to expect from one. I would assume most soirees do not begin with a long-lost aunt showing up on a doorstep to deliver a bedazzled version of the homecoming dress your grandma wore fifty years earlier, only to have your parents drive up twenty minutes later to the shock of their lives, followed by lots of questions and tears and deep discussions as everyone hurriedly cuts the celery and stirs the punch and, yes, sticks toothpicks in all the party food.

The stuffed mushrooms, as you can imagine, are a little anticlimactic after that.

Candace is at the door, hugging my dad, hugging my mom, hugging *her* mom ... You get the point. It's hug city.

My mom has already taken twenty pictures of Candace, one of just her hands entwined with Grandma's, which I'm sure is going to be the feature in her next blog post. Dad keeps patting Candace on the top of the head like she's a newborn infant left on our doorstep.

"We'll see you in a few weeks!" Mom calls as Dad pulls Candace away for a private good-bye. When he first met Candace, he bawled like a baby, which made the rest of us tear up at his open emotion.

Grandma sticks her head on my shoulder. "So this list you told me about the other day. Did you finish it?"

"Almost."

"I know you had this ideal of what you thought my youth was like. I hope my big secret didn't spoil that for you."

Spoil isn't the word. I'm a little bothered that my hypothesis wasn't entirely right. I thought The List was going to take me back to a simpler time, but in some ways it's just made my life more complicated. "It's not that different now, is it? Being sixteen?"

"Adolescence is the same tragedy being performed again and again. The only things that change are the stage props."

I finger Grandma's ring, tucked under my shirt. She's right. The props—my computer, my phone—they're not the main conflict in this play. I mean, fifty years ago my grandma experienced these same messed-up emotions. The Internet might not have existed yet, but love and heartache did.

Do I even need to finish The List? What am I proving now?

Dad shuts the hatch to Grandma's Mini Cooper. "You better hurry, Mom."

Grandma kisses the top of my head. "Candace is flying out of LAX, so I won't make it back in time for your grand reveal."

"I'll take pictures."

"It's just as well. Not sure if I can handle much more déjà vu."

"I'll do your dress proud," I say.

She smiles, eyes wet. "Mallory. You do me proud every day."

Hug central convenes, and then they're driving down the street, and Ginnie and I only have thirty more minutes. I shoo her upstairs to get ready and finish up the final preparations. I'm still in my white oxford and gingham capris when the guests start to arrive. Grandma already did my hair in a slick chignon, my fake eyelashes and black eyeliner heavy on my lids, but getting a stain on a vintage dress, even with vintage food, is a housewife's horror in any decade.

Besides, the soiree is for Ginnie's friends. Paige, Yvonne, and Cardin come. I never got around to inviting Oliver. Our most recent conversations have ended rather abruptly.

When Bennett gets there, corsage in hand, Ginnie stages an entrance down the staircase. Bennett gawks, obviously a fan of my sister's short green dress. Or maybe just her legs in that short green dress.

Cardin finds me in the kitchen cutting more vegetables.

"Where's your dress?" she asks.

I chop off a celery limb. The cream cheese sticks were a surprise hit. "I don't want to have a run-in with the punch. You look awesome."

Cardin brushes something off her chest and shrugs. "I

wore this two weeks ago to a dance in Laguna. It's the fourth homecoming I've been to this year. I need more dresses in my rotation."

"Or less boys in your rotation. I don't know how you do it."

"You've been on the shelf for the last year, honey. If you got out there more, the boys would be dropping left and right."

"Doubt it."

"I saw Oliver Kimball drooling over you by the float yesterday. What's that about?"

"He just gave me a pom-pom," I say.

"Is that what the kids are calling it these days?"

"It's not like that."

"Sure, sure." She sticks her elbows on the counter. "I'm still dying to hear about that fight he had with Jeremy."

"Don't ask *me* about it. I wasn't there."

"Well, I was." She dips her celery into the cream cheese. "And it wasn't pretty. Lots of yelling and defending of Mallory's honor."

"Really?" I stop arranging the food. Half of me finds this news horrific. And the other half...the other half wants to know every single detail. Oliver could have told me more, but that whole kiss-in-the-shed episode got in the way of the full recap. "What did you hear?"

"Well, first there was the basic stuff. Oliver was mad that Jeremy would take another girl to homecoming so soon after your breakup because it wasn't respectful to you. And Jeremy said he wasn't taking that girl from Iowa—"

"Illinois." Or was it Indiana? Weird that I would forget.

"And then Oliver said it was only because she couldn't get off work to fly out, so then Jeremy got—"

"Wait, what? So Jeremy didn't cancel on her, she canceled on him?"

Cardin is quiet. "Didn't Ginnie tell you that part?"

I can't be mad at my sister. She didn't tell me for the same reasons I haven't told her about Mom. Love. Protection. And we were fighting, and…So was I Jeremy's default girl *again*? Jenny couldn't make it, so he told me the whole lie that he'd never really asked her? This is getting to the point where it's almost comical. Almost.

"It doesn't matter," I say. "Jeremy and I broke up. He can do whatever he wants."

"And so can you." Cardin aims her celery stick like a gun. "All I'm saying is you're single and Oliver Kimball is a hot boy who—"

"Is Jeremy's cousin," I finish.

"No. A hot boy who is interested in you. The relationship you just got out of was a dud anyway. If you're feeling it with Oliver, do something about it. Cousins, friends, brothers… there are no rules when it comes to love."

"There are rules to everything," I say.

Cardin's date pokes his head into the kitchen. "They're doing pictures."

She waves him off. "I'll be there in a second, sweetie."

"He's your sweetie?"

She winks. "They're all my sweetie."

We head into the empty living room, which looks like a

Dixie cup graveyard. Ginnie rushes in, all made-up and glowing. I want to pinch her cheeks, say something about how womanly she looks. She scrunches her nose at me.

"Mallory. You have cream cheese in your hair. Get ready. I have a surprise for you coming in ten minutes."

"Better not be Eduardo," I joke, but Ginnie's already back to her friends. Seriously. It better not be Eduardo.

I run up the staircase before the couples start taking pictures, which I'm glad to skip. There's a deep sense of dread filling my stomach. This dance has been the end of my plan for the last two weeks. Two weeks is nothing—there are colds that last longer than two weeks—but I've been going on survival mode this whole time, and tonight was always unofficially The End. I just hope there's a *happily ever after* beyond this point.

Grandma's dress is much tighter as I shimmy into the poof, pinching my shoulder blades together so I can do the zipper. Once I'm in place, I peek over my shoulder at the full-length mirror behind my door. The girl looking at me, with the freckled back, slim arms and mysterious eyes, could be out of a *Seventeen* magazine fifty years ago, it's that authentic. The look is finished off with some red drugstore lipstick that I'll never wear again.

"Mallory!" Ginnie yells. "Hurry! Your surprise is here!"

I could borrow Mom's pearls, but I opt to keep on Grandma's necklace. It's become a symbol of The List, even if The List technically doesn't represent whatever I thought it did. Maybe I'll see the real benefits from the other side. Or maybe I'll feel like a loser all night long and remind myself to not be so nosy next time I go through Grandma's stuff.

The odds are in my favor that Ginnie will get her steady, and it doesn't take much thought to do something dangerous, so I dig my cell phone out of a shoe in my closet. Ginnie didn't find it during her tech sweep, and I'd been hiding it there so I'd have it when I complete The List.

I find my family outside, staring at a white limo parked in front of our house. Dad has his hands behind his head; Mom is giggling like crazy.

"Did Bennett get you that?" I ask.

My family turns around. Mom gasps, Dad dissolves into *more* tears, and Ginnie beams. "There's the vintage queen."

"You look beautiful," Dad gets out.

"Hurry, let me get a picture of the sisters," Mom says.

Even though I know this picture is going online, I pose and smile. I can get into it with Mom tomorrow. I'm nervous enough about this dance, and there's only so much my heavy-duty deodorant can combat.

"Where's Bennett?" I ask.

"He forgot to gas up his car. He'll be right back."

"Why does he need gas when you guys got a limo?"

"The limo isn't for me. It's for you," Ginnie says.

"What?"

Dad slings his arm around our shoulders. "Ginnie surprised your mom and me with a special date. We're dropping you off, then hitting the town."

I shoot a look at Ginnie. She shrugs. "I reserved it for Bennett and me, but the more I thought about it, the more I figured we didn't need it. Mom and Dad will get more use out of it."

This is another part of her save-our-parents marriage scheme. An extreme part. I'm going to have to tell her the truth tonight, before she rents out a wedding chapel for their vow renewals.

The driver steps out and opens the car door. I thought there wasn't anything lamer than going to a formal dance alone, but I was wrong. My parents are taking me in a limo.

Thanks, Ginnie.

Chapter 24

Things I would rather do than go to this
dance:

1. Scrub toilets.
2. Eat storage-unit cockroaches.
3. This list could get long if I let it.

I am in a limo, on my way to a school dance, watching my parents snuggle on the bench opposite me. I have already placed the champagne bucket nearby in case I need to vomit.

They've changed into "going out" clothes—Dad in a bow tie, short-sleeved button-down shirt and faded jeans, an ensemble that matches his tattoos but maybe not his age. Mom's in a low-cut black number, and they're giggling like teenagers, wrapped in their luxury vehicle cocoon. Which is exactly what Ginnie wanted, and I should be glad that my parents are getting along, but everything my mom does bothers me since I found out about her blog.

I stare out the tinted window. "Can't you two unstick from each other for five minutes?"

"It's good for our relationship. Cuddles count," Mom says.

"That sounds like a good blog-post title," I say under my breath.

"Mallory." She sighs. "Honey. Now isn't the time to bring that up."

"Oh, why, does Dad not know?" I sit up in my seat. I'd promised myself that I wouldn't get heated, that I would save this until later, but I can't control myself in this confined space. I hate how . . . how happy they look, like they're the perfect couple, when they fight in front of us all the time and have no idea what Ginnie really thinks or what I saw online. "Dad, do you read Mom's blog?"

"Well." Dad shoots Mom a look. "I know she has one. I don't usually—"

"It's okay, Kevin. I know you don't read it." Mom shrugs.

"Well, maybe you should," I say, angry at my dad now for being so clueless. "Then you'd know she wrote a post about my breakup and said I have low self-esteem."

Mom twists her hands in her lap. "You're taking it out of context. I wrote that post because I was worried about you."

"Then talk to your best friend about it. Don't tell thousands of Internet strangers about me." I shake my head. "Did you know I gave up all modern technology for the last two weeks because of what happened with Jeremy? Because everyone was online talking about my personal business? And then I have a moment of weakness and get on your computer, only to find out that you're talking about me online too, only worse. You had no right doing that."

"Why were you blogging about Mallory on a coupon blog?" Dad asks.

Mom turns to Dad, then to me, unsure what issue to address first. She finally casts me a desperate look. "Mallory, I'm so sorry. I wasn't trying to hurt anyone. I think of my readers as friends, and I did want advice. That blog…it's something else besides being a mom or a wife or Dad's job. It's my thing, you know?"

I rub my lips together, remembering too late I'm wearing lipstick. Should my mom have blogged about my relationship without consulting me? Absolutely not, and we'll have to set some online boundaries about what I feel comfortable with her discussing. Is she entitled to have "a thing," something to grow and connect and expand? Absolutely, and I can't believe this is the point that ties me to her, makes me understand. Being online is something real for her, something valuable. "Yeah, okay."

"Sometimes I forget how big the blog is now, forget that I have…an audience."

Dad shakes his head. "How big are we talking?"

Big enough that she can lie about selling those cuff links, I think. I wonder if Mom will bring that up, since Dad clearly has no concept just how successful *Totally Hot! Totally Thrifty!* is.

"I mostly blog about coupons, but I also have deals of the week from your antiques business," she says. "Your cuff links were actually last week's deal."

"You sold antique cuff links on your blog for fourteen thousand dollars?" Dad asks.

"Maybe for less than I told you."

"How much less?" Dad asks.

"I don't know." Mom pauses. "Minus seven or eight thousand."

Dad's jaw hardens. "I see why Mallory got so upset. You've been lying to this family."

"Kevin, I—"

"I already spent that money you said we made on advertising." Dad's voice is rising. They're headed to that awkward fighting place, and there's no out from the car. "I bought that trailer on credit, thinking we had the money, extended my booth size—"

"Dad," I cut in, unsure why I'm coming to my mom's defense. Maybe because I understand wanting a "thing," maybe because I realize her intent wasn't malicious. Her post was a mom asking for help. Help from whoever happens to do an Internet search on coupons, but help nonetheless. "I'm sure Mom still has the money."

She nods. "I added sponsors to my blog a few months ago, and I make an income on that now. Please don't be mad. I know you like to be the breadwinner, and you are, but I saw a chance to make extra money and—"

"I would think that I'm secure enough in my manhood

that you would realize that doesn't matter. You don't need to lie about how much I make financially to cover up how successful you are," Dad says, dazed. "I don't know if I should yell at you or kiss you."

"Please neither," I say.

"You've been working so hard on your business," Mom says. "I didn't want to take away from that."

"The only reason this business is *in* business is because of you," Dad says.

She nuzzles into his shoulder.

I interrupt before they can pull another one eighty and sap out on each other. "There's something else," I say. "Do you guys know why Ginnie got a limo?"

"So you won't feel bad about going to the dance by yourself, sweetheart," Dad says.

"No. First she thought you were having an affair, Mom, because of all your computer sneakiness."

"Why would she—" Mom starts.

I hold up a hand. "Doesn't matter. She also thinks you two are headed to a divorce because of how much you fight."

"We don't fight that much," Dad says.

The limo slows into the school parking lot. I unroll the tinted window, letting in some brisk air. A group of kids in formal wear run in front of us, their laughter cutting the tension.

"Honey, we're fine," Mom says. "Better than fine. We just express our emotions very openly—"

"I'm not the daughter you should be having this talk with." I slide out of the limo and poke my head into the open door. "Ginnie's the one who rented the limo. But obviously something is going on that made her worried. So maybe spend the ride figuring that out."

Mom sighs. "You sound like the parent here."

"Ah." I smile. "Make *that* your next blog post." I slam the door and turn to the large high school gymnasium looming before me. The limo starts to drive away, and Mom and Dad pop out of the sunroof, yelling things like "We love you!" and "You make us so proud!" but their voices are soon lost in the wind.

I'm glad I rode with them. Their relationship isn't perfect in a lot of ways, but it's something real. And real should probably be the goal, not perfection. Every relationship is flawed; you just have to figure out how to make it work. Keep trying. That viewpoint might have saved things between Jeremy and me. Could *still* save things with Oliver. If I want that. Does he want that?

I square my shoulders and shake out the poof of my dress. Going to a dance all by myself, without even latching on to a group or walking in with friends, *seemed* like a good way to prove how strong and independent I am. Just like I'm sure twelve-hour child workdays *seemed* like a good idea during the Industrial Revolution. Wow, a real-life curriculum application. I should ask Mr. Hanover to give me extra credit.

The only warmth I have is a black cardigan, so I scurry into the dance and thrust my ticket into the hands of two ASB underclassmen.

"Just you?" one girl asks, totally matter-of-fact, but the question still cuts.

"Yep."

"All right." She flashes a smile. "Have fun!"

Fun? This isn't about fun. I spend the next five minutes in that hallway, literally talking myself into going inside, and I don't care that the ASB girls are staring at me. They're selling tickets at a table outside of the dance, so who are they to judge?

I can't believe I'm doing this, showing up at a dance by myself after all the Jeremy shenanigans. This isn't just stupid, it's ... dangerous. Socially, that is. And wasn't this whole list a social experiment anyway? I should count this as doing something dangerous. No, seriously, I *will* count it. Mallory Bradshaw, woman of danger and ... datelessness.

I am so close now, just final steady confirmation from my sister, and I've actually started and *finished* something important for the first time in my life. It is that shot of confidence that finally pushes me through the open gym doors.

They've made a white-and-silver balloon arch, and tiaras and stars hang from the gym ceiling. The decorations committee carried over the cartoon theme well with a nod to Disney princesses. Living so close to Disneyland, someone must have had a hookup, because I recognized the thrones for queen and king from the Disney parade last summer.

One more beat, another deep breath, and my legs are moving, my heart is hammering and ... that's it, really. I'm here. The music doesn't stop to signify my arrival. I'm at my junior homecoming dance alone.

Alone.

Stag.

By myself.

And the most surprising part?

It's okay.

No one is watching me or judging me or even thinking about me. It's like this is my very own moment. If I were here with a date, I'd be worried if he was having a good time, I would be thinking about what he thinks about me, if he likes my dress. *I* like my dress. That's more than enough.

Alone looks good on me.

But of course, there's my sister, sitting at a table, stirring a water cup with her finger. Bennett is nowhere in sight. She grunts when she sees me, which isn't the warm sisterly welcome I would have hoped for.

"What took you so long?" Ginnie asks.

"Talking to Mom and Dad in the limo."

She breaks into a grin. "Oh yeah? How'd they like it?"

"They loved it." I watch Ginnie's finger as it swirls around in the water. In Grandma's day it would have been punch, but the administration has finally learned it's more difficult to spike water. "Ginnie, Mom isn't having an affair."

Ginnie's finger goes motionless. "How do you know?"

"The reason she's online and secretive and all the other things you were worried about is because she has a blog."

"A *blog*?"

"I mean, it's more than just a blog. It's a business. Couponing, deals . . . I found it the other day, when I had my technology relapse."

"So what does that mean?" Ginnie scrunches up her eyebrows. "Do Mom and Dad fight because of her blog?"

"Mom and Dad fight because Mom and Dad fight."

Ginnie wipes her finger on a napkin and folds her hands in her lap. "So will they get a divorce?"

"Ginnie ... no. I think their relationship seems worse than it is because they're into public displays of emotion—the kissing *and* the fighting. But they do recognize how much you're trying to create family harmony, and I think that's going to make them try to communicate better."

"Really? They're good, then?"

"Fine. I'd label it a fine."

"So I shouldn't buy those turtle doves?" she asks.

"Maybe save your money."

Ginnie takes this with a nod. "Well, in that case, I should have kept the limo too. Then I'd have a way to bail on Bennett."

"Oh no, is the date awkward? Did you guys kiss again?"

"Oh, we kissed. But then he practically attacked my pieces on the way over here, so ..." She smiles wickedly. "I punched him in the nose."

"You're kidding."

"No. And he totally flipped out." Ginnie lets out a sigh. "It didn't bleed *that* much."

I slump back in my seat. "So I guess Bennett is not going to be your steady."

"Um, no." Ginnie's laugh starts as a small giggle, but rolls into a loud snort. "But he's still in the bathroom if you want him."

I laugh with her, bent over, shaking. This is what my match-making has led us to, my sister hitting her homecoming date in the face. Which would be the opposite of a healthy, steady relationship. So much for The List.

"If you want a steady, I bet you could still find one." Ginnie points to the dance floor. "Oliver is over there."

I pull down her hand. "Don't point!"

"Why? He's looking over here."

I jerk my head around. Oliver's in a large group, jumping to the loud music. He's the only one here wearing a bow tie, or a cummerbund, for that matter, red and shiny to match his date. Carmen looks darling in a short number, something rock star that only she could pull off.

Oliver sees me and waves me over, but I answer with a helpless shrug. We're really mastering our nonverbal communication this weekend. Oliver is on a date with another girl, and whether or not they like each other romantically, I'm not going to interrupt. And I'm not going to suddenly try to find a steady just because Ginnie didn't deliver.

I stand and scan the room.

"Are you going to go dance with Oliver?" Ginnie asks.

"No. Jeremy."

"Now you're taking this too far. Look, you won, you advanced. Mallory, you conquered. We'll get all your technology out, fix your Friendspace page for good—"

"Oh, I expect everything you confiscated back in my room in the morning, including the bobbleheads. But I still need to do this."

"If you care so much about this stupid list that you'll go back to your old boyfriend just to check something off, I'll grab Bennett out of the bathroom right now and make out with him."

I pat Ginnie on the shoulder. "I appreciate the gesture, but I don't want you to get blood on your dress."

Jeremy is the reason I'm here, really, although I didn't know it until I was in the moment. I squeeze over to his table, watching him as he watches me approach. He has his arm around the seat of the girl next to him, so this must be his date. He brought a date. I can't believe he really brought a date.

"Hey, Jeremy. Can we dance?"

Jeremy leans over to the girl next to him and whispers something. She smiles and gives me a nod. This is *her.* Jenny. The other woman. She's really here. He brought her.

She's not prettier than me. Her hair is stringy and black, her dress a yawn-inducing blue sheath, but she has good teeth and nice skin. I should hate her. I should want to tear her eyes out. It's not like I offer her a winning smile, but I'm kind of ambivalent to the girl. She wasn't the problem with me and Jeremy. She was just one manifestation of our problems.

It's not my fault that Jeremy went cyberpimping. It's not my fault that he didn't see the other sides of me, the more important parts. But I settled for a long time, convinced myself that what we had was more than it was. And of course I did. He was my first love. I didn't know any better. I don't think he did, either.

It's a slow song, something by a past *American Idol* winner, although I can never keep them all straight. Jeremy is respectful of my space as he slips his hands onto my waist. Although the respect might be for his date, who's watching us.

"She's pretty," I say.

"Sure."

"I thought you weren't flying her out."

"Flying?" Jeremy's hands relax a bit on my sides. "Oh, that's not... that's not her. That's Heidi. She lives in Irvine. Her dad knows my dad, it was a last-minute setup thing."

"Oh. So Jenny couldn't get off work after all."

"Do we really need to talk about this?"

"No." I pull farther back. "We don't need to talk about anything."

"What do you want me to say?" Jeremy blows out a breath, and his hair flops to the side. How I used to love that hair. "I've tried. I've said everything. It is what it is."

"I hate that expression. Basically means 'things suck, so deal.'"

"No, I mean... nothing will change. Between us." He shuffles his feet. "Right?"

"I just... I came here so I could tell you something." I squeeze my eyes shut, my fake eyelashes tickling my cheek. I can't say this and watch him at the same time. "I forgive you. For... for caring about another girl like that. And for all the online stuff."

He pulls in a breath. "And I forgive you for the online stuff."

My eyes fly open. "You started it!"

"You called me a tool on my own page!"

"Because you *were* a tool."

"Yeah. Okay. I was."

The song is ending, and so are we. This us. It's done. Really done this time. The breakup doesn't feel like a wound anymore, more it has scabbed over and is starting to scar. That scar is going to heal, eventually, but I'll still carry it. Like Oliver said, I'll remember what happened, but I'll forget the pain.

"One more thing. Did you cancel on Jenny, or did she cancel on you?"

"I mean, she was going to come out, but after we talked a couple times, it didn't seem worth the effort. She said we should just go our own ways or something like that." He lowers his shoulders. "I felt the same way. She wasn't you. I think I was sharing myself with an icon, not a person."

It's probably the most profound thing I've ever heard Jeremy say. "So you got dumped by your girlfriend and your cyberwife in the same month."

Jeremy cracks a smile. "That sounds so pathetic." The song ends. He keeps his hands on my waist, but I pull away. "Mallory, I get that we're done. But just so you know, you look hot tonight. Kind of old-school, but hot."

"Thanks."

He lowers his voice. He can go pretty husky when he wants to. "And if you ever want to get back together, even just for a hookup, I'm down."

He's down. So . . . not the most poetic guy on earth. I reach over and give him a hug. A friendly, platonic, you-are-now-my-ex-and-dream-on hug. "Probably not going to happen."

"So what about Oliver?"

I pull away, leaving a large space between us. A space that will stay. "Oliver's been a good friend when I needed a good friend."

"And that's it between you two?"

"Whatever there is between me and Oliver is between me and Oliver. You don't get to ask me that anymore. Good night, Jeremy."

My heels click across the gym floor. No one else hears because everyone else is dancing and flirting and homecoming…ing. The only one who notices my noises—my shoes, my dress, my breath—is me.

I make it to the hallway and lean my forehead against a locker. It's weird how Jeremy's deception led me to The List, which brought out everyone else's secrets. But I guess The List was my own secret, a valuable one that I wouldn't give up now. My hand goes to my chest, to Grandma's necklace. I yank off the chain, the symbol that she belonged to someone else, to her steady, to Candace's father.

The list item was to find a steady. Despite our different paths, I think we both did this. Because it turns out Grandma made a little typo. I didn't need to find *a* steady, and neither did she. I needed to fine *my* steady.

I am steady. I'm okay being alone, I'm fine edging out of my comfort zone, and I have a list of things that make me the girl I am.

It's too bad I don't have the actual list here, in my clutch, so I can click a pen and ceremoniously add a check to each item. Pep club? Pepped. Soiree? Hosted. Dress? Fabulous. Steady? Solid. Dangerous? Stag.

Without The List to get all symbolic on, I take out my cell phone. I don't look at the messages or texts, the past two weeks of communication. I'm sure I've missed out on plenty without technology, but I don't think I've lost anything. Well, I might have lost that online Scrabble game Ginnie and I had going, which is too bad because I was about to put a *z* down on a triple-letter tile.

I click on Dad's number, sliding my foot in a circle against the tile as I listen to the rings.

"Mallory?"

"Can you guys come get me?"

"Already?" Dad asks. "It's only been twenty minutes."

"I know. But my date just keeps stepping on my toes."

"Your date?" Mom shouts into the phone.

"Oh yeah, Prince Charming showed up with some other girl's shoe that happened to fit my foot. So I'm eloping. Hope you're okay!"

"Mallory, you don't need to feel bad!" Mom shouts again. "We're proud of your independence—"

"Just come to the school."

I hang up. Yeah. Don't want to rush completely into the twenty-first century quite yet.

I plop down, careful that Grandma's dress doesn't snag on the locker. The poof sprays around me. I'm done with the dance. It's too cold to go outside, so this empty hallway is as good as any place to sit and wait for my parent-drawn carriage to appear.

My phone rings again. I don't even glance at the caller ID, just pick it up. "Mom. I was joking, okay? I'm waiting in the hallway. Are you guys close?"

"I'm really close, actually," Oliver says. "Just tell me which hallway."

"Oh. I can't," I deadpan. "I don't talk to strangers."

"How rude! Hello, this is Oliver Kimball. May I please speak to Mallory?" Dance music blasts through his phone.

"Didn't your scoutmaster ever tell you not to call people when there is loud music in the background?"

"Hold on." There's shuffling on the other end, like he's walking. "I kind of lied about that. Phone etiquette was not included in the etiquette merit badge." His voice echoes down the hall. In seconds, he's above me, holding out his hand to help me up and doesn't let go once I'm standing. His bow tie is undone, his adorably hideous cummerbund off. Oliver grins, both sides up. My heart nearly explodes.

"What happened to your cummerbund?" I say into the phone.

"Lost it in a hand of poker. It's been a wild night."

"Then why are you calling me? Don't you have a dance to get back to?"

His grin fades into a soft smile. "I called to tell you how beautiful you look tonight. No, wait. Ethereal. I'm going with ethereal."

There are no witty replies. He's too sincere. It's miles away from Jeremy's hookup offer earlier. I lower my phone and lower my gaze. "Thank you."

Oliver shoves his phone into the inside pocket of his tuxedo. "So I've called this number every day for the last week."

"Really?" I hold the phone away from me, stare at it, decide that later I'll rifle through all the missed calls. "Why?"

"To see when you would start using it again. Guess you're back on the technology horse?"

"Guess so."

"So now we can text each other and take funny pictures and post them on Friendspace!" Oliver's voice sounds like a twelve-year-old girl's.

"Slow down, turbo."

His expression goes serious. "I can do slow."

I believe him. I believe he can do anything. Which is why it's so hard to say, "But I need more than slow. I need a full-on freeze. For weeks, months, I don't know, just time to myself without having to worry about storage shed encounters."

"I told you I wasn't sorry about that."

"But *I* am. You're right. It was stupid. I want something better." I run my hands up and down my bare arms, trying to warm up. I'm already feeling the freeze I asked for. "Now you have a really nice girl inside that gym waiting and I have my parents picking me up in a limo. So...thanks. Happy homecoming."

I turn to leave alone, to finish my night of danger and focus on growing from steady to solid. To bury Grandma's list and begin my own. A list of Mallory's things.

Oliver touches me, just two fingers on my forearm, quite different from the grab in the shed. I don't pull away as he leans in and brushes his lips against my cheek. "Mallory, you want a freeze? I'm a glacier. You want slow? I'm a turtle. But I'll also be waiting by the phone every night, no matter how long it takes until you're ready. Scout's honor."

He drops his hand and backpedals down the hall, back to his friends, back to his date.

And I'm left with time to ruminate, time to solidify, and time to prepare. Prepare for what exactly, I can't say. But if Oliver Kimball is involved, I know it'll be worth the wait.

Epilogue

Junior Year: 3 months later
Mallory's list of things:

1. Cataloging, selling, and bartering antiques.
2. Collecting bobbleheads. Now expanding to NBA basketball players.
3. Sewing (okay, maybe not).
4. School spirit...ing.
5. Eating sister's cooking. Have switched to organic food. Half of the time.
6. Thrift-store shopping.
7. Touring Disneyland with my family— finally converted Mom to a fanny pack.
8. Creating fake Friendspace groups.
9. Playing tennis, but only with Grandma so I can actually win.

10. Telling jokes that make people laugh. Real laugh.
11. Inventing fake merit badges for Oliver Kimball. He's already earned his conversationalist, phone singing, and wooing grandmothers badges. Kissing badge? That boy could be a scoutMASTER.
12. Conquering very complicated and important lists.

Acknowledgments

This book is here because these people and places exist. Thank you to:

My editor, Caroline Abbey, for your kindness, calm, and understanding during the revision process and for helping me transform my ideas into words into pages into books. Yes, plural! You're golden.

My agent, Sarah Davies, for helping me figure out what this novel should be before it was anything at all.

The entire team at Bloomsbury. Cindy Loh, Regina Roff, Michelle Nagler, Melanie Cecka, Alexei Esikoff, Melissa Kavonic, Regina Castillo, Christine Ma, Katy Hershberger, Bridget Hartzler, Kim Burns, Rachel Stark, Beth Eller, Kaitlin Mischner, and Linette Kim. Also, Alice Swan and Scholastic UK. Book people are the best, and y'all are proof.

The city of Orange. I was in search of a setting for at least the first half of this book, and once I researched this charming town, everything clicked into place. Thanks to the students at Villa Park and Orange High Schools, whose feedback helped me create the fictional school Orange Park. Also, the San Clemente High School homecoming parade, the brilliance of which I incorporated into the Orange community. Lastly, the fine business owners in the Orange Circle at Olde Towne Plaza for answering my random questions, often randomly.

Readers who responded to my queries on various social networks. Ironically enough, these sites helped me research Mallory's tech-fast and her escape into the early sixties. Some works that helped me to connect to this time period include *Seventeen* and *Life* magazines from 1959 to 1964, as well as *The Feminine Mystique* by Betty Friedan, *The Best of Everything* by Rona Jaffe, *Boom!* by Tom Brokaw, and *Mad Men: The Illustrated World* by Dyna Moe.

Brett and Kelly Taylor, for answering California questions, not to mention Zach and Jana Taylor/Spencer and Rachel Orr for wild California adventures. Heather Fife, for additional California wisdom. Morgan and Kaylee Taylor/Sinclair Johnson, for help with kiddos. Irene Latham, for your invaluable feedback on early drafts and poetic tips on the secrets we keep. Lisa Schroeder, Rachel Hawkins, Becca Fitzpatrick, and Emily Wing Smith for title brainstorms and plotting tips.

Mom and Dad, always. Curry, forever. Rylee, Talin, and Logan, stop growing up, already.